Jeanette
Love can break
us apart and
us together
us
love to
Maria
Macdo

Finally UNBROKEN

Finally Unbroken Series Book One

MARIA MACDONALD

Finally Unbroken

Finally Unbroken Series Book One

Maria Macdonald

ISBN-13: 978-1530271948

ISBN-10: 1530271940

Formatting by Swish Design & Editing

Editing by Swish Design & Editing

Cover design by Francessca's Romance Reviews

Dedication

This book is dedicated to three special souls.

I started this book when I was still writing the Entwined Hearts series. I've had a lot of support throughout this last year. None more so than from the beautiful Beth LeMilliere. Therefore, she's the first person I thought about when a dedication was needed.
Beth… I butterflying love you! You are the skittles!

There were two others that were at the forefront of my mind, mainly because these two have championed this book since the beginning. Loving the characters and the story endlessly.
Annmarie Thomson and Kerry Adamson.
You both loved this book even when I wanted to give up. When I was drained, you spurred me on. Always asking for the next chapter and telling me how much you loved this story.

Danny and Anabel belong to you.

Sometimes the stories suffocate us.
By writing the words for others to read,
We let the stories fly free...
Allowing us to breathe again.

Finally UNBROKEN

Chapter ONE

Anabel Vincent

"Anabel, where the *fuck* is my beer?" I hear bellowing through the house. I use the term house loosely, it's more like a ramshackle hut. It had belonged to Keith's parents before they died. Now, I guess, it's ours—well, his.

Wrapping my arms around me, I feel cold all over as I hang my head, staring at the bubbles in the sink, watching them slowly pop in the dirty water. Shivering, I wonder now how my life became this, and if, one day, I might be like one of these bubbles and just pop, ceasing to exist.

"*Do I have to get it myself!*" he shouts again.

I jump into action, not even drying my hands before opening the fridge and grabbing his beer, almost jogging to get it to him as quickly as possible.

The house is only tiny, so it's not far to go, it's more about the abuse I'll get if I don't act quickly.

"Here you go," I murmur, handing him the beer. He doesn't even glance away from the television.

"About fucking time," he grinds out, followed by, "Have you done the dishes yet? I told you earlier to clean my car as well, don't forget."

I sigh silently. "Nearly done, I'll get on your car real soon, I promise." At my reply, he mumbles something that can't be deciphered. Twisting around, I rush back to finish washing the dishes so I can start on his car.

It wasn't always like this. We were actually once in love. If you can believe that. Keith used to be the quarterback while I was the quiet, nerdy girl. Our school life should have dictated that we could never be, but in the end, the popular girls didn't get him and I was the one that *'won'*. The one that beat the cheerleader to get the guy. The one you always read about and assume there's a happily ever after. Looking at Keith now, the only parts of him that remain the same are his eyes and height. He's still tall at six foot two, his dark blond locks have grown into a gray, blond, greasy mix over the years. His build although large is less defined, stodgier. His teeth have yellowed from the tobacco he smokes, and he rarely smells of anything other than beer these days.

The thing is, none of that bothers me. I would have loved him anyway, just for his bright bluish-gray eyes and his reciprocation of love. But even his eyes are hard and cold now, and that teamed with his personality over the last ten years, I know I'll never love him again.

Keith's never hit me, never raised a finger to physically hurt me. I should be thankful of that. However, I've learnt over the years, there are many ways to break someone. So many other ways to pull someone down, to make them bleed, just not on the outside.

Emptying the water and bubbles from the sink then walking over to open the back door, I grab the bucket and sponge. Spinning around, I catch myself in the mirror. My long thick blond hair hangs lank and lifeless. I really need a good cut and style, it could use a color too as I'm getting the odd wispy stray gray hair dotted along my hairline. I kind of think it's pretty, I'm probably the only woman that does. Still, it's a sign of aging and there's nothing wrong with that. My green eyes look sad surrounded by pale skin with the odd wrinkle. I'm lucky my appearance isn't as bad as it could be.

I got the guy at high school and he married me. I don't feel lucky, though, not really, not with what he's turned into. It could have been worse, at least, most of the cheerleaders that still live in this town look a lot more haggard than me.

That really shouldn't make me feel better, someone else's hardship isn't for me to comment on. It's not like the way he treats me isn't common knowledge, they probably have a good laugh at my expense.

Little Anabel didn't actually win in the end, huh?

When we were younger, Keith would drive around town with me in his truck, proud that I was on his arm. He used to tell me how beautiful I was, he used to stroke my face and kiss my temple softly when he was dropping me home. We would lie in the truck bed and watch the stars in between making out.

Before I realize it the tears are softly falling, slipping down my cheeks and dropping on the floor looking like raindrops splashing from above. Bending down, I wipe them away with the sponge. I'm not crying because I still love him, I'm crying for everything I once had but lost. He used to hang the stars for me. I can't believe I could've been so wrong about someone I willingly gave my heart to. It shows how well I judge people. I've wanted to leave him for years. There's just no way of achieving that goal now.

My pop died twelve years ago, my mom ten months later, leaving me with no family—except *him*. My friends from high school all left this town one by one, moving onto better things, things I missed out on because Keith wanted me to be a housewife and nothing more, and I allowed myself to believe his dreams were my dreams. Now all my friends are his friends, which basically means I have nobody.

No job.

No friends.

No family.

So I'm stuck.

Some would say, that's not a good enough reason to stay. That I should be brave, but I'm not brave. I used to be. Even with being the quiet girl in high school, there was a reason I won Keith, a reason he noticed me. It was because I was brave. I would talk to him. It was frowned upon by the popular girls. How dare someone in my social circle be so brazen as to talk to one of the jocks? Gasp! But I'd do it anyway. He would come into my parents' ice cream store with his friends and he was always nice to me, unlike most of the others.

I remember one of the first times he noticed me. I was working by myself, as it was a Saturday and the weekend manager, who was only four years older than me, had called in sick. I'd decided not to call my pop, who worked all week and deserved a break. It was heading toward two in the afternoon when the popular crowd filtered in. Throwing my shoulders back and raising my head, I readied myself to serve them, without feeling inferior or blushing.

When I got to Danny Quinn and asked him what he wanted, he smirked. “How about you, there must be a room out back?”

“Sorry, not for sale,” I replied with a wink. He’d always joked with me, so I knew that with Danny it was light-hearted fun.

“That’s not what I heard,” Ashley Summers whisper-yelled to the group, who were all standing to the right. Of course, the girls all tittered, a couple of the guys laughed, the rest just had smiles on their faces.

Danny frowned and I was about to ask him what ice-cream he wanted when Jenny Yates chipped in with, “Yeah, it’s always the quiet ones you have to watch out for. They’re usually the biggest tramps.”

Before her sentence was finished one of the other girls, Samantha Watkins added, “I always wondered how this place stayed afloat in the winter.” At this point, the tears pooled in my eyes. I turned to Danny, his face was a picture of stone, I was about to tell him to get his friends out of my shop when Keith piped up, “Shut up you douches. I like this place, stop acting like jealous bitches just because blondie over there is hot.”

“Anabel,” Danny forced out but nobody listened, and I briefly wondered how he knew my actual name.

“Oh, but Keith, baby, we were only playing,” Ashley purred to him with a smirk.

"Well then, say sorry to Blondie and let's go," he replied to her, then looked over at me and winked.

From that wink, I was gone for him, or I thought I was. I couldn't see anyone other than Keith—my hero. Pity his hero status didn't last a year past us getting hitched. Still we had three relatively good years. Two dating and then the one married before it started turning to complete shit.

Of course, I know why it went the way it did, and really it's not Keith's fault. We tried, unsuccessfully, to have kids. At first, we tried a lot, over time that died, along with the passion. It didn't happen, I couldn't seem to get pregnant. After a while Keith became bitter, he had always wanted kids and he believed I couldn't give him them. We'd been trying for about three months before the wedding too, so in total it had been about nine months. I didn't think that was very long, but he did. So he used me as his emotional battering ram when he was depressed. I took it because I felt bad. He still looked after me in most ways, and we were still having sex. Then my pop had a heart attack and died and that caused me to spiral downhill. When my mom died from a stroke just ten months later, I lost it completely.

Keith wanted me to sell their shop. I wanted to keep it, but he won—as usual. I felt like a piece of me was torn away the day I finally accepted I was losing my small haven. I still feel that emptiness.

The shop sold almost straight away, but I never knew who had bought it. The sale was done through a realtor, nobody ever moved in. It's still empty now. The realtor and Keith have no idea that I still have a key, and sometimes, I slip in the back door and sit in the kitchen, remembering all those years ago. A time long since passed.

When Keith's parents died in a car accident a year after my mom that was the end of whatever shreds of a relationship we had left. There was no more lovemaking, there wasn't even sex. There were no more tender kisses, there were no kisses at all. No soft words just bitterness and resentment fueled by alcohol. Although, he was like it even without the help of alcohol, just not quite as bad.

I've lived no life for ten years. The only orgasm I've had is from my own hand. The little human contact I'm allowed is with Keith—if you can call it human—or his friends who are almost as bad as he is. There's Pastor Wilson and his wife. They knew my parent's really well and are lovely, but they are also seventy-five years old at least, so they can't do much to help me, and they aren't the partying type. Although, these days, I don't think I'm the partying type either. I've missed out on so much that life has to offer. It's like I should be eighty-five and in retirement. When in reality I'm only thirty-one. *That's not that old...is it?*

Keith still has his friends, well some of them. Danny left town right after high school and is an athlete, but I don't follow sports, so have no idea what he's doing or where he is. Rubén was another of his friends. He left town and went on to college, he's some big business owner doing àdvertising or something. Keith and his friends regularly bitch about them, though. Apparently, you're not allowed to leave this town and make something of yourself.

The women of the group didn't fare so well. Ashley got pregnant within two years of high school ending, which put a halt on community college. Whoever the father was, he didn't stick around. Jenny married Keith's friend Tommy. She likes a drink and to sleep around, which means Tommy lays into her. Not just verbally either. Samantha works as a hairdresser. She's never married but is a serial dater. She's probably better off than me, though.

"Are you washing my fucking car yet? Or are going to be a lazy bitch all day?" Keith shouts.

I forgot.

I was reminiscing about everything, and it slipped my mind.

I forgot my place.

Chapter TWO

Danny Quinn

"Mr. Quinn your wife is on line one."

Looking up from the pile of paperwork that I was trying to sieve through, my answer is sharp. "Not my wife, Layla."

"Oh yes, sorry, sir," she says, her cheeks pinking as she backs out of the door.

The truth is technically she is still my wife, but I haven't considered her as such for a long time.

"Shannon," I say, my voice flat as I answer the phone

"Danny, what the fuck!" is the reply screeching down the line. Pulling the phone away from my ear, I stand up and walk toward the floor to ceiling glass wall. Placing my arm above me, against the window for support, I rest my forehead on the cool glass. Staring outside, I look over the lunch hour rush of

San Francisco city while mentally preparing myself for whatever nasty words she's about to vomit. "I've just got a letter from your attorney. She's saying you're going to pay me fifty thousand dollars, and that's it…" she pauses, but I know it's just to take a breath before she carries on, "…that's it? What the fuck, Dan?" I hate her calling me Dan and she knows it. "You're worth millions. And I'm not getting any alimony either because you so cleverly made sure I signed that damn prenup before we married. If you think you're going to get me off your back for fifty K, then you're wrong Dan… so wrong!" She waits for my reaction, but I'm not going to give her any.

"We shouldn't be talking, other than through our attorneys, Shannon. If you have an issue, from now on, I suggest you talk to Ms Deakin."

"Oh, I bet you'd love that wouldn't you? Are you fucking her? You fucking ass!" she screams down the phone then hangs up.

I stay still, unclenching my muscles and trying not to crack the phone as my fingers spasm around it. Closing my eyes and sighing, I take a minute to calm down, then walk back to my desk. Pressing the intercom, I buzz for Layla. After a few moments, she knocks and walks in.

"Sir?"

"Layla, could you arrange for me to have all the documentation for the archived project please." She nods and rushes away. Within a few minutes, she knocks again bringing the paperwork. "Thank you, Layla. I'll need travel arranged. I want you to get me the first flight out. Book a hotel, too," I tell her looking through the documents. When I don't hear the door close, I glance up but she's still standing there. "Layla?"

"You're going back?" she asks cautiously.

"I am."

"Are you sure?" she queries.

"Layla, if I wanted your input I would have asked for it," I tell her returning to my documents with a sigh.

"Yes, sir, my apologies. I'll organize that now."

I say nothing and she leaves.

Meticulously I look through each piece of paper, wondering if I'm doing the right thing. It's time to move on, but some things are hard to let go of. With that thought, something drops from the pile to the floor. It's a photo. Picking it up slowly and staring, I remember this picture, it was taken when my face was much younger. I didn't have so many lines. My life and career were just beginning. As I stare, it's there in my eyes—hope. I had it in abundance then. Always thinking I would come out on top. That was what I believed, well, when it came to most things.

My fingers travel over the photograph that shows a group of carefree young kids outside the shop. It stops when I reach her face. She was beautiful then. I have no idea what she's like now. Probably has a few kids, little girls that have her eyes and smile, with long strawberry blond locks, just a touch darker than their mom. Little boys with her wicked sense of humor and fun. I just hope that she got everything she wanted. She deserved to be treated like a queen. That's one of the reasons I left. To let her just *be.* We were becoming closer, closer than was right, so I had to pull away. I slap the palm of my hand against my forehead, as an ache spreads through my chest. "Get a grip Danny." I murmur to myself. "It's time to let the past go."

Anabel Vincent

"Of course you use milk, it makes the potatoes creamy."

"Actually no, you just use more butter *that* makes the potato even creamier." I feel the breeze hitting my back as the door to the store opens and I'm jolted out of my stance. This is what my life has become, watching two little old ladies argue about the best way to make mash potato. Still I smile. I love volunteering, helping the old folks is the one thing that makes me feel like my life has some meaning, some purpose.

"Come on, Agnes, Meredith, we're in the grocery store, it's probably not the best place to be having this argument," I say, trying to appease them.

Agnes spins around to me, a look of disgust on her face. "This is exactly the place to have this conversation. We're in the dairy aisle, do I want to go home with too much milk, because this one thinks milk is what we need, when we actually need butter," she tells me with a huff but her eyes are shooting daggers at Meredith. I roll my eyes at her.

"Don't you roll your eyes at her young lady!" I get shot at me from Meredith now. Looking over to her, she has her hands on her hips and a frown on her wrinkly face.

"Young ones these days… I tell you Mere, there's no respect," Agnes says from my other side as Meredith nods enthusiastically in response.

Linking her arm through Meredith's, Agnes says, "Come on, let's get butter *and* milk, then we can make both." They nod their heads together and walk off to pick up the ingredients that they've spent the last ten minutes arguing about. I lean over the shopping cart and run my hand down my face. Shaking my head, I walk toward the old ladies with a smile, hoping I'm just like them when I'm older.

I can hear them laughing out in the back garden. Well, the patch of grass that's considered a back garden. Sometimes I fantasize that it's just me living here. This place is a dump, but still, I think about all the things I'd do to pretty it up. At the very least, I'd mow the grass patch and plant some flowers, something that I refuse to do when Keith and his friends insist on sitting out here drinking, throwing empty bottles everywhere and relieving themselves on the grass when they're drunk. Not surprising it's turned brown. I would if it was just me, though. I'd save up to get someone to paint the outside of the house while I tackled the inside. I'd paint the outside myself, but I'm so scared of heights that I'd probably fall off the ladder.

Walking toward the back door, I can hear them all chatting, hooting and hollering and generally acting like the asses that they are. "I can't believe you haven't got her working yet?" I hear Tommy say.

"Nah, man, I need her to be at my beck and call." They all laugh at Keith's statement. I already know that it's me they're talking about. Years ago I used to stop and listen, then have it out with him after they went home. It took years, but eventually I realized there was no point. Keith didn't respect me anymore. Hell, I didn't respect myself anymore, so how could I demand it from him? Hanging my head, I walk out there with beers in my hands. While passing them out to the guys, I notice, as usual, not one of them says thank you. Declan grabs the bottle with one hand while trying to shove his other hand up my shorts. I step away with a frown and look to Keith, who has his back to us and so doesn't see anything. But I know… *I know*… if I tell him what happened, he wouldn't believe me when Declan denies it. It's not the first time it's happened, and it probably won't be the last. One day I worry that Declan will push it too far and I'll have nobody to help me. Quickly, I move back inside the relative safety of the house.

"Did you pick up more beers when you were out?" Keith shouts into the kitchen. They've been out there for five hours now and they're all drunk. It's like looking after a bunch of toddlers.

"Yes, of course," I reply shouting out into the garden.

Forty-five minutes later and they just seem to be getting louder. "I don't know why she has to volunteer any time to those old fuckers, they're gonna be dead soon anyway," he tells his friends and my grip tightens on the iron. I've been standing here ironing his clothes for the last half hour, listening to him berate me. It makes me so angry but I realize, every time my anger surfaces, that there's nothing I can do about it so I might as well let it go. Looking down at the now small pile of clothes left, my skin hot and prickly with irritation, I wonder why I bother. I think it's a thing that's just bred into me. *Plus, if he noticed I wasn't doing it anymore I'd just be giving him ammunition to shoot me down.*

"If I had her I would bang her all day long," Declan slurs to Keith.

"No, you wouldn't. Trust me, it's not fun now she's passed it." They roll about laughing. My shoulders sag as my vision blurs and I feel the emotion that I usually hide so well, bubbling to the surface. Pushing it back down for the moment while grabbing my jacket and purse, I creep out the front of the house. Keith and his friends will be there all night, and they're too drunk to really know what's going on. If he asks tomorrow, I'll just say I went to bed with a headache. He'll chew me out, but I need to get away. Some days it's just all too much.

It's a three-mile walk into town, but it's one that I need right now. I'm glad I grabbed my jacket, as although it's the end of August and the days are hot, the nights are cold. It's eleven p.m. now, and it's only going to get colder by the time I'm ready to walk back. I smell the crisp night air, and can feel the dew on my face. When I reach town, I walk briskly past the local bar so nobody will see me. Scooting down the alley behind Main Street, and digging the key out of my pocket, I look around taking a final sweep of any possible signs of life, before concluding it's just me. Opening the back door to my parents' old ice cream parlor, as soon as I'm in I lock the door, then lean back against it, closing my eyes as my heart thumps in my chest. It's strange to think back to only twelve years ago where I would have come in here every day to open shop. It's the last piece I have of my parents—the final piece of me that Keith has destroyed.

I walk through the back of the shop. I can't sit out front anymore, the glass windows will give me away. Although I have, on occasion, still gone in the front door at the dead of night and sat in my favorite spot, remembering when I would come in after school and Pop would bring me out my favorite ice cream—mint choc chip. I'd sit and watch as he and Momma danced around to the old music, which they always played in the shop while serving customers. Always happy. *God they loved each other so fiercely.* I only ever wished to have a love like theirs. Something all consuming, and for that person to love me back in the same way.

They would be disappointed in me now. I know it. Disappointed that I've let myself become so worn down, that I've allowed my self-esteem to drop enough that I'm broken. I feel a tear slip away from my restraint and I quickly wipe at it, making my face dry once again. I don't want to allow myself to go down that path, I don't want to open the floodgates. Reaching out, I touch the photos that still hang in the back room. Photos of my momma, my pop, and me as a young girl in my teens. Keith didn't want those photos in the house, he says we don't have room, and that the memories are all in our heads anyway. I've managed to hide a few photos away, but as for the rest I had nowhere to store them, no one to ask to keep them for me. Then while I was trying to work out what to do with them, I realized that it didn't matter—nothing mattered. If I stayed with Keith, they were never going to be allowed to go up on my wall. I cried that day, for my parents, for their shop, for their photographs and for my loss. Then two months after selling this place—once Keith had spent all the sale money on drink—I realized there was still nobody doing anything with the place.

The night of my twenty-first birthday was the first time I crept into the shop. It was my first birthday without both my momma and pop. I had come home from a day saying goodbye to my best friend, Amanda. We'd been inseparable growing up. I loved her like a sister, still do. She was my next door neighbor, our parents had been close too. Unfortunately, her mom had passed when we were in high school from cancer. After school, she went on to college. When my pop died, she came back to visit me, but then, when my momma died she came back to town and stayed longer than she should have. She had just finished both a French and English Degree at Dartmouth College. Amanda was heading to Paris to be an English teacher. As an only child her father had sold everything and was going with her, but because she loved me, she pushed back her plans to come and prop me up knowing Keith would be useless, even back then. We had spent practically the whole day crying. Then she was gone. I had gone home in bits hoping that Keith would, at least, give me a hug and maybe give me a birthday card. Instead, I didn't even get a hello, just a *'Where the fuck have you been, and just because it's your birthday I still need dinner.'* I made him dinner, then I walked out. He was livid when I got home. It was the first real undeniable and irreparable hole in our marriage. After that, it just got worse.

I sigh as I walk into the kitchen. The big freezer is still here. It's empty and clean. The whole place is spotless, I made sure of it before it was sold, and now I clean when I'm here, which is becoming more often as time goes by. Grabbing the cloth and cleaning spray under the sink, I wipe all the surfaces that don't need wiping, just to do something.

Picking up the radio, I wish I'd remembered to bring batteries. It died the last time I was here. I love listening to music, but it's just another thing Keith doesn't like at home. Now I only get the chance to do it when he's at work, which isn't often. Since he hates any kind of labor and won't let me work. We live below the breadline, but we always have beer, especially for his asshat friends. I put the cloth and spray back and check the clock on the wall, which still works. I can't quite believe it's after one in the morning. Grabbing my jacket and purse, I creep out the back door to the shop and lock up, walking down the alley and back onto Main, turning right and starting the journey back home. Dragging my feet, with a heavy heart and wondering why I call it home, when in reality it's nothing like what I'd consider a home. Halfway there it starts raining and I just stop and hold out my hands looking up to the sky, like a completely crazy person with a smile. Before I carry on walking, I scream up into the night, releasing whatever tension my body retains from the day. Telling me I'm still alive.

Chapter THREE

Anabel Vincent

I have moments of peace. They don't happen often, but when they do I savor them. This is one of those moments where I have freedom today. Keith's currently at work at his job at Selma's, the local bar, which he manages two days and two nights a week. The peace I feel right now comes from digging out my secret box of photos and knick-knacks, which I keep at the bottom of my closet. I sit flipping through my hidden keepsakes. The photos, from a time long since passed, bring me an equal mixture of happiness and sorrow. But, more importantly, they also remind me of who I used to be and sometimes I need that reminder.

Skimming past anything relating to Keith—moving those items to one side to throw away—my first stop is a photo of Amanda and me. We must have been sixteen. It was before Keith and I got together and about a year after her mom passed. She was just starting to come back from the downward spiral that saw her acting out and hanging about with the wrong crowd. That year had tested our friendship, but I never gave up on her. She was and still is my soul sister, and I would have walked to the ends of the earth for her. So I kept holding on, gripping her with only my fingernails sometimes, but it was worth it, *she* was worth it. Then Amanda got out of this place, and she made something of herself. I miss her so much sometimes that I can't breathe. She calls me once a week when I visit Pastor Wilson and his wife after church on Sunday's. We don't have a phone in the house and the cell is held by Keith. Lack of my own money ties me to him. He likes me there, under his control. As much as he tells his friends I'm not worth anything—and I know he really truly believes that—he likes that he has someone to dictate to.

When I think about the way he turned out, I'm glad we never had children. I wonder if we did, how he would have tried to control them—what lengths he'd have gone to. I shiver at my own thoughts. I can't even imagine having sex with him anymore, I'm just grateful that he doesn't try. I sleep in the spare room now and he doesn't care. He asked me to move in there years ago. Said I was getting fat and taking up too much of the bed. I've stayed in that room ever since. But it doesn't give me a false sense of security, I know my place, and I have no doubt that he probably looks through my room regularly. Checking for God only knows what. Still, he either hasn't found this box yet or he just doesn't care enough.

I'm glad tomorrow is Sunday. It means he works today and tomorrow and it also means I'm able to speak to Amanda. She hates Keith, we talk about my situation sometimes, but to be honest, not much changes on my end and I prefer to listen to what's going on in her life. She got married three years ago to Pierre. The man who won my best friend's heart. She'd been dating him for five years and she seems totally in love. So, I live vicariously through her, learning about relationships all over again, reminding me what I saw with my parents and hers. Maybe that's where we went wrong, Keith looked to his parents. They weren't happy, you could see that a mile away, but they stuck because they came from a time when you didn't divorce. It just wasn't the done thing. So Keith and his brother Robert, who's three years his senior, grew up in an unhappy home. Their dad was strict and would regularly beat them. It's one of the reasons I've always felt grateful that Keith isn't like that with me. Robert went to prison for assault and rape eight years ago, and although I suspect Keith talks to him I steer clear, he always gave me the creeps when we were younger. Thankfully Keith was never like his brother.

I take a moment to ponder my thoughts, and when I manage to clear them, I pull out my paper and pencil. I open my folder carefully, containing layers of paper, some empty and waiting for beauty, and some I've already used to draw. I sketch my dreams. It's how I still function, by having dreams. I dream that someday, I'll be rescued. Someday, someone will love me with their whole essence. One day I'll be somebody's everything. I look at my favorite sketch of the Eiffel Tower. I picture laying on the grass, staring up at the beautiful masterpiece in front of me. Amanda would be with me, and so would our respective husbands—Keith would not be in that picture—and we would all be deliriously happy. The only thing missing is the unicorns farting rainbows, right? Well, I guess that's why they're called dreams because most people don't get to achieve them.

I fold the papers up and tuck them back in the box. Returning to the photographs, I pause at a group shot. I'm standing next to Amanda smiling wide, we were obviously giggling just prior to the photo. Keith is next to me with Tommy and Declan, at the back stands Rubén and the girls. Then there's him… *Danny.* He stands at the other end to me, and while everyone is looking into the camera, he isn't. Instead, he's staring right at me, looking straight down the line of people to my smiling face. I didn't know it until I had this photo developed. Then I kept it for myself. Kept a piece of Danny to have with me. We'd gotten close since I started dating Keith, at times I had told him things, problems or worries I had, whether they were about Keith or about life in general. I found him easy to talk to. He didn't treat me like the others. He acted like I was worth something, even if I wasn't from the popular crowd. We became really close, actually too close. Well, back then it was too close, for someone who was already in a relationship. I asked him once whether you could love two people. He told me he thought that it was possible to love two people, but you couldn't be *in love* with two people. He held my hand, looked into my eyes and said, '*The strongest love, the love that was meant to be, that's the kind of love that will stand the test of time. That's the love that will still sit in your heart fifty years from now... even if it's a dormant love, remaining useless and unused. It will still be there and will always exist throughout time.*' I get what he meant now I'm older. He was mature beyond what eighteen-year-old boys should be. I wonder if he has that love. That same one I do, the one that sits dormant in my heart unused, because the person it was truly meant for left and has never come back.

Danny Quinn

"Welcome to Wentworth by the Sea Marriott Hotel, Mr. Quinn," the over enthusiastic receptionist says as I check in. "Christoph will take your luggage up to the Presidential Suite, Sir," she continues and I just nod. Weary from my flight and four days of phone calls from Shannon. Calls that I could have done without. I make my way to the suite, ready for sleep. The moment the door closes my cell buzzes and vibrates in my pocket. My heart is heavy as I pull the phone out, dreading another round with Shannon, but the day brightens slightly when I see it's not her calling.

"Layla," I answer.

"Mr. Quinn, I have spoken to Ms. Tinder. She wants to come and meet you to discuss the new venture and possible locations," I sigh. Gabrielle Tinder is the best person to locate the real estate I require, but every time we have a meeting she practically throws herself at me.

"Layla, can you arrange for Ms. Tinder to have the details of where I'm staying. Advise her I'm not sure how long I'll be here, but if she wants to come to my location, then she'll need to contact you when she's arrived. Then we can set up a meeting. Oh, and Layla… can you organize to fly out here, too."

"Sir?" Layla questions.

"Since arriving, I've realized I'm not sure how long my stay will be. You're needed here with me, and if Ms. Tinder insists on coming then I may need you to play chaperone." She giggles at my statement and my thumb moves clicking the phone off knowing Layla will get everything squared away. She's the best assistant I've ever had, which is why I've held onto her for over five years. I know she's had offers, people who've tried to steal her away from me. She's always turned them down, though. I'm not sure why, but I'm thankful to her for staying loyal. I throw my suit jacket over the chair and loosen my tie. I want to have a shower and get my head straight. Tomorrow I'm going to face the first town I lived in, the first town I had friends, the first town I played football for a team, and the first and last town where I had my heart broken.

I get up from the bed and pull the curtains back looking out over the harbor, opening the doors, I step out onto the balcony and take a deep breath of ocean air. It reminds me of summers spent down at the beach. Leaning on the balcony railings, the melancholy creeps up my throat as I watch the boats bob up and down in the water. I loved high school, had lots of friends and was on the football team.

Grades came easy to me, but because of my height, build, dark hair and looks, I was easily ushered into the popular crowd, even before I got picked for the team. It didn't take me long to realize the rules of high school - *the do's and don'ts*. It took me a couple of years to really understand that those rules were bullshit, and by that time I'd already lost the fight. The one girl I had really wanted only had eyes for my friend. I had my fair share of girlfriends and hookups, but they were all pretty meaningless, even if they didn't realize it.

I moved away to go to college when I was eighteen. Mainly for my own sanity. Watching someone else's happily ever after—with the person that your heart believes belongs to you—is like being slowly suffocated, and I didn't want to live that life. Good job too, because after college ball I got drafted. But it only lasted a few years, though, then it was all over when I broke my ankle. Luckily I'd saved most of my money, so with that I opened my first restaurant. I was blessed because it was a success. Now, I have over thirty across the US and am hoping to expand into Europe within the next couple of years. I didn't tell anyone back home that I kept tabs on the place. When I was drafted, I moved Mom, Pops, and my younger sister Molly out with me. But now they live in Florida, my parents deciding to retire there and my sister likes the almost constant sunshine. I never told them that I left my heart in our hometown, or that I'd invested there either. I've only visited the town once. Went to a realtor, and asked about houses to buy. There wasn't anything that caught my eye, and I cursed my stupidity, not really understanding why I would punish myself by living in the town, watching her with him, knowing she would never be mine. I decided to leave and never look back and for good this time.

But as I was walking out of the realtor's office, I spotted a property that caught my eye. Asking about it, the lady explained that it was about to go on the market. I bought it, then and there. I think the realtor nearly wet her panties when I gave her full market value. I took the keys and visited—just once. I realized that Bel hadn't had time to take any of the photographs down from the walls, and it felt like I was intruding. Still, while I was there, I couldn't help but stare at her, so vibrant, so beautiful. I locked the door after that and moved back to San Francisco.

Now, it's time to do something I've put off for so long.

I have to let it go.

For good.

Chapter FOUR

Danny Quinn

I look over the note for the fourth time. After going out for an early morning run, I needed to shake off the unease that had spread through my body when I woke. Being back here makes me feel like that young kid who never knew what he was throwing away. It makes me lose hold of the rigid control I apply to my life these days. Nearly an hour later, I was walking through the foyer when one of the receptionists called to me. She told me there was an urgent message for me from Layla—not especially unusual. She knows I run about this time in the morning and would be unreachable. The part that threw me slightly was that she wouldn't normally leave a message with reception. She would text me on my cell. When I read the note, though, I understood why.

Mr. Quinn, I couldn't reach you on your cell, please be prepared. Ms. Tinder is on her way. She found out where you were before I could call her, and upon speaking to her assistant, I've been informed that she'll be arriving at your hotel within the next few hours.

Fuck my life.

Now I've showered and dressed in jeans and a T-shirt and am reading the note once more like the words might suddenly change. This was supposed to be time for me to say goodbye, to process everything. I wasn't meant to have company, and now I'll have Gabrielle and Layla.

Shit, now the need to run again is like a beacon flashing in my brain.

I make my way out of the hotel entrance and get into my rental car. Driving out of the gates is a stark reminder that I'm leaving the safety and shelter surrounding me. But making my way up and down familiar roads, ones I haven't traveled for many years, the feeling changes from unease to warmth. The familiarity, it seems, is not altogether unwelcome. I'd forgotten how much I loved this place as a child, especially being so close to the sea. I'd never had an unhappy childhood, so I'm not quite sure why I've been so reluctant to come back here, and why I would think visiting would evoke pain. Then I remember, it's not pain I'm trying to avoid. *It's love.*

Anabel Vincent

"Thank you, Martha!" I smile taking the china cup filled with tea from Mrs. Wilson. It's been years since she's let me call her Mrs. Wilson, and she still reprimands me if it slips out. I enjoy my Sundays with these people. They took me under their wing when my momma and pop died. They never had children, so I think I fill that place in their hearts. Which is amazing, because I need them, much more than they need me.

"So has anything changed this week?" she asks me softly. I know what she's really asking, and she knows what she's really asking too, but the actual words are always left unsaid. It's always unspoken, the *'Keith'* that sits between us.

"Nothing interesting has happened this week, Martha," I reply with a smile.

"Well, it's about time something did," Pastor Wilson says walking up behind me. Martha looks up at him with a beautiful smile. He lights up her world, and I know he feels the same way about her, it's blindingly obvious. It's almost magical. I just wish that kind of love existed for us all.

The phone rings and I startle. Martha chuckles, "It will be for you, Anabel." As I get up to cross the room toward the phone, she grabs my hand and squeezes, so I stop to look down at her. "Dreams can become reality, Anabel. For some of us they just take a while longer to happen." I smile back at her and my heart swells for how much I love this lady in front of me. Squeezing her back, I release her hand and take the phone from Pastor Wilson, who's answered it.

"Mandie Moo," I squeal down the line, bursting into a little jig. Pastor Wilson chuckles and wanders away as I sink into the armchair wearing a huge grin and feeling the ache, the one that's always there in her place, subsiding.

"Bellie," she squeaks back. "I've missed your voice," she tells me, and just those four words brings all my carefully held in emotion to the surface.

"It's only been a week." I laugh trying to beat back the pain in my stomach that I feel hearing the sadness in her words.

"Yeah, I know," she answers. "I have some news."

"Oh?" I reply.

"I'm coming home."

"What? I mean… what?" I splutter the excitement escaping me. Amanda giggles on the other end of the line

"I wanted to come and visit you, show Pierre where I grew up and finally, you could meet each other. I'm just working my notice at my current job so I can come in a few weeks," she tells me and I bounce up and down on my toes with glee.

"Oh! I can't wait. All this time of keeping in touch on the phone, I'm finally gonna get to see you again and I'll be able to hug you," I say wrapping my free arm across my chest imagining it's her I'm holding.

"I know," she whispers and I know that she's crying. She's the crier out of the two of us. I can't be a crier, if I were, by now I'd be drowning in a river of tears.

After speaking to Amanda and then having dinner at Pastor Wilson's house, it was time to go home, but I wanted to visit the parlor today. I wanted to feel my history, rather than face my present. So I took the short walk to the old shop.

When I turn the last corner to enter the alleyway, I notice there's a car parked outside the back entrance. "Shit," I whisper to myself. Power walking as quickly as I can, without setting my butt cheeks on fire, I arrive at the back door and can see it's ajar. Pulling it open slightly and peeking in, I can't see anyone, but obviously, someone must be there. I'm about to take a step inside when I hear something crash and I jump backward.

I shouldn't be here. This isn't my place anymore.

I take another step back and feel my heart drop. It dawns on me that if someone is finally here to do something with the shop, then I can't come here for peace anymore. Something else that I'll just have to let go.

Danny Quinn

I sigh and close my eyes. I never knew coming back here would make me feel like a teenager again. The moment I opened the back door and walked inside, it was like my body recognized this place. What amazes me even more is that all the photos still hang on the wall. It's eerie like the shop has been kept in its former state, but with nobody living it, no one keeping it vibrant and alive. I stand and take in each photo, giving everyone the time it deserves. I can't help but feel a vise-like grip on my heart when I look at the photos of Bel. I wonder why she never took these photos with her. Grabbing one of her and her friend Amanda when they were about sixteen off the wall, I curse as I catch my finger on the nail. Spinning around, still cursing, I slam into the metal bin sending it toppling over. I stand still and look at the ceiling, then back to the frame in my hand.

Maybe the universe is trying to tell me something? Maybe I should just leave this photo? But If I'm going to sell this place, then I don't want someone to come along and throw it in the trash. Just one photo, another one to remember her. That makes my total now three. All kept filed away. The memories, though, they assault me more often than I would like. I place the picture frame on the counter and grab the bin. Walking to the back door, I'm sure I hear footsteps. Swinging the door open I look out, up and down the alley, but no one's there. Placing the bin outside the back door, I close my eyes and will myself to go back inside. To bare my heart again. I've come to realize that being in there opens up all the old wounds afresh. I enter and go straight to the serving counter at the front of house this time. I spy a radio and flick it on. It doesn't come to life so I pick it up, turning it over, and realize there are no batteries. *Of course, there wouldn't be.* I head out the back again, this time determined to do something useful, something to soothe me today.

Locking the door, I jump in the car and drive the three minutes toward what used to be Jim's hardware store. Surprisingly, it's still there. Not surprisingly, there's nobody working there that I know. I grab the batteries and get in the car heading back to the shop. Stopping at a red light, I think about how this town hasn't changed much. A fleck of light bouncing off something catches my eye, looking at it I see the back of a woman. She has a slender figure and blond hair. She glides as she walks, although by her movements it's pretty obvious that she doesn't realize this, as she's almost trying to hide, attempting to make herself insignificant. She fiddles with her fingers in an endearing way, and when she reaches the end of the street she stops under a ray of light. She must feel the warmth from the sun as she holds her hands out to her sides and raises her chin toward it. In that moment, I just wish I could see the bliss that I know is probably on her face as the warm rays caress her. I wonder when we all stopped enjoying such basic things, something as amazing as the sun on our faces. Suddenly, I'm rudely honked at by the horn of the car behind me. "All right," I mutter turning around to glare at the other driver who shrinks back into his seat. Heading back into the shop, this time I stride in going straight for the radio, placing the batteries in and wondering why I'm not just emptying the place and leaving. Switching it on and bringing life back into it, I get my reward when Nickelback - *Far Away* comes on the local station. I move to sit in my old booth which always faced the counter so I could watch her. Closing my eyes and listening to the words, I remember a time before my heart was ripped from my chest.

Anabel Vincent

The loud beeping of the car horn jolts me out of my moment. I've learnt in this life, to try and take every small blessing that's showered on you, however irrelevant you may think it is. I feel the warmth of the sun, it's like someone is trying to tell me that everything will be okay. But I've been known for my unwavering hope before, and I've crashed and burned because of it. Even so, I can't stop smiling, knowing that Amanda is coming home, coming back to me. I just don't know why. It's been ten years and as much as I love her, she's never come home before. I've never had the money to visit her. I got a passport once. I thought I'd try and save. Eight years later and I still have no money in that pot. She was struggling for a while to manage her bills correctly. Her pop helped out, but she's stubborn and wanted to manage on her own. It's expensive to fly back here. She couldn't afford it. But more, I don't think she's ever wanted to come back here.

The whole place reminds her of her mom—her loss. So I wonder why now? She always told me when she had the money she would pay for me to go to her, rather than coming back here. I shake my head at the errant thoughts and am about to continue my journey home when I suddenly decide that it's about time I got batteries. If there's a new owner and they're going to sell the shop—the only real home I have—then I want to make the most of the limited time I have left. I buy the batteries and walk back out of Jim's Hardware Store with a smile on my face and warmth in my chest. Even the thought of telling Keith doesn't upset me today. Nothing can rain on my parade.

Chapter FIVE

Anabel Vincent

I didn't think I would feel this happy again. Can you imagine? Resigned to the fact that I was going to spend the rest of my life miserable. Then the moment a ray of light shines on me and I feel that long since lost emotion, I suddenly find myself wondering how I'd ever lived without it. Even Keith can't turn my mood sour right now.

He's sitting in his usual spot in front of the television when I get in. Obviously not going to work today. "What the fuck are you whistling for?" he snaps.

I stop confused. "Was I? I didn't realize." He doesn't say anything, so I make my way into the living room and sit on the chair next to his. He doesn't even turn his head to look at me. "Keith," I say.

"What," he answers not pulling his eyes away from the television.

"It was my weekly chat with Amanda today." He snorts his disgust, he never liked her, telling me she lead me astray. He was happy when she moved to France. Even through my pain, he could only see it as a win on his part. So I can't wipe the glee from my face when I tell him, "Yep, she's coming back."

Snapping his head around to me with narrowed eyes he moans, "What the fuck does she want to come back to this shithole for? I would've thought she'd be too good for the likes of us? I figured she only spoke to you each week to brag about how amazing her life is, and how much better she is than you. She always was better than you." With still narrowed eyes he looks me up and down as his lips curl. Even that can't bring me down. He must know by now that I'm hardened to his shit. Most of the time, at least.

"Whatever you think, Keith, I'm happy," I tell him, the smile never slipping from my face.

"She better not come over here. She's not welcome," his angry mouth spews out. He turns back to the television, raising the volume of the football so I can't be heard over the drone. I realize I've been dismissed. Getting up and moving into the kitchen, I pull out the things needed for dinner. I catch myself in the mirror again, as I often do, but this time, there's something new to see—a smile on my face. It lights me up, and for a second I get a glimpse of the eighteen-year-old me, the one that was left behind, the one I gave up on. Only when I remember that does my smile slip.

Danny Quinn

"Mr Quinn." Rousing to the noise of someone calling me joined by tapping on the door, I throw my arm across my eyes not wanting to move. Moving means facing whatever is out there.

"Coming," I croak unhappily. Clearing my throat, I glance at the time, six twenty-five a.m. I groan and drag myself out of bed. Looking down my body I can see that I'm still wearing the same clothes I had on last night when I was looking through paperwork on the bed, it's the last thing my brain remembers. I glance back at the bed. *Yep.* The paperwork is now everywhere, including the floor. Walking to the hotel door and pulling it open, I immediately turn around and walk back to the phone calling room service to ask for coffee. I didn't even look to see who was at the door, but I'm more than aware, however, that it'll be Layla, even if initially I didn't recognize her voice. Nobody else is crazy enough to wake me up this early in the morning.

Layla walks in and sits at the table. She doesn't say anything and I know why. She's waiting for me to be caffeinated. With that thought, there's a tap on the door and Layla jumps up letting the waiter, and more importantly, my life-force into the room. Thankfully, she deals with him as I'm not sure my brain has the capacity to at the moment. I devour a cup of coffee then pour another.

"Talk," I mutter and Layla raises an eyebrow at me but doesn't respond to my rude demand. She knows what to expect before eight a.m. even though I asked her to wake me early.

"You may have noticed Ms. Tinder hasn't arrived yet. She was unexpectedly delayed and, therefore, won't be arriving until tomorrow." I release a breath and nod my head at a smirking Layla.

Two hours later, and slightly more refreshed and awake, I find myself at Rye on the Rocks Beach staring at the surf. This is a pretty local place. It's not that easy to find half decent surf in New Hampshire, and this spot is perfect with the right weather. I haven't surfed for years. Sometimes I miss the freedom that was taken for granted with youth. I used to come down here a lot. It took my mind off things—Bel mainly.

I was lost back then, and if I'm being honest, I still am. My feelings confused me. I always wanted her, but when she got together with Keith that was the end of everything. The truth was that their relationship made our friendship stronger. I had watched her from afar. Always wondering how to approach her. She was so happy and free, never seemed burdened by everyday life and I assumed she'd go on to do great things. I never saw her with any guys, I figured she didn't want a boyfriend. Not wanting to drag her into our circle of friends, because the girls were bitches and I knew they would tear her apart.

As it turns out, when she got together with Keith, she could actually hold her own—she was a strong little thing. Then when she and Keith became an item, he doted on her. Their love was apparent for all to see. It was only about six months into their relationship, as Bel and I spent more time together, I started to realize that maybe a lot of what Keith felt wasn't love, but more lust. I'm not sure Keith was as totally devoted as I first thought, and I wondered if he ever strayed. I never knew. He distanced himself from me as I got closer to Bel. He didn't like the closeness we shared. We'd fought over it, but because I could kick his ass he couldn't make me stay away. He knew how strong Bel was back then, and that if he pushed her, she would probably walk away. So he played the dutiful boyfriend—to her face. I can't say for certain what he did behind her back. There were always rumors, but nothing substantial.

Nothing that was concrete enough that I would willingly cause her sadness.

As Bel and I got closer, we did a lot of things that could only be described as old-fashioned courting. That included no kissing, but everything that came before, such as the touches, the looks, the secrets shared and the hard *'what if'* conversations…

"What if I wasn't with Keith?" She looked up at me from the grass she was sitting crossed legged on.

"You know, if you weren't with Keith, I would make you mine," I told her staring into her green eyes, blood whooshing in my ears.

"You would?" she whispered, her eyes wide.

I didn't understand how she never realized this. "Of course," I said no more. Instead, we stared at each other and I could feel the tension. It was something I'd never felt before. It was sexual. Primal. I wanted her to be my first. I wanted her to be my forever.

"Maybe I should run Keith over with my truck," I said, keeping my face impassive, even though my hands were clenched. Then I let a smirk tickle the corner of my mouth and her eyes darted to it. She smiled back and then snorted, which made us both laugh. The laughter covered over the previous conversation. But it was

strained laughter, and I know that was because we were both ignoring the pull we felt.

Whatever we shared it was thinly veiled by the cloak of friendship. I knew, even back then, that eventually we would get to a point where a decision would have to be made.

I made that decision.

Sometimes regret makes you her bitch.

Anabel Vincent

I pace my bedroom, worried that Keith had decided not to work today. As it turns out, they wanted him to work tonight, not today. Asking him instead to do a day shift during the week. I must admit I was momentarily thrown, and even felt guilty for like a second, because I'd just assumed he wasn't going to work being the lazy jackass that he is. I soon gave myself a good telling off for feeling guilty about anything to do with that man. The time has long gone that I have sympathy for him, in any way, it got washed away with the countless tears he's caused.

I hear the tell-tale click of the front door and force myself to stand still for five minutes, just listening to the car start and drive away, making sure he's gone.

Taking the few steps into the bathroom I stare at myself in the mirror. My mood has lightened in the last twenty-four hours, and I can see the change in my face. I don't look as old as I once did.

The hair dye box in my hand tempts me as I contemplate whether to use it. I don't think Keith will notice, he rarely looks at me anymore, so it's doubtful he'd notice that my gray hair has gone.

Forty minutes later and I have hair dye all over the bathroom and a very dubious looking white towel. Still, my hair is much better, which in turn makes me feel more confident in myself than I have in years. Making quick work of cleaning away most of the evidence, I find the dye washes off the bathroom tiles easily. My skin, however, that's a different story altogether. By the time I have all the remnants off, I feel like I've been to one of those evil spas. You know the ones that try and massage you with instruments, and you feel like you've had a going over with sandpaper. Then they try and convince you that it's good for you.

Still, I've decided to put a plan in place—*Operation Fixing Myself.* Okay, so the name's not original, but I don't need to put up banners. I just need to have a plan, to find the real me again. I want to be the person I was before *'she'* was ripped from me, through years of abuse, neglect, and loneliness. Amanda telling me she was coming was all the wake-up call I needed. After the euphoria of her surprising me when the news had worn off, I'd sat and thought about it and started to worry. I know it's silly, Amanda has never been the type of person to judge anyone, especially her best friend. But let's be realistic, it's been ten years. She has friends in France, and she's spoken about them—Joelle, Celia, and Estelle. I bet they are all elegant Parisians. All designer gear and impeccably turned out at all times. They wouldn't let gray hairs appear in their perfect locks. They wouldn't wear jeans that were frayed at the leg ends and had faded through years of wear. I look down at my tattered jeans, a tightness in my throat.

"Well, not unless they were designer and supposed to look like this," I mutter and sigh. Sitting down on the toilet lid, I allow myself a moment of self-pity, before I roll my eyes. Knowing what I need—a visit to the shop—I pull my still wet hair back into a plait and put on my chucks. Shutting the front door behind me, I start the walk to the only home I still have left. Nearly tripping as I falter thinking about my own words, thinking that I'm not going to have it for much longer as someone has decided to claim it. After all these years, I'm going to lose it, like everything else. I stop walking and bend over, placing my hands on my knees, while taking a few deep breaths. Then getting up slowly, I pull myself together once again. This is the time I wake up, this is the time I make myself more, this is the time I start fighting… *for me.*

Chapter SIX

Anabel Vincent

I meander inside the shop with ease this time. Unlike earlier today, all is quiet, but that's what I expected as it's nearly midnight. I don't want to turn the lights on, so instead I blindly fumble under the kitchen cupboard until I locate my torch. Pointing it toward the floor, hoping it will go unnoticed, I follow the light with my feet until I get to the radio. Turning it over and opening the battery compartment, I'm momentarily thrown when I notice the batteries inside. Switching it on, I jolt as Bonnie Raitt's – *I Can't Make You Love Me* blares from the small box. It nearly slips out of my hands as I panic, trying to turn the volume down. Once I've managed to bring the beautiful song to a reasonable level, I stand still staring at the dials as the lyrics penetrate the wall I've built around me. I gasp at the pain, which is like a fresh wound in my chest, like a physical thing crushing me. I quickly feel inside my back pockets until my hands grasp my small wallet, the one that keeps more of my memories locked away. Carefully, I pull it out and unclip it. Taking a deep breath, I dig out the photographs that I keep locked away in there. Stumbling in the dark to the nearest table, one that's at the back of shop, I'm hopefully not spotted as I stare at the photos. The first one is of Amanda and me, we're posing before a night out. We were so young and free back then. We had so much fun together, always laughing, smiling, and feeling alive. Sighing and dropping my shoulders, I realize I let that life go too easily.

Placing the photo on the table in front of me, I close my eyes and take a second to pull in the strength I need for the next one. Opening my eyes again, I greedily drink in every part of this photo. It was taken about a month before Danny left. I took it on a night out. The whole group was together. We were out at a bar a few towns over. Keith had gone missing about an hour before, and I was passed the point where I still looked for him when he disappeared. We'd been together about eight months, and the honeymoon period was definitely over. He often went missing on nights out, and I'd stopped tackling him about it. The truth was that I don't think I truly wanted to know where he was, and or, what he was doing. Or *who* he was doing, which was more likely. *Ignorance is bliss, right?*

Danny, Amanda, Tommy and I had been playing pool and getting drunk. We were all laughing about something and I whipped out a disposable camera, which I took everywhere with me back then. I was scared to miss out on one glorious moment we spent together and not willing to take the chance that I'd ever forget. I think I knew our time was coming to an end, college was beckoning those who were going. The photo was a fond memory for me. Danny had a subtle grin playing at the corners of his mouth, Tommy was doing a stupid thumbs up sign, and Amanda was leaning on the bar trying to avoid the camera. They were all sick of me and my camera, snapping them at the best, and usually the worst of times.

I let my index finger graze across Danny's face. Just looking at him, even now, I feel like a Mack truck has been lodged in my throat. Swallowing twice, I pull in my restraint.

He left me.

He never loved me.

Like the song said, I couldn't make him love me.

I remember the week before he left, Keith and I had been arguing. We were spending less time together. I'd been thinking more and more about the words Danny had said only a few weeks before.

"You know, if you weren't with Keith, I would make you mine."

He had said it with such conviction that I'd believed him. When we were at school, before even the idea of Keith had existed, there had been Danny. He had, however, always ignored me, except the playful banter we shared. I had tried the eye fluttering and the twirling of my hair. I'd even tried playing the damsel in distress once, pretending I couldn't get a jar of sprinkles open when he had come into the shop. He had laughed at me, then rolled his eyes and smiled, dazzling me. He came behind the counter un-popping the lid. The rest of the group then started to filter in and Danny quickly made his way back to the other side, ignoring me. Eventually, I'd given up hope on Danny and decided to just fawn over hot guys from afar, but the moment that Keith defended me, and done so by saying I was hot was enough for me to fall for him. In my defense, I was young and stupid and hadn't really had a boyfriend before. The little interest he showed in me was all I needed at the time. It took my focus from Danny, and it was all about Keith from then on.

Still, I'd always had a soft spot for Danny, and from the moment I got together with Keith I was able to watch Danny up close and personal. The dating was the hardest, especially the parties. We would all go together and Danny would have whichever girl of the moment hanging on his every word. I laughed and smiled with them all, and almost convinced myself I didn't care. *Almost.*

At first it wasn't so bad, I was getting to know Danny and although I was attracted to him, my feelings didn't run deep. I didn't know him enough for them to run deep. Keith was showering me with attention and I thought I was completely in love with him. However, Danny and I spent more time together in the confines of the group, and I found we always gravitated toward each other. Having a similar sense of humor amongst other things. We ended up spending more and more time together. Then from that, our own friendship blossomed. It helped that he and Amanda got on so well too. I'd once suggested to Amanda that she might want to date him. I forced that little nugget out of my mouth, almost choking as I did. She laughed and told me she saw Danny like an annoying brother, which made me giggle and instantly feel better. I ignored the latter.

So when Danny told me how he felt, I'd gone home feeling torn. Amanda and I had decided to go to the beach that morning and after sunbathing for a while, and dozing on and off, I felt drops of freezing cold water all over me. Sitting bolt upright in shock, and gasping at the coldness, it had taken a few moments for my brain to catch up to what was going on. I quickly realized Danny was standing at my side, laughing his head off. Rubén was there too, all surfer looks with his scruffy blond hair. Standing close to

Amanda, his laughter almost drowned Danny's out. However, Amanda had a look on her face, that said, *'I'm gonna kill you while you sleep.'* The guys had been surfing and were now, instead, trying to piss us off. After certain words were exchanged and the boys knew exactly how we felt, they offered us a ride back home. On the way, we passed a fair in the next town and decided to stop for a bit. As we ambled around, Amanda saw the Ferris wheel and was desperate to go on it. Being that I was scared of heights, I flatly refused. Rubén had taken the opportunity to grab Amanda's hand and drag her onto the ride. He'd always liked her, but again, she only saw him as a brother.

I often wondered what it was that she was looking for.

While they lined up waiting for the ride, Danny and I walked over to the empty grass behind the stalls. As we sat there, the conversation had turned to the girl he was seeing—Whitney Bass. She was pretty and actually quite sweet. But she seemed more hung up on him than he was on her. He told me that they weren't serious and that he was ending it this week. I asked why and all he had said was, *"Why settle?"* I stared at him for a moment and then replied with words that I hadn't ever uttered aloud, not even to myself.

"What if I wasn't with Keith?"

I hadn't ever meant to say them to Danny, it was just a thought process that I was having. I'm not sure if Danny assumed I was asking him the question directly, or if I was trying to say something without actually saying the words. The moment they were out, though, I knew I wondered. When he answered that he would be with me, I was shocked. I tried to deny the butterflies that suddenly came alive in my stomach. The next day, I had fussed over Keith, feeling like I'd somehow betrayed him. I didn't know what I was doing. I was a young, confused girl. That's all I was—a girl.

After that I'd avoided Danny for a few weeks. Until, one day, I felt I needed to be honest. Danny's parents owned a big farmhouse just outside of town. I borrowed my pop's car and drove over. His mom answered the door and told me he was working out in the barn. I ambled toward the big barn which was further down the lane. I could see the light from the old building in the distance and it was like a beam, trapping me and drawing me toward it. As my feet approached the barn, I could hear *Higher* by Creed blasting out, waking up the night. I walked inside and there was no way that Danny could hear me over the music. He was across the other side of the barn, doing pull ups on some makeshift frame and he was mouthing the words to the song. I watched him for a few seconds, taking him all in. As I got closer he noticed me, jumped down, grabbed his towel, and wiping his face he turned to the stereo and muted the volume. He cocked his head to the side, pulling his eyebrows in quizzically.

"Bel?"

"Danny." I breathed his name out huskily. My want right then was very obvious.

"What are you doing here?"

"I was... I..."

"Bel? Are you okay? Is everything, okay?" He walked forward grabbing my upper arms gently.

As I stared into his eyes, I was drawn into them. I leant forward my heart beating rapidly. "I just want to know..."

"What?" he asked confusion clear on his face.

"This," I whispered, then closed the last few inches between us, placing my lips on his. Gently I moved my mouth, and although at first he seemed stuck, frozen in place, within moments his lips met mine, synchronizing and fitting like puzzle pieces only ever meant for each other.

"No!" he suddenly shouted pulling back from me. My eyes widened and my heart drummed across my whole body. "This is wrong! Keith's a friend."

I felt winded at his words. When only weeks before he'd told me he wanted to be with me. "I thought... you said... at the fair—"

He cut me off. "Forget what I said at the fair, I was still drunk from the night before. You and me? It's never gonna happen."

"But..." I didn't know what exactly I wanted to say, just that I needed him to be clear. I was so confused, and it was partly his fault. I crossed my arms over my chest as anger bubbled inside me, I could feel it prickling just under the surface. "What was all that talk about running him over then? Was that just to see my reaction? Did you want to see if you could 'get the girl' then when I come here to give myself to you, I'm suddenly boring? The chase is over... is that what this is?" I spat out.

He looked at me not saying anything. For a moment, I thought I saw something soft flicker in his eyes. Then all at once they frosted over. "There's nothing here, nothing between us that's romantic. You belong to Keith. I'm not going to tell him about this. As far as I'm concerned this conversation never happened, Bel."

"Don't call me that," I hissed. "Don't ever call me that name again. Nicknames are reserved for real friends. Not for people who lead you on, give you hope, act like they want to offer you their heart just so they can trample on yours." I didn't give him a chance to respond, and I didn't see the pain in his eyes. I stormed off, forcing myself to not look back. To never look back.

I still remember that time clearly, and whenever I think about it, I get a sick feeling in the pit of my stomach. Because I moved on, well, I tried to. Distancing myself from Keith at first, thinking that I needed to make a clean break. But he must have sensed something was wrong with me because he played the perfect boyfriend, something he hadn't done for a while. So much so he was almost suffocating. I avoided Danny for three weeks until he left for college. I broke when he moved away. Only Amanda ever knew the truth. Slowly, over the next few months, I got better. Keith was actually pretty amazing back then, things were changing and I felt like we were all growing up.

Keith stopped spending time with the bitchy girls that had always unfortunately made up a large part of our group. He got a job and showed me what a great boyfriend he could be. It was like it had been in those first few months once again laying on the back of his truck and watching the stars.

Then he proposed and I agreed.

My fate was sealed.

We planned out our wedding to be in seven months. Three months before the wedding, we started trying for children. A week before the wedding, Keith and I had a massive argument. He accused me of still being on birth control and of not really wanting a child. He told me to cancel the wedding. Of course, he came back that night and apologized. I wasn't sure whether I was relieved or not. It had been the first big argument we'd had since before we got engaged. But I noticed he'd been acting strange for that last month, and I had wondered if he still wanted to marry me.

The day of the wedding I asked Amanda to take me to Danny's parents' house. I was confused since our argument Keith had been frosty and when I asked him if he still wanted to get married he'd snapped my head off. Something I was sure about for the last few months had suddenly become unstable. I put all my doubts, all the feelings I wasn't supposed to have inside a black box and locked it tight. Since our argument that box had broken open, and I was filled with unease. I needed to get my head straight and I couldn't think of a better way than to be near Danny, in any way possible.

I'd known the Quinn's for my whole life, even so, I was sure they were shocked when I broke down on their front porch in my wedding dress. Everything came out. His mom was amazing, she comforted me. She told me I shouldn't be getting married. Not if that was how I felt. After releasing all the built up frustration I had inside, I asked her if she had Danny's number, I said maybe I should call him.

She patted my hand with pity or sadness in her eyes, I couldn't quite decipher which it was. "I'm so sorry, Anabel. He'll be playing a game right now, and, well, my dear, he's dating someone, and he has been for the last six months." She smiled sadly at me and I tried to do the same thing back. Nodding, I got up and made my way back to the car. Finding myself, ten minutes later, back at the chapel.

Amanda turned to me. "I've brought you here because it's time, Bellie. It's time to get married or to cut loose. You can come with me, you know?" She had hope in her eyes, I could see it as clear as glass.

I thought about my life, about her life, about all of us. I was one of them, one of those people that would live in this town my whole life. I had no real future. Not like Amanda. The only thing I'd ever been good at was drawing and that wasn't going to get me anywhere. I didn't have money for college, so I needed to face my future. Keith loved me. I loved him. We might fight, but most couples fight. It's normal. Natural. He hadn't always been a good boyfriend, which is one of the reasons I was second guessing, but I hadn't always been the best girlfriend either. I convinced myself of it all.

I *was* a devoted wife, though. From the moment I made my decision to marry Keith, I was dedicated. I pushed Danny and all thoughts of him out of my head. I removed all the photos I had. I never destroyed them, I believed too firmly in memories and how important they are. But I stored them at my parents so I could begin married life with a clean slate. Keith never seemed to put *his everything* into our relationship, though, not until a month or so before the wedding. Things never got better, they only went downhill.

I tried. I truly believe that. Eventually, though, you have to admit defeat. Once my parents died, Keith was almost unreachable. Then whatever we still had, stopped being husband and wife and turned into master and servant and nothing more. That's when I brought all my memories back. When my parents died, I had a few boxes of belongings from their house that I had stored in our garage but never looked at. When things turned irreversibly sour between Keith and me, I opened those boxes. I took out the things that made me cling to a happier time. They were all I had left. Only memories but memories have kept me going for all these years.

I smile at both photos and place them back, then I take out the last memory that I keep in my wallet. Carefully unfolding the worn piece of paper I look at the drawing. Different shades of gray, soft and hard edges. Shadows bounce across the paper in the darkness, but I can still make out the tenderness etched across his face. His striking face still makes me catch my breath. My shoulders drop as a heaviness settles in my stomach. I remember why I drew this. It was because I realized I didn't want to forget anyone I loved. *Ever.* So I drew Danny. I drew him and I kept him. It was my silent rebellion. It was my hope. Then I folded him up and hid him away. Now I know he's always there when I need him.

Looking up at the clock I shine my torch on it and gasp when I see it's almost one in the morning. Keith will be home before me. *That's not what I wanted.* Not that I can do much about it now. Sighing, I stand and stretch. When I was at Pastor Wilson's house earlier, he mentioned that the fancy members-only club on the edge of town wanted a waitress. He said that the owner—one of his parishioners—had mentioned it to him and he had, in turn, said that I might be interested. Pastor Wilson had secured me an interview for tomorrow. He told me it was my choice if I wanted to go, but there was a chance for me if I wanted it. I knew what he was doing. Both Martha and Pastor Wilson have become impatient waiting for me to leave Keith. They, of course, can't say as much. The Bible says, *'What therefore God has joined together, let no man separate.'* I know how they really feel, it's in every look, every hug and most of their actions. This is them giving me their help by way of a stepping stone, allowing me to branch out, find a job, and earn some money. It's a start. I'm not going to let them down. Dying my hair was just one step. The next will be facing Mr. Cumberland tomorrow at The Hatfield Club.

I smile while putting the torch away already feeling stronger. This might be the start of something. I hope so. *Hope*. It's an incredibly powerful emotion.

Walking out the back door I lock it as quietly as possible and tuck the keys into my pocket. As I turn, there's a figure in front of me about a foot away. I gasp and jump backward slamming into the door I just locked. I feel my body starting to shake. I can't open the door. I have no cell because of Keith. I have no money. What the hell else could this person want from me? I don't want to think about it. I try to take in as much of him as I can, something to pass onto the cops if I ever get away. He's tall, six foot or more, but I can't see much else. He has a beanie on and his clothes are dark.

"I don't have any money," I whisper, my voice shaking.

"Bel?"

I hear the word muttered and I stop moving. Stop shaking. For a moment, I stop breathing. When my breath gushes back into my body, I start coughing, leaning over to catch as much air as I can. I feel a hand rub my back. "Bel, are you okay?"

Managing to even out my breathing, I stand up and look, really look. The person in front of me has bright blue eyes. Stubble across his beautifully etched chin, one just like the drawing I have in my back pocket.

"No," I splutter.

"Bel?"

Shaking my head, I pull away from the hand I didn't realize he had on my arm. I walk away already feeling tears stinging my eyes.

"Bel!" he shouts behind me and I pick up my pace. "Bel!" This time, I run… run until I can't breathe. I run from my past. I run because I don't want to be here, but there is nowhere I want to be anymore. I can run, but that's only any good if I have somewhere to run to. I drop to my knees the moment I reach my back garden and sit on my haunches, my heart beating wildly, as my hands shake.

"What happens now?" I ask looking at the sky, waiting as always, for my parents to give me an answer. Knowing they won't. They never do.

Chapter SEVEN

Danny Quinn

Staring at the dark empty alleyway, I feel like I've been winded. Anabel Adams in the flesh. Well, I guess she's Anabel Vincent now. The thought brings me back to reality with a thud, and I find myself sinking onto the step outside the shop door. She just came out of that shop, and now I can't quite bring myself to go inside. Not just yet anyway.

I have so many questions circling my brain, all desperate to be answered first. I can feel the pressure behind my eyes and I close them for a moment. My thoughts betray me when all I can see is her face—shocked, scared and horrified.

She ran.

Why did she run?

I know why, there's no point kidding myself. That night in the barn, I stopped her declaration of love, or whatever she was going to tell me. I stopped her for her own sake. She doesn't know. But how could I have told her the truth? I couldn't explain how I really felt. Let her end things with Keith to be with me? In a fantasy, that sounds perfect. Like a dream. The problem with that idea? It *is* a dream. What would have happened? I know she didn't look further than her feelings, I can understand that, but someone had to. I did what was best for her. The moment she walked into the barn, I was aware of her. I pretended I didn't know she was there… took the time to steady myself. My heart and head were at odds, and I needed to take control. I knew why she'd come, maybe even before she fully realized.

The minute she walked in, I'd wanted nothing more than to rush her and then keep her forever, I had grabbed her arms just to rein myself in. I was going away to play ball at college. She was staying here in this place. *With them.* If she left Keith to be with me and then I moved away to play college ball, she would have been here, on her own with Keith, his friends, and those bitches. No. It was too much, the wolves would have circled. As strong as she was, I'm sure they would have ripped her apart, worn her down and broken her. I didn't want that, not for Bel. So I decided the best thing to do was to leave her alone. The only problem with that was I broke my heart in the process.

And it's never recovered.

Anabel Vincent

Blinking against the light, I finally manage to open my eyes. As they start to adjust something suddenly blocks the sun from my face.

Keith.

"What the fuck are you doing out here?" he shouts down at me.

I try to take in my surroundings, I'm in the garden, laying on one of the two recliners he bought years ago. This one he leaves out in the garden, so he can relax while drinking beer. The other is in front of the television. He never offered one to me and he doesn't like me using either of them.

"Oh, I must have fallen asleep," I reply, my voice still tired as I yawn.

"Do you intend to lie on your fat ass all day?" he questions, but there's an undercurrent to his words.

"No, of course not, I have some work to do in town," I answer too quickly, not thinking straight and almost giving away what I'm supposed to be doing today.

"What work?" he snaps

"Oh, Pastor Wilson asked if I would help out with the old folks a bit more this week," I lie, plastering on a saccharine smile.

He glares at me, then replies with, "Old fuckers." He says no more and stomps away only turning around when he's nearly at the door to shout, "Get the fuck out of my chair." At his words, I scramble out of his chair thinking about what I can do to get him back for being a dick. For now, I need him out of my way, I have things to do today. Hopefully, these things will keep my mind away from thoughts of last night. I can't think about it because every time I do I want to throw up.

"So Mrs. Vincent, Pastor Wilson tells me that you're looking for a new challenge. You think this is it?" Mr. Cumberland asks me.

I look around the opulent dining room, wood and glass stare back at me, surrounding lovely French doors that lead out to a patio area. I've always wondered what the inside of The Hatfield Club looked like. There was a time my folks would come here. Once a week on Saturdays, their date night. They had good friends. They made good memories. I used to listen to their stories and feel like I'd been right here with them.

Looking back at Mr. Cumberland, I reply, "I've never worked Mr. Cumberland. I've been a housewife. Any job would be a new challenge for me, but somewhere like the Hatfield, somewhere special…" I pause as I watch the confusion pass over his face. Then I explain, "…special, because of the memories my parents made here. Memories they shared with me." I see pity briefly in his eyes and it makes my stomach sink. I hate pity, but it's the most common emotion I receive these days. I look around again. "I feel like I know this place just from their stories."

Mr. Cumberland coughs making me turn back to look at him. "Wednesday," he croaks out and I swear there's a glisten in his eyes. He stands up repeating himself, "Wednesday… that'll be your first shift. I know you've never been a waitress before, so I'll give you some time. Two weeks, I think. Then we'll meet again and review the arrangement. See Stella on your way out and she'll sort out your contract. Salary, uniform, hours and all that good stuff."

I stand with my mouth open, amazed that he's willing to give me a shot. Quickly shutting it again I offer him my hand, which he swiftly takes shaking it with a smile, but I just keep shaking forgetting to let go. In the end, when it's become slightly uncomfortable, he rips his arm away looking at me like I might be slightly mad.

My first stop after leaving the Hatfield is Pastor Wilson's house. I thank him over and over until the point comes that Martha has to pry me off him. They both have big toothy smiles as they see me off. It's only as I walk home, walk past Pop's shop, that I let the night before seep into my skin coating me with the truth that my mind has been trying to avoid.

Danny's back.

What does it mean?

Danny Quinn

"Mr. Quinn, Ms. Tinder has arrived," Layla tells me with reservation in her voice. She knows that I don't want to see her. She also knows that there's something off with me today, I think she can tell my mood has soured somewhat since yesterday, and it was already circling the drains.

"Thank you, Layla. Has she made an appointment?" I ask not looking up from my laptop. Since last night, I've tried to dive headfirst into work. Attempting to keep my mind trapped in a far safer subject, and failing in an epic way. No matter how hard I try, Bel is all I can think about.

"Shit," I growl and then realize as quiet descends on the room, that Layla has been talking and I've completely zoned out. Glancing up, I see the concern in her eyes. "My apologies. Please repeat what you were saying, I was reading something on here and missed everything," I lie, pointing at my laptop and laying the blame on the inanimate object.

Smiling, falsely, she repeats her words, "Ms. Tinder suggested dinner with you tonight. I subtly suggested a light late lunch this afternoon may be a better choice as your schedule is very busy," Layla relays her lies this time. We both know my schedule has almost been cleared at my request, but I appreciate her putting Ms. Tinder off. I'm not sure a viper at my dinner table is what I need tonight.

I feel the corners of my lips tip up. "Thank you, Layla. That brings me some relief. However, I still have to face her. So what time should I be downstairs to meet the voracious Ms. Tinder?" I ask feeling my energy draining already.

"You have an hour," Layla answers, then adds, "I'll call your room ten minutes prior to remind you." She then leaves me sitting staring at my laptop like a douche, wondering how I can get Ms. Tinder to understand that I'm not interested, without having to find another real estate agent.

"Fuck," I curse then go take a shower. I need to get ready for a few rounds with Gabrielle Tinder, the woman who never gives up.

"Gabrielle, these locations are great, but I have already told you what I want. This isn't it," I say handing back photos and paperwork she gave to me with details of possible new sites.

"Surely, Danny, there's something here that floats your boat?" she asks, casually touching my arm. This is no casual movement, though, even if she wants it to seem that way. I gently pull my arm away, hoping not to offend. If I have to make my point clearer I will, and I won't be making any apologies. But I believe in trying tact first. A frown appears in her eyes, I believe it's a frown, but it's hard to tell what's happening on her face as it hardly moves due to being over botoxed.

"I'm sorry that you seem to have wasted your time coming out here Gabrielle."

"It's never a waste when I get to see you, Danny. Would you like to meet for dinner tonight?" she asks almost offhandedly I would think if I didn't know better.

"Sorry, I have a prior engagement," I reply making no more of an explanation.

"Tomorrow?" Now she sounds almost desperate and I can feel the annoyance buzzing around in my head.

"Gabrielle, you need to find more sites. When you've found them, please let Layla know and we can arrange another meeting. Until then I really don't see what we have to discuss?" I tell her keeping my face impassive.

"Oh, yes, very well," she snaps getting up to leave. She walks away from our table and then seems to hesitate before turning around and coming back. "You know, Danny, I just wanted to have a meal with a friendly face. I came out here, obviously with the wrong intention, I can see that now, and maybe I'm a little overbearing but, at least I'm trying. Everyone knows that Shannon had to chase you for two years just to get you to date her. And now look, you're divorcing her. *You carry on this way and you'll die alone*," her voice rises with every word, the last part is shouted and now everyone in the dining room is staring at us. I stand up and Gabrielle blanches, her breathing heavy after the outburst.

"Ms. Tinder, I'm very sorry you feel that way. But I'm glad you were able to air your views, even if it was to everyone in here." I say, gesturing to the room. "Now that the air is cleared between us, and we both know where we stand, maybe you could get back to sourcing me a site for my new restaurant?" I question and then stride out the room to gazes of astonishment at the lunchtime show that she, maybe we, just provided.

"Ahhh," I let out a low rumble of pleasure as I stroll out of the sea. I feel refreshed, invigorated like I've washed the first half of the day away. Dropping my board and grabbing a towel, my day gets rocked for a second time in the space of a few hours when I finish drying my face and look up to see Bel sitting on the beach. It's obvious she hasn't spotted me as she stares out to sea, with what looks like a thousand things on her mind. I peer down at my board grabbing the back of my neck to take a minute. Gabrielle was right earlier. It did take Shannon years to even get me to date her, but not because I don't want to have someone, but because nobody has ever been her—Bel. Even so, Gabrielle doesn't really know me, none of them do. I'm used to getting what I want, and although I never really date and only married Shannon because she told me she was pregnant, I've had my fair share of women. I've never been shy of taking what I wanted. Bel, though… she brings out a different side of me, a loving side. A side no other woman has ever really experienced from me.

"Fuck," I whisper.

As I walk toward her, she lifts her head and I watch the second her brain registers who I am.

Anger, followed by sadness, then fear swim in her delicate green eyes. I stop at her feet.

"Bel." *I still can't believe I'm saying that name again.*

"Danny," she mutters and looks down at the sand.

I want to throw something and scream with happiness at the same time. I've thought about this moment for years. Never really knowing how I'd feel. Now I know. It's a mixture of anxiousness, anguish and hesitancy, all coated with a layer of hope.

Chapter EIGHT

Anabel Vincent

I'm not sure what I thought would happen by coming down here. He always came to the beach to surf, whenever he needed to relax. Everyone thought football was his thing, but I think he was born to be on the water. I didn't plan on seeing him here, although now he's back in town, the chances were fifty-fifty. I wasn't sure if he would still surf, but the passion he always had for it tells me I'm kidding myself by saying I didn't come down here for the sole purpose of seeing him. Now he stands in front of me and with my heart lodged in my throat, I don't know what to say. I catch his eyes then turn my head back to the sand, trying to gather my thoughts. Sighing he sits down at my side, pulling his wetsuit down to the waist. I can't see him as I stare at my toes immersed in the sand. I don't want to look, but I can feel him there, right next to me.

"Bel," he says my name again and a shiver runs down my back. That one word brings pain and comfort all at the same time. "What are you doing here?" he asks.

I pick up the sand and watch the grains run through my fingers. Heat radiates through my chest as I answer "I don't know why you're asking me that question. I live here. What the hell are you doing here?" my reply is filled with bitterness and I hate it.

Danny snorts, "Fair question. I came for business."

"You own my pop's ice cream parlor." It's not a question, I know the answer. Since running away from him I've pieced it all together, there's no other reason for him to have been there.

When he says nothing, I finally look up at him. He stares at me and nods, sadness or melancholy crossing his face, I'm not sure which. I don't know his looks anymore. It's been too long. Now that I'm staring at him, I can't tear my focus away from his face. His eyes are still piercing blue, and apart from having slightly gray bags underneath them, they look exactly the same. The features of his face burn a hole in the pocket that I keep his drawing in. I miss him. *Fuck, but I miss him.* I don't think I've realized how much until this very moment. It's easy to shut someone away. Put them in a box and lock it tight, when they're not in your life, refusing to go unheard. When they're there, in front of you, in all their glory… well, that's a different thing. He's still beautiful.

Fuck my life. Why couldn't he be fat and balding like Keith?

I look up to the sky. "Why have you cursed me?" I whisper.

"What?" he replies to my momentary loss of mouth control.

"Nothing," I mutter, annoyed. "Why?" I say the one word softly, hoping he'll understand. I'm not sure my voice is capable of saying much more, with each word the wobble in my throat gets harder to control.

"I came back once, years ago." His words make me look out to the sea, hurt that he didn't come find me. But at the same time knowing that he couldn't have. "I was thinking of buying a house here, after all, it is my hometown." He stops and I chance another look at him. His head hangs, he props his elbows on his knees which are bent up, and rubs his head with one hand. "I was only in town a day. I heard some things, things about how happy you were, I didn't want to see it, I was a coward, so I decided not to stay and to never come back. When I told the real estate agent to quit looking, I noticed your pop's shop. She said it was about to go on the market and I knew," he stops and takes a breath, turning toward me, "I knew, Bel…" the words spill softly from his lips, "…I had to buy it. I had to have a piece of you. I'm sorry, this is inappropriate, but you have to know the truth. You deserve it." His gaze swings back out to sea.

"Who said that?" My voice is barely audible.

"Said what?" His face is pulled in, lines etched across his forehead, showing his confusion.

"Who said I was happy?" At my words, his body rocks back slightly.

"You're not?" His question is like a bullet in my heart.

"Never…" is all I reply. Again afraid at the words, both good and bad that might slip out.

"Bel, I didn't… I never—"

I cut him off. "It doesn't matter. It didn't matter back then, so it sure as hell doesn't matter now." I stand up abruptly, feeling suddenly out of place. Brushing the sand off me, I walk away.

"Bel… Bel…" I continue moving. "Shit, Bel, don't keep walking away," he shouts and I spin around against my better judgment.

"Me!... Me walking away? That's rich coming from you!" He's made up most of the distance between us with his long strides, but I take the last step toward him. "You!" I point my finger towards his chest. "You left me. You fucking left me!"

Grasping the back of his neck he swallows, pain in his eyes. "I did what was best for you back then."

"Who are you trying to convince, Danny? Me or you?" I bite back.

"Bel… I… you would've been left behind."

"Whatever the choice it was mine to make. We both got closer. *Both of us.* We knew it, there was no denying what we felt back then. You could have talked to me. Instead, you made me feel worthless, like I was a game, a bit of fun while you were biding your time waiting for college."

"That was never how it was. If you didn't feel so bitter right now you'd see that," he argues back.

"Bitter? What exactly do you expect? You come back here, successful, still gorgeous. I'm sure the world would drop at your feet. What do you want from me? An ego boost? Well, here you go. I loved you back then. You know I did. If you were any kind of a man, you would admit that. You turned me away. Told me you didn't feel that way. You were a coward, and because of that I condemned myself to the life I got. Don't worry, that's not your fault, I'm taking full responsibility for my own fuck ups. You should do the same." My voice is starting to break and I need to get away from here. My whole body feels weak. I thought I was stronger than this, but I'm not. I'm getting there, but this is too much. It's an emotional overload and not in a good way. I take him in, I can't help it, there's something that will always draw me to him. His head is bowed, hair wet, and I watch the droplets of water chasing each other down his chiseled jawline. The pain etched across his face causes an ache in my chest. I need to escape before I'm crippled with his pain as well as my own. Leaving him standing there, I once again start to make my way from the beach.

"Bel, I wanted to be with you. You have to believe that. You're the only woman I ever really wanted. I would always choose you," he tells me, his voice tight.

Looking over my shoulder as I continue walking, throwing my parting shot, "That's good for you, that you would choose me *now*. But know this, Danny, you didn't *choose* me that night and you took *my* choice away, when you sent me from you as a hormonal teen, believing what you said was gospel. You took my choice from me. I can't forgive that." I try to ignore the look on his face as I turn back and commence walking. Knowing he can't see me. He can't see the tears free falling, he can't hear the moment my already battered heart stops beating.

Danny Quinn

"Fuck… fuck, fuck, fuck!" I watch her leave. I can't do this again. I can't watch her walk away. I can't try to be the good guy. Shit, this time, I know I won't be the good guy if I let her go. With my wetsuit half off and water still dripping, I run after her. The wind feels cold on my face as I jog across the beach. Fuck! I'd forgotten how hard it is to run in sand. I keep my eyes on her back as she darts across the road and then skirts along the sidewalk until she reaches the bus stop, then I watch her sink onto the bench. Leaning forward she pulls her legs up resting her heels on the edge of her seat then buries her head in her knees. Even from here, I can see her shoulders shaking. She doesn't know I'm chasing her as she allows the emotion to overtake her. I get closer having no idea what I need to say, but knowing I need to say something. I move over to her, watching as her back stiffens then relaxes again. She must think I'm just someone waiting for a bus. I take another step until I'm in front of her and crouch down, looking up into her eyes.

"Bel," I whisper and her back stiffens again but she says nothing.

"Go away," she sobs. "Please. Allow me *some* dignity." I grind my teeth at her words. I want to know what's happened in her life. Why she hasn't been happy? At the beach, I had time to take her in. Her beauty has grown. She's naturally stunning. I've never forgotten her eyes, and although they are so much sadder now than they ever were before, they can still mesmerize me.

"Bel," I plead. "I just want to talk to you," I murmur, my hand lingers in the air above her knees, but I pull it away before allowing it to touch her. Knowing that will be a step too far. She barely wants to talk to me, she's not going to be happy if I lay my hand on her, as much as my body naturally wants to.

"I can't do this right now. Please leave me alone." She sniffles, and although her head is buried, I can hear her voice yielding. Like the fight has left her. And it hurts. Bel always fights, she's a survivor. Now she sounds pliant and it doesn't suit her.

"Okay, not now. I'll leave you alone right now, but tomorrow I'm going to the shop. I'll be there from ten until eleven in the morning. Then I'll go back in the evening, four until six. Come see me, Bel. Please? Even if it's only for ten minutes. Please come see me," I beg her. Still she says nothing, so I sigh and walk away. *Again.* I can't keep leaving this woman who holds my heart, even if she doesn't realize it. Every time I do, it breaks me a little more.

"Sir?"

The word sounds muffled like I'm underwater. Or maybe they are.

"Sir, are you okay?" The words are nearer now, but as I attempt to move my head in the direction of the voice, the whole of my body suddenly becomes a lead weight and I find myself stuck in place. I feel a warm hand on my shoulder before I register the voice again. “Mr. Quinn, I’m usually reluctant to advise you on your drinking. However, in this case, people are staring, and I’m not entirely sure this is the way you want to be seen.” My brain finally connects with the voice.

“Layla.” I will myself to raise my head, which I realize now is laying cheek down on top of a bar. The moment I move my face toward her the room spins and blurs. I know Layla is closer when I smell her scent. Then she talks and her hot breath flutters across my cheek.

“Mr. Quinn, I need you to assist me, I’m trying to guide you to your room. The hotel staff have asked me to remove you from the bar area, other guests have complained. Especially as some families are now trying to dine. An evening meal with their children and you’re completely intoxicated and trying to sleep on the bar.”

“Only my face,” I tell her unnecessarily.

“Okay, Sir, only your face is resting on the bar. Either way, you need to leave as they don’t want someone as intoxicated as you asleep on their bar at six on a Monday evening.”

Forcing my body to stand, pulling my muscles tight and stretching my tingling legs, I realize most of the people at the bar and in the restaurant are staring at me. I take them all in with a slow perusal, stopping on the ladies and letting the corners of my mouth tip up in a grin. Their eyes change quickly from scrutiny to hunger, a few even lick their lips. I allow Layla to move me through the restaurant until we reach the bank of elevators.

"She hates me," I explain uncharacteristically once we get inside.

"I'm sure she doesn't," Layla replies pressing the button for my suite.

"I broke her," I continue, ignoring her words and hanging my head as I lean against the wall.

"You can make it up to her." She sighs, and my brain somehow registers the exhaustion in her voice.

"How do you know what I'm talking about anyway?" My mind has managed to pick up on the flow of conversation and piece it together.

"You kept talking about it at the bar. Just to yourself from what I could make out, but still, there was enough information for me to piece together and I know the history, remember Danny?" She only uses my first name when I've worn her down so much that her professionalism goes out the window. It's rare, and it makes me take notice. "For her to react that way means she still loves you. She may be hiding it, even from herself. But it's there. There cannot be that much hurt, pain, and anger for someone who means nothing if she'd moved on then you wouldn't matter. And you obviously do."

Her words try to pass through the mess that is my head right now, and I wonder if I still have a shot.

Looking at Layla and whispering, “I still love her.”

“I know,” she replies, but I don’t miss the sad smile that lingers in her eyes before she clears it.

I close my eyes and wonder what to do. I can’t watch her walk away again, but there are other things to consider. Will I make her life harder if I push? She’s fragile like she’s holding herself together by sheer willpower alone. I’ve caused Bel enough pain already, I don’t want to be the reason that the sadness surrounding her, finally destroys her.

Chapter NINE

Anabel Vincent

There are times in your life you make *the right decision*. The decision that's best for everyone. The choice that you feel needs to be made like someone is guiding you and steering you down the path that was always meant to be *just yours*. Then there are the decisions that you make for yourself. Either because you don't have to worry about anyone else, or maybe, because for once, you'd like to choose something to make *you* happy. Sometimes you make those decisions because you're sick of making the other choice all the time, always taking the same route. None of it really matters, we go on a journey, whether it's hard or easy, triumphant or failing, long or short, it's a journey all the same. As long as we learn from it, become better people for it, grow and evolve and someday impart our wisdom to someone who needs it, then we should class it as a win. *So why do I second guess everything I do?*

When I pulled myself out of bed this morning, I momentarily thought about making Keith his breakfast as I have for all these years. It's routine, not so much a choice as it is a chore that's been drummed into my subconscious. My responses are automatic, just like the way I deal with him and have dealt with him for all these years.

I married him.

That's on me, it was my choice.

A decision I made.

I was stronger back then, I could have stopped it—said no. I chose to marry him because I was hurt. I realize now that what happened was just Danny making his own choice. He thought what he was doing made things easier for me. But I'd already made my decision, so when he told me that what I wanted was no longer a possibility, I crumbled. I was led easily after that, mainly by my fear. Looking back at my young self, I realize I was still trying to work out the world and my place in it. When Danny rejected me, I assumed it was because I was unworthy. Keith was a sure bet, so it made sense to stick with him. A few years, and some experience later, my life outlook has changed dramatically. I've always been treated like a second class citizen by Keith, but it's not really his fault. He wouldn't be able to treat me that way if I hadn't enabled him to.

I've made this my life. There's no one else to take the blame. The fault sits squarely on my shoulders. That was my realization this morning. So when I finally pulled myself out of bed, I decided to do something different, something for me. I ignored Keith's breakfast and walked out. In times past, I would have made my way to the shop, hiding in my own head, debating with myself over what I should do. Then after hours of internal chatter, I would go home, mentally exhausted and no further forward. Nothing changes and I've been a coward for so many years it's hard to know if there's anything else in me anymore.

So this morning, still not really having any answers, and aware that I couldn't use the shop as my escape, I chose to walk down the unused, dusty road opposite the house I share with Keith. Deciding to see where it took me. Years ago the path would have led to the Millar farm, but they moved away, selling the land for development. It never became anything, other than a natural jungle, if the overgrowing grass and weeds were anything to go by. The path did lead into a forest area, which meant I was walking somewhere that probably hadn't been walked on for years. Somewhere I was unlikely to be found. What worried me, was that I didn't care if something happened to me, if I was never found. I wasn't scared, it was excitement that I felt, the idea that I could slip away. Now, two hours of walking later, I want to clear my head, and I find myself sitting by a lake I didn't know existed, with my head more messed up than ever.

I'm not sure how long I've been sitting here, staring at the almost still water of the lake.

Water shouldn't be still, should it?

Water should move and flow and continually dance. This water seems stagnant, and something about that sits uneasily in the pit of my stomach. Like it's a metaphor for my life. I left the house early this morning, I've been gone for hours and have no idea what time it is. What I do know is that I need to go to the shop and speak to Danny, I just hope I haven't missed that opportunity.

It takes me ages to get into town. Taking the long way and weaving in and out of the overgrown bushes and through the forgotten fields. Even though I may be too late, I still walk slowly, watching the birds as they circle in the evening sunshine. I need to take my time and I drag my feet doing just that. I don't really know what I'm doing. The explanation that Danny wants to give me is both important and irrelevant at the same time, if that's even possible. I feel like the reasoning behind his decision has already been aired, I'm not sure what else he can tell me, or where he wants us to go from here. But there's a need in me, a desire to know all, to hear the soft words fall from his lips. I haven't had soft loving words spoken to me for years, and although it's selfish, I want that—what's more important is that I want that with Danny. *Only Danny.* Today, I'm making a choice just for me. My gait speeds up as I hit the town and the hard asphalt brings me back to the here and now. Reaching the door, I pull on the handle with purpose, glad that it's still unlocked, it means he's still here.

"Bel," I hear the soft word and look straight up into startling blue eyes once again.

"Danny," I whisper so quietly my own ears barely register the name as it spills from my lips.

My eyes graze his features, etching them once again in my memory. His face is older, but he's only got better with age. Danny reaches his hand toward me, before widening his eyes and allowing it to drop back to his side.

"I'm glad you came," he says gesturing to the kitchen area. It's private in there, and I let out a relieved breath. I don't want to be out the front of shop where people can see me, especially in the daytime. Moving through the place I know so well, seeing nothing is different, gives me a sense of peace. Now Danny is here, I figured he'd be changing things, or maybe he just hasn't started yet. I meet his eyes and quickly avert mine, every time I look at him it burns. He still does it for me. Chiseled features, piercing eyes, and although I haven't really seen it yet, his captivating smile, still adorns him. As I study Danny, my heart picks up speed. He must still keep himself in shape if the Henley he's wearing stretched across his chest, showcasing every ripple hiding behind the material, is anything to go by. I have to stop before I feel nothing but lust. Right now, I need a clear head.

"Amanda's coming back," I blurt the words and drop down into a chair. I have no idea why I told him that, other than having something to say.

"Where has she been?" he asks. I notice his voice is solid, level, he's keeping his feelings locked down. Something I need to get better at doing.

"She's lived in France the last ten years, teaching English. She got married a few years ago. Pierre and Amanda dated for five years. It seems strange telling you this stuff, Danny, I feel like you should already know it." I turn away feeling my face heat at the same time wanting to cry, knowing how far removed we have become from one another.

"Hey," Danny's voice pulls me back to him as it always did. "I *should* have known it, I *should* have been here. I wish I'd never left." He shakes his head and moves away, looking out to the shop floor. "I never wanted to, you know that now." He sighs and looks back at me. "I felt it every day, you have to understand that."

I frown, not really sure what he's trying to say. "What did you feel?"

"Broken. Without you, I've always been broken." My lungs seize and for a few seconds there is no air, no blood pumping through my system, nothing, just shock. Then all at once the words slam into me and I stand, walking over to him.

"Danny…" I have nothing else to say, I'm not sure what any of this means, we're not eighteen anymore. I step up to him and grab his upper arms. "Danny," I breathe his name out, heat prickling my skin. He looks down at me and I feel the emotion creep up my throat. "I wanted… I always needed… you were…" My words get caught, but it doesn't matter. Danny leans down pressing his lips against mine. They're soft but firm. I close my eyes as I feel his big hand wrap around the back of my head, his other hand moves to my back between my shoulders, and he pulls me into him. I feel his thumb stroke the back of my ear and down my neck as his lips move over mine, softly, reverently, caressing me. It's a kiss that doesn't ask for any more. Just the need to be close, to touch. I press my body against him like I'm trying to sink into him altogether. I've missed Danny, everything about him. The truth, which I can't allow myself to ignore anymore, is that I will always want this man… I'll always love this man. I pull back and look into his surprised eyes.

"Bel, it's always been you and me. Don't run, please don't run," he pleads, I can hear the break in his voice as he wills me to stay. My hands shake and I look down at them, catching the glint of the cheap wedding band on my ring finger. I know what I need to do, but I have to do this the right way. If I'm gonna be free, then I firstly have to be me, just me.

"I can't, Danny. Not now. You don't have to wait, but if you do, then I'll be your friend. It's all I can offer right now," I explain, before turning and walking out, moving further away from all my broken pieces. Every shard—Danny holds them all in his hands.

Chapter TEN

Anabel Vincent

I can't sleep. I've been lying here for two hours now, looking out the window at the silver moon, casting its light across my bed. I wish I could blame my lack of sleep on Keith, on him and his stupid friends making noise. But unusually, he's quiet. When I came home today, he was pissed.

> *"Where the fuck have you been?" His words assaulted me the moment I stepped through the back door.*
>
> *"I went for a walk." I heard my own words and they sounded as though they came from someone else. The tone was flat, bored even.*
>
> *"Listen, woman," Keith snapped and grabbed my arm, hauling me back into his space. His eyes were threatening, and unlike I'd ever seen before.*

The whiskey was wafting from his mouth, carried to my nostrils with every breath. "You do not leave this house without making my breakfast. How the fuck do you expect me to go to work if you haven't made my food?" He was breathing hard and the momentary flash of fear ebbed away as I looked at him. The only emotion he emitted from me these days was repulsion. I snatched my arm away.

"You're a grown man, Keith. You can make your own damn breakfast. I needed a walk, some fresh air."

His hand raised before I even realized it. As it swooped down, I thought about how in all these years, I'd always considered myself lucky because he'd never hit me. Suddenly in mid-air he stopped, letting his hand drop to his side. He shook his head, sneered at me and stalked off. I spent the rest of the day–and night–in my room. Both confused and deflated.

I knew before today that I had changed. Before my new job, before Amanda's revelation, before Danny arriving, and before Keith raised his hand to me. Today's events have just made me face the fact that I need to step up my game. This needs to be done quicker, and I need to get a plan together.

My first day at The Hatfield Club goes better than I expect it to. Although I must admit, waiting on people who mostly look down their noses at the wait staff throws me slightly. It momentarily makes me question whether my parents acted this way. I certainly never noticed it if they did. But even with a few superior acting customers, my shift mostly flies by. I get to meet Duncan and Selma. They're both older than me and friendly enough. Just before I clock out we have a few minutes to chat. I tell them why I was happy to get this job, and how my parents used to come here. It comes to light that they knew them. Suddenly, I'm enveloped in kindness from virtual strangers. I bask in it. I'm not too proud to let someone show me kindness, I only hope one day I can show someone else the same. As I walk home distracted by the day, I don't notice until the last minute that I'm walking toward Declan. I always avoid Keith's friends when he isn't there. Declan is something else, though, with his wandering hands and innuendos.

"Anabel, looking good sweetheart," he oozes like slime and I feel a shiver creep up my back.

"Declan." I move to walk past him, wrinkling my nose.

“Where are you going?” he asks grabbing my wrist.

“Home,” I lie.

“You have two minutes to stop and chat with an old friend.” He smirks at me. I rip my arm from his grasp. If I won’t let Keith tether me anymore, then I’m certainly not going to let his awful friends do it.

“You’re not my friend, Declan. You belong to Keith, and if I had my way you wouldn’t step foot anywhere near where I am.” I move to walk past him, but he grabs me around the waist this time and pulls me flush into his body. He’s so close I can feel his breath on my face.

“Now *you listen to me*,” he spits. “Keith might let you answer back, but I’m not Keith. You’ve been giving me signs for years, and you know you want me.” He tries to pull my waitress dress up. In that moment, every bit of vulnerability I’ve shown to Keith and his friends over the years runs like a movie reel through my head. I’ve had enough.

I’m not a possession.

I’m not a slave.

I’m not worthless.

And I’m not helpless.

Not anymore. I move my leg back slightly, and just as Declan pushes my dress up my thigh, I use all my force bringing up my knee straight into his balls. He drops instantly, crying out in pain, and although I can see he probably wants to cuss me out, he can’t, his face is red as he struggles to cry and breathe at the same time.

"Don't ever touch me," I seethe then turn and walk away. I come to a halt the instant I see Danny walking around the corner. He stops, stock still, on the other side of the road. I quickly walk on, not knowing what to say or do. I haven't stopped thinking about him since our kiss, and although I offered him friendship, I'm not entirely sure how I can give him that. Not until I get out from under Keith's footprint.

"Bel." Danny runs up beside me and matches my gait as I continue walking.

"Not now, Danny."

"Later then?"

I shake my head. "We'll see, I'm not sure," I mutter distractedly.

"No, Bel," his demand is growled from beside me.

I stop, which makes him jolt to a stop too. We stare at each other for a few seconds and I can feel myself bristling from everything that's happened recently. "If you think I'm going to realize my worth, finally, after all these years where Keith's concerned, only to have another man try to command me, then you are very much mistaken," I snap. Only then do I realize I'm pointing my finger at his chest. Pausing, I look at my finger then back at his chest, slightly stunned that I'm being so aggressive.

Shrugging, then turning around to leave, I stop when Danny says, “Please, Bel.” I deflate slightly and turn to face him once again.

“I didn’t really see what just happened with Declan, but I could clearly see your anger. Are you okay?” I don’t answer right away, thinking through what just occurred.

“Yeah. I actually am.”

He nods. “Okay, that’s good enough for me. I wasn’t trying to push you, Bel. I’m aware that you need space. That you need to sort your head out. But seeing the look in Declan’s eyes, even if he was writhing around on the floor…” he stops clenching his jaw. I watch, fascinated, as his blue eyes narrow and a cold look slithers across his face. “I wanted to go back and teach him some manners. I second guessed myself, because I’m sure Keith doesn’t know I’m back in town yet, and I don’t think for one second he’d be pleased if he thought his wife was spending any time with me.”

“I’m not, though,” I point out, throwing my hands in the air.

“Do you think that nugget of information would stop him being pissed if Declan told him you were with me? Would he believe you over Declan? I’ve been listening since your revelation at the beach, saying you weren’t happy. And as far as I’ve overheard through town gossip, you don’t have a good relationship." He crosses his arms over his chest.

My thoughts scatter. The young girl in me wants to tell Danny everything, I want him to be my knight in shining armor, my hero. But the woman I want to be—the one that knows, in order to survive and to succeed must be able to look at herself in the mirror with pride—she needs to come forward to be the hero and the savior. "My relationship isn't good. I'm pretty sure our kiss proved that. That shouldn't have happened, no matter what. I still live under his roof and we're still together." I watch anguish flicker in his bright blue eyes. "I told you I could offer friendship and I can, but I need time. There are some things I need to sort out." I glance over my shoulder, hoping we haven't been spotted. I only moved into a side street when I left Declan, there's always the possibility that he could appear any second.

"I won't be here forever, Bel." His words surprise me, not because I expect him to wait around, but because he's the one who wants more from me this time, and he knows the situation I'm in.

"Nice of you to let me know," I snap at him. "You come back here *after you left me*. You now know what that did to me? I'm shocked that you're back at all, let alone telling me how you feel and what you want. You're aware of my situation. That I'm married. So you could cut me some slack," I puff out my frustration, and only then I notice Danny's jaw working, his body taut, and the whites of his knuckles showing on his clenched fists.

"I get it," he grinds the words out through his locked jaw. "I hurt you. You're angry. You have every right to be, and yes I can give you time. But I won't give you forever. I'm not going to wait around like a puppy. You're so angry about the past, something I did when I was still a boy, something I thought I was doing for you. I get that. You're still hurt, I understand. What *you* have to get, is that I'm also hurting still. I've been hurting every damn day since I let you walk away, ripping my heart out with every step you took." His words are like machine gun fire, pushing holes through every part of my body. Spinning around, Danny walks away, and I can't move until he's disappeared from my sight, until I feel less like I might throw up the contents of my stomach at any second.

I'm still reeling from everything when I walk into the house that evening. Keith is in front of the television. "Get me a beer," he says by way of a greeting as I shrug my jacket off.

Sighing, I look at the ceiling. "Get your own," I tell him as I move toward the stairs. I make it to my bedroom before the door is thrown open, smashing against the wall.

"The fuck you say?" Keith spits to my back.

I close my eyes then turn to face him. The man who I've allowed to have so much control over my life for all these years. This man who doesn't really love me, but instead feels like he owns me. "I'm done."

His eyes widen for a second then they narrow and he clenches his fists. "We're done when I say we are, and not a second before."

"You have no hold over me anymore. I told you, Keith. I'm done."

"And I don't think you're listening. This isn't a choice you get to make. We were married in God's house. You agreed to obey me, so fucking obey!"

"*No!*" I scream. The word is raw and painful and freeing all at the same time.

Keith launches himself forward and grips me around the throat, pushing me up against the wall. It shocks me, but not as much as it should do. He places his mouth near my ear and speaks quietly, menacingly. "I fucking own you. You think I'm going to allow another man to screw you? That I'll let the whole fucking town laugh at me, or say, *oh look, there's Keith, the one whose wife is a whore.* You will do as you're told. Fall into fucking line or I *will* make you."

"If I mean so much to you, if you supposedly own me, then tell me why you've never told Declan to back off me. You can't pretend you've never seen him touching me?" I growl out. I'm scared, my heart is thumping against my ribs, but still, I need to say this and I can't go back now. I will *not* allow myself to be his doormat for another decade.

He steps back from me. I take him in. His anger hasn't completely subsided as he tries to stare me down. I feel the white hot rage penetrate me. "He hasn't… he wouldn't. Nobody would want you these days." His voice wavers as he continues to rein in his self-control.

"*Fucking let me go then!*" I scream. I can see he's taken aback. I breathe heavily. "Just let me go." The hushed words are ripped from somewhere inside my soul. The pain and sadness I've endured for years, rises to the surface, giving me the resolve I need, while causing my body to feel heavy, but strong.

"I can't! You need me, you're nothing without me." His sentence ends on a sneer.

I sit on the bed and watch as his chest puffs out, he thinks he's defeated me again. "See, Keith, that's where you're wrong. Look at me, take a good look. I'm not the same woman I once was. Something has happened in the last few days. I know what I'm worth, and it's more than you. You can't break me down anymore. I've done enough of that to last me a lifetime, and I finally realize what I need to do." I stand up and take a step toward him. "I need to be alone. Keith, you don't love me, be honest with yourself." I haven't stood this close to him in years, and I really look at his face. Although his looks have been lost, mainly through drinking, he could easily get them back if he took more pride in his appearance and stopped with the whiskey. His friend choice might need to be revised. But he could move on, find someone else, because if he met the right woman I have no doubt he wouldn't be this way, this unhappy. When he says nothing, I continue filling the silence, "You could be happy with someone else. We've always been a mistake. I think we know that. We've always known. Aren't you sick of living this life, unhappy and empty?"

I'm shocked when I watch a tear slip down his face. "I loved you." His voice is croaky. "I really did, but I knew I wasn't who you wanted. I wasn't him. Even back then, I did some things I wasn't proud of. Then when you came back to me, I knew I had to make you mine. But the truth is, you were never mine. I kept you like I'd won a prize." He moves to sit on my bed and rubs his hand down his face, sniffing. "I treated you like crap all these years… when I should've treated you like a gift, because you are." He looks up at me and I know my mouth is hanging open, I just can't do anything to shut it. All the years I wanted to hear him say these things and now it's too late.

"Keith..." my voice fades as my words clog in my throat.

Keith stands up pulling me into him and holding me. "Just be happy, Anabel," he whispers in my ear. I don't move as I listen to him leave the house. Ten minutes later I've packed up the small amount of things I own, and I make my way to Pastor Wilson's house.

Knocking at the door, I wait hearing shuffling.

"Who is it?" Martha calls out through the door.

"It's Anabel," I say softly.

She unbolts the door and swings it open, obviously concerned as its past ten in the evening. I hold the storm door open and she looks between me and my suitcase. "Finally." She smiles.

Chapter ELEVEN

Anabel Vincent

"Calm down, sweetheart," Pastor Wilson tells me. Looking over at him I smile, but don't calm down even a little bit. Amanda is arriving today. When speaking to her last week, she gave me the final dates. After I told her that I'd left Keith and she shrieked with glee non-stop for a solid three minutes, I offered to meet her at the airport. It would have taken every penny I've managed to save so far from my job, but it would have been worth it. Amanda told me not to worry, she was arriving with Pierre and would come to me. I wasn't sure exactly when she was arriving, she'd been kind of sketchy on the details. I'd wondered if it was because she thought that after arrival they would be jetlagged, obviously needing a couple of days to recuperate, and maybe she was concerned that I'd be upset at not being her first stop. I mull that thought over for a second.

"What's wrong?" Feeling Martha's hand touch my shoulder as her words reach my ears.

Turning around, I drop my gaze to the floor. "I don't know, I mean, there are things I'm worrying about…" I look back up and meet her eyes. "Things I never would've even considered years ago. It's just been so long. What if the friendship we had isn't there anymore?" Sighing, I sit back down in the chair next to the window.

"Oh, Anabel. Your feelings are understandable, you haven't seen her for many years." I glance out of the window again. "Still, don't forget how you were. I know you've both grown up and changed, but in your soul, you'll always be those young girls. I believe that your soul is at its truest form when you're a child because that's when you can be who you genuinely are, who you were always meant to be. Your souls will recognize each other, it may be awkward, but it will still be you two. You still talk every week. You still love her. She's your sister… even if not by blood, right?"

Grabbing Martha's hands, I squeeze them in mine and whisper, "Yes… you're right. Thank you."

She smiles at me as I hear a car pulling up outside, jumping up with a squeak, Martha chuckles then I run outside. The car door doesn't even close behind Amanda as I rush her, pulling her tiny body into mine and clinging on for dear life, all the awkwardness I was worried about only moments ago completely forgotten.

"Bellie," she whispers.

"Mandie-moo," I reply. After holding her for what would probably be considered inappropriate if it were anyone else, I pull back taking her in. Her body is smaller, she's lost weight, although she was always tiny, but now she seems even smaller. "You look great," I whisper, although I'm not entirely sure if *great* was the word I was searching for. She certainly looks different, though.

"You're kind to me, Bellie," she says blushing. "Come on, take me in to see Pastor and Mrs. Wilson." I nod, grasping her hand as though she might disappear at any minute and drag her inside the house.

"Do you remember this place?" I glance back at Amanda, waiting for her answer.

"Of course, why wouldn't I?" she replies stopping in her tracks.

Sighing, I take a seat on the swing. It's really too small for me now, this registers as I try squeezing my butt in between the chains and kick one foot off the ground, starting the back and forth momentum.

"You've just been gone so long, Amanda." I stop talking and stare down at my feet. A shadow passes over me and my swing jolts to a stop as another pair of feet come into my eye line. I look up as Amanda crouches down in front of me.

"I've been gone for a long time, you're right, but you're in my thoughts every day. You've always been here," she tells me pointing to her heart. "You know it was always you and me against the world. We have so many memories, both good and bad. They belong to us, no one can ever take them away from us, baby girl. Never forget, Anabel." She grabs my hand. "Never forget." Her voice is a whisper, and I close my eyes as she moves in to hold me. I take in her scent, it's different to what she used to wear, but her signature citrus and vanilla smell still drifts from her skin, the same way it always did. The bubble of emotion I've been holding in for so long finally breaks within me as a sob erupts from my chest.

"I've missed you. I've been so alone." The words are like ripping a Band-Aid from my heart.

"Shhh, it's okay. I'm here now. I'm staying." Amanda's words jolt me and I lift my face from her tear-stained shoulder.

"You're staying?" I hiccup while speaking and she smiles.

"Yeah. I gave up my job. Pierre, he's not coming here." She turns her face away from me and I have a sinking feeling.

"Hey," I say softly placing my hand on her cheek and guiding her eyes—which now hold her own tears—back to me. "What's happened?"

"He's having a hard time at the moment. There's stuff that's happened in his past, and because of that, we're struggling. I don't think he's going to be joining me, but it's okay, my pop is coming back with me," she says with a small, lopsided smile.

"Really! Where is he? I can't wait to see him." My excitement washes away the sadness that surrounded us only a moment ago. My heart hasn't felt so full in such a long time.

"Relax Bellie, he's going to be here in a few weeks. There's some stuff he has to settle in Paris. I have so much to tell you. First come with me, I want to take you somewhere." Standing up from the swing, the seat comes with my butt. "Guess we should think about a new hangout now, you know, somewhere our butts fit in the seats," Amanda tells me winking.

"Yeah, that would be great. Although it has been just as nice coming here," I tell her, looking back to the park as we walk away. "You know, in all honesty, I've avoided all of our places as much as possible over the years. When you left, my heart broke," I admit and Amanda reaches over grabbing my hand briefly.

"I hated leaving you, I wanted to drag you with me." She shrugs her shoulders and the corner of her mouth twitches.

"I know, but you were making a better life for yourself," I reply. "I wanted that for you. It's just… you've been my sister, not just my best friend since we were born. Our parents, then us, your dad is like an uncle," I explain wrapping my arms around myself protectively. "It was harder after Mom and Pop died, because you came back, and left again." I look up at the sky thinking about my parents momentarily, then shake my head and look back at Amanda's face. "Sorry… I sound like I'm complaining and I'm totally not. It's just, I've never loved someone in the way I love you." I chuckle to myself sadly. "When you're here for me to talk to at any time my world sits straight. Having you to hug, or for me to make things better for you. For us to laugh and joke and have fun. Even talking about boys or the bitchy girls like we used to. Without you, my world is tilted. I've been tilted." Releasing my arms, I thread my fingers through hers. "You give me strength and make me more like I'm worth something. I've gotten so heavy and you've only been back for a few hours." I giggle and watch as a tear escapes down her face, over her perfect cheekbone and resting at her chin before falling to the floor.

She takes my free hand in hers. “You were the first person outside of my parents that I loved Bellie, that’ll never change. I’m sorry I’ve been gone so long, but I’m here now, so let’s make up for it, yeah?” I nod and watch her smile, then she leads me to her car.

“Where are we going?” I ask once we’re on the road again.

“You’ll see.” She turns and winks before facing forward. “I put some music together,” Amanda says and I can hear the happiness in her tone, which in turn makes me happy. She fiddles with some buttons then suddenly *Cover Girl* by New Kids on the Block blasts from the speakers. Amanda laughs then throws one hand up hooting, before singing the song to me, while glancing over and pointing at me, in-between watching the road. Laughing, I join her in singing the song. We both loved NKOTB. We were total fangirls. We had our favorites, Donnie being Amanda’s, Joe being mine. This song was supposed to be for a boy to sing to his girlfriend, but Amanda and I always sang it to each other, just a little way in which we said how much we loved each other. I’m guessing from her beaming smile, she still loves me just as much as I love her. As I study her the realization hits me, I have no idea how I’ve lived all these years without her by my side.

Twenty minutes later and we’re pulling into a road I’ve avoided for over a decade. “What are we doing here, Moo?" I ask, using the nickname I gave her in third grade.

"When I say I'm coming back… I mean right back. Right to the beginning." Her words stop as we pull up outside her childhood home. The only home I've ever known sits nestled next to it. I look between the two houses and feel a swirl of emotion burn in my chest. I haven't been back to either of these houses since my mom passed. I left Keith to deal with everything after I took what sentimental things I wanted. The only place I've ever actively visited is the store. Staring at the houses means I miss it when Amanda gets out of the car. But a moment later she's swinging my door open and looking down at me. "Come on. I want to see how much my old home has changed." Amanda's smile lights up her whole face and I immediately drop my fear and take her hand, knowing when we're together we can conquer anything.

"Hurry up, slow poke!" Amanda's voice carries up the stairs and I rush to put my lipstick on. After an emotional day spent at her new... um, old house—something I haven't even begun to process yet—we visited our old school and the beach. Then we went to some of the other places we used to spend time at, like the skate park. Now we're about to head out to dinner at a nice restaurant the next town over. Having all my belongings—which isn't much—in suitcases at the Wilson's is proving to be a pain. But I can't afford rent at the moment, and Pastor Wilson says that paying for a hotel is money down the drain, when I could, instead, stay with them and save for a deposit and the first month's rent. Applying a light dab of pink on my lips and grabbing my purse, I hurry downstairs.

"Finally!" Amanda moans.

"Stop complaining. God, I remember this, always hurrying me," I reply.

"Well, I wouldn't have to if you were ever ready on time!" she shoots back. We stop and look at each other before both dissolving into giggles. "Ah! I've missed this!" she squeaks excitedly.

"Yeah, me too, Moo… me too." Sighing I grab her arm, threading mine through hers. "Come on, take me in your carriage and feed me, woman," I demand and she grins. I glance back to Martha. "I might not be back tonight, so please don't leave the door unlocked. If it gets too late, I'll sleep in Amanda's double bed at the hotel."

"Don't worry dear, you just go and enjoy yourself. Heaven knows you need it!" Smiling at Martha's words I move to kiss both her and then Pastor Wilson on the cheek before Amanda ushers us outside and onto our journey.

"Do you remember the time that Declan got drunk, then tried it on with you?" Amanda asks.

"Vaguely," I reply.

"Yes, you know, he tried it on, said he was a great kisser and that you needed to give him a test run. You shot him down. Poof!" Amanda shoots an imaginary gun with her fingers and giggles. Having had quite a few to drink, I can only assume she's trying to beat back the sadness she must feel at whatever's going on with Pierre. "Then Jenny sidled up to him, but even in his drunken state, he turned her down. She was not happy. Like a cat in a bath, she got those claws out." Amanda giggles again, obviously remembering a funnier version than me. "Then she tried to be nasty to you, but Danny shut her down… like immediately." My body locks at the mention of his name, but she doesn't realize. Instead, looking past me and signaling the barman. We've been here a while. We ate, laughed, caught up, and honestly, it's like she never went away. I'm once again feeling thankful that we have such a genuinely amazing relationship. After dinner, Amanda wanted to sit at the bar, so that's where we've been. She's been drinking like it's going out of fashion, which made me decide to remain sober. "I wonder what happened to him." Although her words are directed at me, she isn't. "Can I have another?" she asks the barman, holding her empty glass in the air. He nods and sets about topping up her vodka.

"I saw him," I tell her and watch as she sobers up in a matter of seconds.

"You did," The whispered surprise in her tone makes me smile, then she leans forward and grabs my arm. "Tell me everything."

I think about Danny for a moment. "God, I never stopped loving him, Moo." I release the words I've been avoiding even thinking to myself for so many years. "He kissed me." Her eyes widen at my statement. "He bought my pop's ice cream store." Her jaw drops. "He wants to be with me… I think. I mean, he hasn't said those exact words, but he did say he's felt broken without me every day since he let me walk out of that barn."

"Wow," Amanda murmurs.

"Yeah. The thing is, I want to be with him. I do. I just can't yet."

"Why not?" she asks shaking her head at me.

"I… I don't know. I guess before it was because I was still with Keith—"

She cuts me off. "Bellie, you haven't *been* with Keith for years."

"Yes, but I'm still his wife."

"So what?" she argues. "He hasn't treated you like it. You owe him nothing! For goodness sake, even the Pastor and his wife wanted you to leave him. It's not like you got out of one relationship and into another within a week. You haven't been in any kind of relationship with Keith for years, but you've loved Danny Quinn since you were thirteen years old. Give yourself a break!" I let her words sink in. "I want to see him. I've missed him. We were once, all, really close. We just need Rubén now to make up our foursome." She winks at me.

"Okay, I'll sort it out. But go easy on me. I've only seen him a couple of times so far."

Nodding she grabs my hand. "I'll give you my strength." I smile and hold on to her, just like I always did.

Danny Quinn

"If I have to read another report on suitable locations for a new restaurant again, I'm likely to give up on the whole idea," I growl at Layla.

"Sorry sir, it's unfortunate that Ms. Tinder cannot look for real estate anymore."

"Hmm, unfortunate, not necessarily the word I'd use, but it has posed quite a problem for me. I've had enough tonight. You can finish up now and do… whatever it is you do, Layla."

She nods and grabs the paperwork. "Do you need me to make a reservation in the restaurant, or order you some food?" she asks.

"No, I think I can pick up the phone and call room service," I answer then take a second to consider her. "Have you eaten?" I enquire and she blushes.

"I'm having room service as I'll be Skyping Heath."

I smile. "You're back together?"

"Yes, he turned that job down." The grin lights up her face as she explains, and I'm happy for her. Heath is a friend. I met him back when I played football, he worked marketing for one of the stadiums and has been headhunted quite a bit over the years, which means he moves from place to place. After introducing him to Layla four years ago, he's stayed in San Francisco. It's the longest he's been in a single location, and it's because of her. When she told me they'd split, a little over a month ago, I chewed him out. But I could also understand his need to work, his desire to better himself because that's what I'm like. Seems he's realized what he'll be losing. *Thank God.* I could barely deal with Layla when they first split, all weepy and snotty. Not my area of expertise.

"Okay. That's good. Say hello from me." She nods and leaves, and I remove the laptop, leaning back in the chair. My mind, as always, wanders to

Bel. She hasn't called, it's been a week. I've been living in this hotel like it's my home for too long now. It's time to leave. Bel hasn't called, she's made her feelings clear. I've never been a pussy when it comes to women, but then only one woman has ever affected me. Time to move the fuck on. Grabbing some clothes, I start the process of packing my stuff. Deciding to forgo dinner, I sit in bed and switch on a game re-run.

The flickering comes from the screen in front of me, and I rub my eyes realizing the phone is ringing. Glancing at the clock, I'm surprised when I see it's just after one a.m.

"Hello," I answer not really thinking to look at caller the ID.

"Danny," That voice is like a punch in the gut. I sit up and close my eyes.

"Bel."

"I'm sorry I'm calling so late."

"It's fine. Wait, is everything okay?"

I hear her giggle and it causes me to smile. "Yeah, I just came back from a night out with Amanda. I'm sorry I haven't called, but I've been so busy that I just haven't had time." I'm about to reply when I hear her sigh down the phone. "I'm lying. Sorry. I haven't called because I didn't really know what to say," she whispers.

"There wasn't anything you needed to say right away, Bel. I just want us to spend some time together, remembering each other…" I let my words hang along with my stomach.

"I never forgot you," her voice is so quiet I almost miss it.

"It might make me a jerk, but Bel, I'm glad you never forgot me," I tell her, closing my eyes.

"I left him." Her words make me drop the phone.

"Shit!" I complain grabbing it from my lap and placing it back to my ear. "Sorry, you left Keith?"

"Yes."

"Why?"

"I haven't loved him for a long time. You were right the other day, we don't have a good relationship. Whatever people have told you is probably true. He doesn't love me either, not really, not in a healthy way. I needed to be free of him, but I've always been so scared. So alone." Her words cause a stab of pain in my heart. I've put her through all that pain, she might have been with me if I hadn't turned her away.

"I'm sorry." The words are out, circling the empty room.

"No. I blamed you the other day, which was wrong. It wasn't your fault," she replies.

I hang my head. "We were both young and stupid. Neither of us realized what we had, allowing it to slip through our fingers and losing it for all these years. Bel, understand me now. I've been getting ready to leave, to move on, but I don't want there to be any confusion. I'll stay in this hotel or rent somewhere and stick around for as long as it takes. I want to be with you. That's all I've wanted from the moment I lost you, but I'll settle for being your friend… for now. Just tell me you'll let me in at some point? I need to know this is going somewhere. I'll fight for you, but I have to know that you'll fight for me too?"

"I don't know what's going to happen, we can't predict the future. But I want you here, as my friend and maybe one day something more." She sniffs making me realize she's holding back her emotions.

"That's good enough for me," I tell her, feeling myself relax.

"Amanda wants us to meet up."

"Sounds good. When?" I ask.

"Tomorrow? Down the beach? Maybe we can have a nicer conversation than we had the other day?" She giggles again and inside I'm feeling hopeful. *Finally.*

"Sounds good Bel. I'll be down there at eleven, get some surfing in first."

"Okay… Danny?"

"Right here, angel."

"I've always thought about you. Every. Single. Day. Danny. Every day, without exception. I don't think I ever loved Keith. How can you love someone when your heart has always belonged to someone else?" All the air leaves my lungs at her words. Then I hear a dial tone. Bringing my knees up on the bed and leaning my forearms against them, I hang my head and close my eyes. Sitting there for long moments, I wonder if finally I'm on the road I always should have traveled. The road that will always lead me back to her.

Chapter TWELVE

Anabel Adams

"How long have you been up?" Amanda asks as she stumbles into the living area of her hotel room. Her make-up smeared face and hair sticking in every direction just makes me remember the great nights out we used to have. So I smile but say nothing pointing to the phone against my ear. She nods and continues, dragging her feet as she walks, until she reaches the sofa, where she flops into the seat, laying her head back and closing her eyes.

"Ma'am, did you want me to set up an appointment?" the woman at the Lawyer's office asks in my ear, reminding me of the task at hand.

"Yes, please," I reply.

"Friday at ten, ma'am. Does that work for you?"

"That's great, thank you."

"You're welcome. Have a nice day."

I replace the receiver and look over at Amanda. She opens one eye at me.

"What was all that about?" she asks before closing her eye again.

"I was setting up an appointment with a lawyer."

Her eye opens again. "You were? For what?"

"I want to set the divorce in motion. I'm going to start using my maiden name, too." My explanation apparently warrants a full on whoop as she springs into the air, which is swiftly followed by her grabbing her head and bending over.

"Shit, I shouldn't have done that," she says lowering herself back down.

I giggle, then she giggles. I move to sit next to her on the sofa and we continue our snickers. Suddenly, I sober and the elation turns into something else. My stomach drops as my shoulders sag, and out of nowhere I feel completely hollow for a minute. It's long enough to set off a chain reaction within me. One that sees me crying into Amanda's chest. Heaving as sobs wrack my body and Amanda clings to me. Just like she did when Danny left. When I first broke.

"It's okay, sweetheart," she coos while rocking me and I try to pull myself together.

"I wasted so many years, Moo. Mom and Pop would be ashamed of me," I cry.

"No. Don't ever think that." The hitch in her voice tells me she's struggling to hold herself together—for me. *So she can be my strength.*

"They would. They never wanted me to be with Keith, they said I didn't love him. Not like I should have. Momma told me she just wanted to see me happy. Pop said he wanted better for me. Someone who… who…" The hiccup sob catches my breath, and I close my eyes trying to calm myself while Amanda rubs my back.

"What did he say, Bellie?" she whispers.

Pulling back I grab a tissue, wiping my eyes and blowing my nose. "He said, he wanted me to be with someone who couldn't see anything but me. Someone whose world stopped and started with every breath I took." I smile and sniff, thinking about my father's words. "Oh Amanda, I remember his words, they're always whispering to me, *'My beautiful, Bel. Life takes you on all kinds of journeys, but that's okay, as long as you know the destination's worth it. You should be someone's destination, my sweet daughter. The man that's meant for you should be striving to get to his destination. He should be trying to get to you because you're all he needs.'* My poppa loved me so much, he just wanted the best for me." Sighing, the tears still silently slide out of my eyes. "He held my hand the night before I got married. I never told you, Moo, it's one of the reasons I finally bucked up my ideas and went to

Danny's house. He sat on my childhood bed, in the only place that's ever been home, and told me I should be someone's gift. That he loved me with all his heart, and if he had to give me away at the altar, then he wanted it to be to someone who thought I was their gift. Like Mom was for him. I should have that kind of love. He told me to never live with regret. I didn't follow the path he wanted me to take Amanda. I didn't listen…" my words break off as contemplation takes over.

"Hey, Bellie. Stop." Amanda gently shakes me, bringing my eyes to hers. "You could have joined the circus and screwed the clowns one by one in the back of the clown car at a live show every night, and they would have loved you and been proud. It didn't matter what you did, you had them, unconditionally. That's what your parents were, with each other, and with you. They never put conditions on their love. Think hard, you'll remember. Anyway, you've left Keith now, you're building up your strength. I'm here to see you through that, and today you start renewing your friendship with Danny. He's already been honest with you and stated what he wants. At least he isn't playing games with you. If he does, I'll kick his ass." She winks at me and I snort-laugh. "Very ladylike," Amanda says raising an eyebrow with a smirk.

"Shush you." I smile.

"There's my beautiful, Bellie," she says leaning forward and wiping the still falling tears from my eyes.

"How did I get so lucky to have you as my best friend… my sister?" I ask her softly.

"Who knows? You must've done something right because I'm amazing." She chuckles.

"You laugh, but you totally are. God knows how I managed all these years without you. I don't think I could survive if you left again." My chest clutches as a shadow passes over her face, but before I get to question her, she jumps up.

"Come on, I'm feeling better now. Go, shower, and I'll call room service and order breakfast, we have a hot guy to meet." She shoos me toward the bathroom as I hear her ordering my favorite food.

Danny Quinn

"Danny!" My name is sung across the wind and I spin around immediately spotting Bel and Amanda.

"Ladies," I say and bow. The silliness of youth still lingering when these two are in the vicinity.

"Danny!" Amanda shouts again throwing her body into my arms, hugging me like her life depends on it.

"Mandie Moo. It's so good to see you," I whisper into her ear, using Bel's nickname for her. She pulls back and grabs my upper arms as she looks into my eyes, searching for something. I glance away noticing Bel as she walks a little past us and sits down on the sand. Looking back, Amanda's now smiling at me.

"You love her," she states.

Glancing at Bel once again, before turning back and answer, "Never stopped."

She nods and let's go. "That's all I needed to know. Look after her… always."

I nod. "That's my intention. If she lets me." I feel the muscle in my jaw jump.

"She will. Just take it slow." Pulling away, she moves over to Bel, leans down and says something before walking to the sea. I amble over to Bel and drop down beside her.

"Hey."

"Hi." She glances at me and smiles, and with just that one smile I feel like I've won the lotto.

"Do you remember when we used to come down here, all of us?" I ask.

"Yeah, gosh, I loved those summer days." She giggles and I shake my head.

"You always complained that we spent too much time in the water and you were bored."

"Oh, shoot!" Bel throws her hands over her mouth and stifles another giggle. "I did, right? I used to hate sitting here watching you in the surf. There was always someone around like Sasha or Alice, or whoever you were dating at the time, and I used to hate listening to them fawn all over you. Then you'd come out of the water, an enormous smile on your face and walk straight toward them, before they ran up to you with a kiss." I watch her carefully as her cheeks pink, she's embarrassed at admitting that. Reaching up, I cup her cheek.

"I walked to you. Every. Single. Time." Looking down and smiling, she bites her bottom lip.

"Bellie, you have to come in the water. Just up to your ankles. Come on!" Amanda shouts and I smirk looking down at the sand and letting go of Bel's face.

She gets up and starts walking away, before stopping and twisting to me. I meet her eyes and the connection that's always been there is still just as strong. "I forgot to mention, I'm not sure if you still speak to Rubén, but Amanda wants to catch up with him… me too… if you can sort that out?" I nod and she smiles walking to the water. Bel and Amanda kick the surf at each other and laugh, running back and forth and it's like we're teenagers again.

Pulling my phone out, I make the call and he answers with, "Yo."

"Seriously Rubén? You need to stop saying that. You sound like a dick."

Laughing at me his reply isn't surprising, "Shut up douche. What do you want?"

"You'll never guess where I am."

"Dude, if this is a guessing game, I'm gonna fail. Tell me, or I'm hanging up on you. I've got things to see, people to do."

"Shit, you don't change." I shake my head with a smile. "Okay, so I'm back home at the beach. Bel and Amanda are in front of me, they're splashing each other in the sea."

"Fuck. I'm on the next flight out. Be there tomorrow." Then he gives me dead air. I chuckle and close my eyes, thinking about how my life is so very close to perfection. That's the way I continue to feel as the sun sets, washing away the old and getting ready for the new.

Chapter THIRTEEN

Danny Quinn

"Layla, I need you to source me somewhere to stay. On a longer term basis."

"To buy or rent, sir?" I can see the curiosity in her eyes, but refuse to explain my reasons. That's not something I need to do.

"Unsure. Let's see what you find first." Nodding she moves away, leaving my room and no doubt going back to hers. I trust her to find what I want, she knows my taste, she'll be able to locate what I require with the minimum of information. Glancing at my wrist, the expensive watch secured to it tells me it's only two hours until Rubén's flight lands. I promised I'd collect him, and there'll be a taxi waiting for me shortly. Turning the shower on, I undress and step under the warm flow of water. My life is so complicated right now. Every day I seem to move into the unknown that little bit more. It's somewhere I've always avoided, now I'm jumping in head first.

My cell rings as I get out the shower, grabbing it I forget to check caller ID before answering.

"Dan." The squawk on the line reminds me why I always check who's calling.

"Shannon," I drawl. Not sure why, yet again, she's calling me.

"Your lawyer's a dick. I've told mine to take this back to court." Closing my eyes I try to retain my calm.

"Shannon. Whatever you want to do, it happens through our lawyers. I've told you. Stop calling."

"Danny, you don't want to see me with nothing do you? I just want a little alimony, baby."

Her words grate on my last nerve. "Prenup, Shannon," I spit, then cut the call.

In some ways, I feel sorry for my ex-wife. She did love me, I think, at one point. I didn't love her back, not really, and so I get that things weren't going to work out between us. I had money, so I had an iron-clad prenup. When I found out she was cheating it was the best way to get rid of her at no extra cost to me. Whether that makes me a hard bastard or not, I don't care. They all say I have a heart of stone. They've been saying it since I became famous playing football. I let them have that, all the fame hungry women I've entertained over the years, knowing they all wanted their piece of me. To use me for my money, my ability to get them into any club, for my connections, my looks, my friends—hell sometimes it was just for sex. I didn't mind those times. Shannon worked to get me to place that ring on her finger. Even if I didn't really put it there with love, more out of loyalty. So I had a prenup drawn up and cheating equaled instant divorce with no alimony. Perfect. Cold hearted. Finished. If she'd just get that into her head, then the divorce would go a whole lot smoother. Either way, my lawyer tells me that this shit will be done in the next month. *Thank Christ.*

Pulling up at Portland Jetport, I see Rubén outside. His bag slung over his shoulder, talking to two long-legged women who are dressed as cabin crew. Shaking my head I smile, he'll never change.

He spots me, turns back to them, speaks, then saunters toward the car. After angling himself into the passenger seat, he looks at me. "Been a long time, D."

"Yeah, Rubén."

"Too long. Next time we make this frequent," he tells me moving his hand between us.

"Yeah," I reply smirking.

"Enough with the mushy shit. Take me to the girls," he demands, facing front and interfering with my stereo until he finds a track he likes. *Paradise City* by Guns N' Roses starts playing and I chuckle as he turns up the volume then holds up his hands making *'rock on'* signs with each one. "Fuck yeah!" he shouts as I pull away from the curb and the cabin crew wave.

"What's the deal with this piece of shit car?" Rubén asks as we get out of it and make our way to the restaurant to meet the girls.

"Rental. I was just visiting," I reply.

"And now?"

"Now, I'm looking to rent somewhere."

"Yeah, I bet you are. Heard that Bel got rid of Keith."

"Shit! Word travels fast in that town," I mutter, stopping to take a moment.

"Yeah."

"Your momma?"

"Yeah. She said she'd heard it from Mrs. Wilkes, who apparently heard it from Robbie, who heard it from Mrs. Decaster, and you know she heard it from someone at church. Shit travels at light speed. Can't say Momma's heard anything but glee from people at the turn of events."

"Really?"

"Yeah. She said it's the best thing Anabel's ever done to leave his ass. She can be a stronger woman now, or some shit like that. Seems everyone thinks the same."

"I expect not his friends. Tommy, Declan."

"There was a time they were our friends too, Danny."

"Not for a long time, and not because I moved away, but before that. They stopped acting like brothers the minute Keith did."

Rubén smirks. "Can't really blame Keith, dude, he knew your feelings for Anabel ran deep. That shit was written all over you. Plus, you spent more time with her than them."

Looking down, I rub the back of my neck. "I fucked up. A lot. I know that nothing much I can do will change any of it. Now my focus is on making things better with Bel. I have no loyalty to Keith. That stopped the second I heard he was fucking around on Bel with Ashley."

"True, but you never got any proof and would you have shared with her even if you did?"

I tip my head up to stare at the sky and sigh. "I don't know. I wanted to tell her anyway. Shit, I was a coward. She called it. Told me straight up the other day at the beach. Said I was a coward and she's right. I turned tail, ran, and left her behind."

I feel his hand on my shoulder and pull my head up, giving him the respect he deserves by looking into his eyes. "You were a kid, D. You didn't know what the fuck you were doing from one day to the next. I remember how broken you were when you left town. You thought you were saving her, and in the process you destroyed yourself. The guy you were back then… shit, you left him in that damn town. I haven't seen him, no one has, I bet even you haven't seen him in over a decade. Five minutes with you today, I see he's back, and you're all in. She's always been your perfect fit. The only problem you had, far as I could see, is that you both tried to fit at different times when you should be trying to fit together. In sync. Momma said that for all these years, Anabel Adams has walked around like her world is hollow. You breeze into town and it's like she's in full color again, and filled with hope. Just take it easy and let the two of you breathe. Give it a chance to grow and have some fun. Remember what we all used to be like. Then, you want her to be yours, she will be."

I nod at him. "Never knew you were some kind of Dr. Phil."

"I have that shit in me, save it for the ladies. They love them a romantic guy, and I work that shit well." I chuckle and he turns to look at the restaurant. "Come on, much more talking like this out here and

I might grow a vagina." He spins and heads to the restaurant, with me following behind, still not sure what the fuck I'm doing. But for once, I'm going with my gut.

Anabel Adams

My breath catches as he walks into the restaurant.

"Yeah, totally need to get you some from that man," Amanda says, pulling me back to the present. Rubén precedes Danny and that's when I jump out of my seat and run to him forgetting where we are. He sees me and braces before I jump into his arms, flinging my hands around his neck.

"Anabel." He chuckles. I feel Amanda attach herself to his other side. "You two don't change, always crazy," Rubén tells us squeezing tight.

As I step back, he tucks a strand of hair behind my ear. "Bel…" then he looks at Amanda, "Mands… missed you both. Can't believe it's been so many years. Should never have let it become this." His words sink in and I look over to Amanda taking note that she's looking away, a sheen over her eyes. I have to talk to her, find out what's really going on. I'm not stupid. There's no Pierre and she's not going back to

Paris. Something's up and I have to get to the bottom of it.

"Come on, we're in the way. Let's go eat," Danny says propelling us forward. His hand has found its way onto my lower back, and although his touch is light my skin feels like it's burning like he's branding me. *As if I need that.* I've always belonged to him. Well, in my heart, where it really counts. Rubén offers Amanda a chair and seats himself next to her, meaning I have to sit facing her with Danny next to me. He sits down after offering me my chair and settles, making himself comfortable. His thigh rests against mine and I know I'm bound for the depths of hell, when all I want to do is get closer to him, share his world and drown myself in him.

"So Rubén, what have you been doing with yourself all these years?" Amanda asks and distracts me from Danny's solid thigh for a moment, allowing me a reprieve from my own thoughts.

"Nuh uh. You first, baby girl. What have you been doing? Danny told me that Anabel said you'd been in Paris? What gives?" I can feel Amanda's foot tapping against the floor beneath our table and I frown, watching her face. She looks like she's weighing something up, something not entirely happy. Then just like that, the fog lifts from her eyes and she smiles.

"Well, I wanted to get away from you Rubes," she replies giggling.

"Oh, you wound me," he groans holding his hand over his heart. Just then a waitress appears smiling at Rubén.

"Are you ready to order?" she asks timidly.

"I'll have the beef tenderloin, with a side of you." He winks at her and I roll my eyes. Catching the pain in Amanda's. *You okay?* I mouth to her when nobody's looking. She nods and smiles. It's fake and it scares me.

"I'll have the ribeye please," Danny tells her, gaining her attention. She scribbles on her notepad and looks to Amanda.

"Mushroom risotto please," Amanda says softly.

"I'll have the burger, hold the cheese. Thanks," I swiftly give her my order. I'm feeling suddenly uneasy. I was so looking forward to this catch-up tonight. I've been working at The Hatfield club for two weeks and have managed to save some money. I shouldn't really be spending it, but I haven't been out to a restaurant since before my mom died. I figured I deserved a treat.

I haven't seen Rubén in even longer. It's strange to think that people who were such a big part of your life could just drift away, into nothing. That thought cuts deep, knowing I allowed it to happen. Sure, Keith didn't want me keeping contact with Rubén, feeling he was too big for his britches. He used to run him and Danny down to anyone willing to listen. Although I know with Danny, the reason he was like that was because of me. He knew, even back then, that my heart lay with someone else. Now, I'm here, I'm surviving, I'm stronger than I have been in such a long time. I know a lot of this is because of Amanda, with her constant support, encouragement and love, I've been able to build myself up. But while I should be in the best place ever right now—single, with the true love of my life next to me, admitting his feelings and telling me he wants me—my best friend, my soul mate, my sister, finally back from halfway across the world, after so many empty years without her, there's something not quite right. Something's bothering me and I need to figure it out. Amanda and I always had some kind of freaky sixth sense with each other, and this time it's off the charts, warning me something is very wrong.

Over the next couple of hours we laugh, joke, reminisce, and the years between us all, melt into insignificance.

"So, I'm staying at Danny's hotel for a bit. If he gets a place I might stay with him for a while, but we'll see." Rubén's offhanded comment as we walk out the restaurant throws me.

"If Danny gets a place?" I ask looking between them and over to Amanda, whose eyes, I notice, have widened considerably.

Danny takes the two steps to me so he's fully in my personal space, and I see nothing but him. I tip my face up to him. "When I told you the other day that I wanted to be with you. That was me saying I'm all in. If you want me, I'm here for the taking, Bel. I have patience and I can wait. I'm showing you my commitment by looking to rent somewhere so you can see I'm willing to bring the fight. Now, I need to know if you're gonna bring the fight, too?" His words hang between us, like an invisible wall, holding us both in place.

"Yes," the answer pops from my mouth and surprises me.

Danny reaches out his hand, running his thumb along my cheek down to my chin. "All I ever needed to know, angel." Dropping his hand he studies me for a second, his eyes move over every inch of my face. "I'll go slow, Bel. As long as you're all in for this… for us… I'll take it at your pace." Then he leans forward and kisses my forehead, before turning around and walking away. My feet are stuck, I'm glued to the spot, both scared and ecstatic at what I just agreed to. Danny looks back over his shoulder. "Come on, Bel, the others will be back at the car by now." His words unlock my frozen state and I timidly walk forward reaching out my hand to his, as he slips his fingers through mine, and I'm suddenly sixteen again wishing the boy at school that always had a smile for me, was my boyfriend. Only now, he's holding my hand and pulling me to him. Just like I always wanted.

"I can't believe how handsome Rubén still is," Amanda whispers, staring at the television, but obviously not actually watching it.

It's been three hours since the guys surprised me by dropping us off at Amanda's new—old house. We said goodbye, like a set of double dating school kids. Her whispering to Rubén and me to Danny, it was all pretty surreal. Making plans for two days' time, after I have work, I found out that Danny is looking to find somewhere in town. We still haven't discussed the situation with Pop's store, and I want to try and find time to do just that. He also informed both Amanda and me, that he's still legally married, and I wanted to double over with the pain that shot through my stomach. But Amanda, as always, kept me together. He went on to explain that he was in the process of a divorce, which should be finalized within a month. Rubén had added a *good riddance,* which wasn't needed, but I can't say it didn't ease the pain slightly.

Pastor Wilson secretly brought all two bags of my belongings over to Amanda's earlier today. I hadn't realized that was the plan, but apparently Amanda had arranged it with him. He then continued to be helpful, by collecting her things from the hotel while we were out for dinner. So now, I'm officially living with my best friend.

"You always had a thing for him," I reply, lounging sideways in the chair and sipping my coffee. Her house has already been furnished. She said no place can be *home* unless it was comfortable. So here we are, the fireplace alight, in our jammies, bad television on in the background, sipping coffee, and feeling thoroughly relaxed.

"Yeah, I did."

I snap my head to her. "Only took you fifteen years by my counting to admit it," I snort.

"Yeah, sometimes life puts things into perspective," she mutters quietly.

"What?"

"What? Nothing," she snaps back at me, obviously realizing her slip up.

"No, Amanda, enough. I know something is going on, so fill me in," I demand. Sitting up in the chair, ridding myself of the coffee cup.

"It's just that I see you moving on from Keith. You're starting fresh, building something new, hopefully with Danny. It puts things into perspective." She smiles.

"Oh, no lady. Don't try and brush this off. I know you, remember. It may have been years since we have physically been in the same space, but I still *know you.* When Sarah Lacey, stuck gum in your hair, you tried to hide it frightened you'd get in trouble. Who knew something was up? Me. That's who. And when you had a thing for Billy Spence and he liked Kellie Bow, who knew? Me. When you had your first menstrual cycle and went missing from class 'cause you were hiding in the bathroom. Who knew? Moi! That's who. You know I could reel off a bunch of other times, too. So let's quit this game and just tell me, damn it! I'm worried!" My chest heaves as I calm myself, completely overwrought with worry.

"I have cancer. That's why I came back."

Her words slam into me, and I double over, grabbing the coffee table as I lean forward. I stare into her eyes as a throbbing starts in my head.

"What?" I screech, jumping up from the chair, knocking the coffee off the table.

Amanda whispers, "I have cancer. It's terminal. I'm dying, Bellie."

I can't breathe.

I can't move.

The fog descends.

That's when my world truly stops.

Chapter FOURTEEN

Anabel Adams

“What?” I breathe and collapse back into my chair, the searing pain feels like it’s pushing my ribs apart. “This can’t be… you can’t be—” I choke as a sob finds its way up my throat and I grip onto the arms of the chair, afraid my body is going to give out.

“I am,” Amanda throws the words out like they mean nothing. Like she’s telling me the weather. “I have an appointment with an Oncologist tomorrow.”

Determination flows through me, bringing a warmth to my cold shell. “I’m coming,” the demand in my voice is only slightly stronger than the wobble of my emotions.

“You don’t need to do that, Bellie. It’s—”

“Stop!” I snap, raising my hand, palm up, to her. I look into her eyes as my insides clench and I push my shoulders back. “I will be with you every step.

Every appointment, every sleepless night, every fucking breath I will share with you," I say, trying to keep myself from heaving.

I watch as tears brim in her eyes. "Love you, Bellie," she whispers and I rush over to her chair and wrap my whole body around hers. My legs feel weak as my pulse races. It's an awkward and uncomfortable position, but that doesn't matter. As long as I hold her, then she's still here. I can feel her breathing, her warmth penetrates my skin, but I can see just how frail her body is now. I can't believe I didn't know, I waited all these years to see her again to be able to hold her, all these wasted years with Keith when I could have been stronger, braver. Maybe if I had grown up and stopped allowing myself to be dragged down by someone who didn't love me, then I could have been there for someone who did. Realizing it's only been moments and yet Amanda has fallen asleep, I detangle myself, watching her for a while, trying to calm my heartbeat. Now I know, I can see it. Her frame, her skin. She looks worn. I haven't been able to get past her being here. *So much for my sixth sense.* I didn't even know my best friend was dying. Hanging my head, I allow a few tears to slide down my face. This woman is amazing and I need to be strong for her. My crying will be done alone, as always.

My new phone—the one Amanda bought me, insisting I couldn't live without a cell—beeps indicating a text and my head snaps to her, worried it'll wake her. She's out cold, so I swipe the wet on my cheeks and pull myself together. Grabbing a blanket, I let it glide over her and then grab my phone walking to my bedroom.

> **Danny:** *Had a great time. Glad we both know where we stand. No matter what, I'll always be your friend. I never want to lose that again.*

I'm surprised that he has my number and that I seem to have his programmed in. I can only assume, since Amanda bought me the phone, that she did it. The thought comes and goes smoothly as I find I'm unable to pull my eyes away from the text. It seems insignificant now. The to-ing and fro-ing between Danny and me seems so stupid. My feelings don't need validating, I'm entitled to feel scared or hurt by things that have happened in the past, but Amanda's confession is a wake-up call. Life is so short… *so damn short.* What's the point in holding onto pain, when we can fill our lives with beauty? I'm done worrying about this whole situation, and Amanda is now my main focus. I can't think about anything else.

Going into the phone menu, I hit enter on Danny's contact and place the phone to my ear, it hardly rings before he picks up.

"Bel," his soft voice filled with love is like a balm on my heart, but I can't speak, emotion overwhelming me. "Bel?" he questions, his voice now threaded with concern.

"It's okay," I say, in a whisper, trying to catch my breath.

"Why are you crying?" he asks softly.

"Danny," I'm struggling to get much out, my throat constricting.

"I'm coming over, I'll be there soon."

"No!" I semi-scream, trying to keep my voice quiet.

"What the hell, Anabel?" It's flat out worry in his voice now as I hear him moving about, grabbing keys, obviously getting ready to come to me. My heartbeat picks up pace, while a thousand emotions bubble to the surface.

"Amanda has cancer," I blurt, then close my eyes. I'm not worried about telling him, or him telling Rubén. I know Amanda won't mind that. It's more the way I blurted it, I just can't think straight.

"What?" he whispers, everything quiet in the background now.

"She told me tonight." I admit, the tears flowing freely now.

"What kind of cancer? What treatment is she having? Does she need help? I have money Bel, and it's hers for treatment if she needs it." The offer makes my heart squeeze a little at the knowledge I'm about to impart.

"I don't know what type it is. Or the money situation, Danny. But I do know one thing… brace yourself… it's terminal," I say the words and a chill runs down my spine.

"No," he states like he thinks he can change things with that one word.

"Danny," I whisper again, not really knowing what to say.

"Do you want me to come over?" he asks quietly.

"No… but thank you. She hasn't told me much, just what I told you, then we cried and she fell asleep. I'm hoping to have a talk with her in the morning, but she said she's going to see an Oncologist tomorrow. That has to mean something, right? I mean, surely she wouldn't need to see the doctor anymore if there was nothing he could do?" The hope in my voice hangs in the air.

"Bel…" his soft murmur of my name says everything that I don't want to hear.

"I have to go. I'll call or text tomorrow."

"Okay. Remember I'm here, for her and you. I'm with you. You're not alone, baby."

"Thank you," I answer then click the phone off. Standing up, I stare out of the window, watching the moonbeams bounce off the cars in the road out front. Then I glance up to the sky, to the stars. Knowing, no matter the questions I ask, there's never an answer, not for me. “Why are you taking everyone from me? Was I bad? Am I supposed to be alone forever?” I whisper to an always silent sky.

Waking up, feeling achy, I hear noises in the bathroom and look around me. The reason becomes clear when I see that I spent the night on the floor. “Ugh.” Moving my neck from side to side, feeling the clicks and then stretching my arms does nothing to ease the pain. “Better brush away my morning breath,” I mumble to myself, getting up from the floor. I hear Amanda leave the bathroom and head downstairs, so I slip in there and give myself a quick freshen up and teeth brush before I head to the kitchen for breakfast.

I’m momentarily shocked when I walk into the kitchen and see Amanda taking a bunch of pills.

“What are all those for?” I ask. A frisson of fear running through my veins.

She turns to face me smiling. “Morning to you too,” she says winking and I grin, grabbing a coffee and planting myself at the table. “There’s a bunch of medication I need to take, some for pain, some to make me not feel drowsy and I have these drugs…” she says holding up a blue packet, “…these are an experimental drug, Bellie. I have been testing them, you know, to see if they'll help."

I sit up straighter. A fluttering starts in my belly. "So this means that you might not be terminal?" She smiles sadly and shakes her head, then moves to sit next to me, grabbing my hand.

"Sorry Anabel, these drugs are only supposed to give me longer." My dry mouth doesn't stop me from grinding my teeth, as she continues, "I'm too far past the point of return. Today, I'm going to see if it's worth staying on them, whether I can get a bit of extra time from taking them. But honestly? I can feel it coming..." she looks away then shakes her head so slightly that if I weren't actually paying attention, I would have missed it. Turning back to me she continues, "The end. It's nearly time. There's a lot I haven't told you, and I'll fill you in after the appointment today. If you want to know?"

I nod my head and bite my lip, trying desperately not to cry, feeling like my head is about to explode, while wishing that this was all a nightmare I could wake up from. On the outside though I know I have to keep myself together…*for her*.

Looking at the clock, I don't really see the time, although I know it's late afternoon. I hate doctor's offices. They're so sterile. I guess maybe they should be? But there's absolutely no personality in this room, and when you're telling someone if they're going to live or die, a little bit of personality or, at least, somewhere more comfortable, might be appreciated. My eyes move over to the older man across the desk. His dark hair has flecks of gray throughout, and his brown eyes have enough wrinkles to tell me he must be in his sixties. He's probably seen it all. Doing a job like this, for so many years, that has to take its toll.

"Ms. Warren." He shakes Amanda's hand, and I'm thrown by the fact that he's using her maiden name. "I'm sorry we're here. It's not a pleasant appointment to have to keep. As we discussed on the phone, I have spoken with your doctor in Paris and we have conversed about our findings with you on this trial drug. I'm sorry to be giving you bad news…" He pauses and it must be for only five seconds but it feels like forever.

Why do doctors do that?

For dramatic effect maybe?

Do they not realize how precious those five seconds really are.

"The trial is failing. We gave it the best shot, and I've been told by Dr. Giroux that he pre-warned you that the chances of this drug working and prolonging your life for any length of time would be slim." I look between the doctor and Amanda. I want to hit him.

Hard. I feel like his words have just reached across the small office and bitten me. I can hear the blood whooshing in my ears. My arms are crossed over my chest as my hands grip my upper arms, nails biting in with a force I didn't know I had. I knew this was probably going to be what he told us. Hell, Amanda had already told me, but hearing it from him makes it so much more real. I sit perfectly still, not knowing what to do or say.

Then I hear a soft, "Okay," come from Amanda.

My head snaps to her and then to the doctor and I glare at him. "This is not okay," I yell.

"Bellie," she tries to placate me.

"*No!*" I scream. "Don't say it's okay. Don't even fucking think that! The minute you say that it's okay is the minute your body gives up the fight. And you're not giving up the fight. Not while my heart beats. I'll fight hard enough for the both of us." My words slow as the emotion catches up. "I can't lose you," I whisper as she pulls my body into hers.

"You already knew what was going to be said. It shouldn't be a surprise, honey," she says softly.

"I know." My breath hitches, and my legs feel numb. "I guess I just hoped…" I let my words hang and she says nothing. We just hold each other.

An hour after the appointment with Dr. Doucheface where he gave us the bad news that he didn't know how long, but wouldn't look past a couple of months at the most, I told her that meant we had to fit in as much as we could between now and then. Amanda shattered my world a little bit more when she explained that even if she lived for two months, it was likely she would be in a hospice for the last couple of weeks, and even before that she might not be up to *living large*. I explained that *living large* could just mean, me and her sitting in bed watching *Dirty Dancing* while eating candy. She smiled at that and told me she loved me. Now I know I have to treasure every piece of her I can have, for as long as I have it.

How we ended up at the diner, over on 5th, I'll never know. We used to avoid this place because all the jocks and cheerleaders came here, and we hated watching them act like jerks. Now I realize what we were missing was the yummy food. I munch my way through a fully loaded burger and fries. Then my thoughts go elsewhere as I glance across to Amanda, who's picking at her food but not really eating.

"You don't like it?" I ask softly.

"Oh, yeah, it's nice. I'm just not hungry. I don't eat as much anymore, I rarely actually feel like eating." She glances away from her plate. Suddenly my hunger dissipates, but I push through the sick feeling and keep my game face on.

"That's okay, you eat what you can, and I'll hoover up the rest. Deal?" I wink at her and her smile spreads from cheek to cheek.

"Deal," she whispers.

"So, I hate to bring it up. But before the docs, you said you'd tell me everything later. It's now later, Moo. So spill." I blow her a kiss, hoping to keep things light-hearted, even if I feel like I've been punched in the vagina every time I have to bring up the subject, her face saddens as she tells me everything.

"You know Momma had cancer… breast cancer." I nod again and she smiles. "Me too. It seems I was always destined to follow in Momma's footprints. I had it about two years ago—"

"*What?*" I shout, making myself jolt with the pitch of my own tone.

"Shhh! it's okay, Bellie. I'm so sorry I didn't share, but you wouldn't have been able to come over to Paris, and I couldn't afford to put your ass on a plane, honey. I knew the guilt of me being unwell would have crippled you, and I didn't want that." I can't speak as my nose tingles and my throat feels like sandpaper. A lone tear escapes from the tight hold I'm trying to keep on myself. She smiles and wipes it away. "Don't cry, Bellie. I'll be okay. I promise." We both ignore the lie that just fell from her mouth. Amanda grabs her coffee cup and sips a couple of times before continuing, "Because of the family history we decided to go for a double mastectomy—"

"Oh my God! What? How do I not know about so much of your life?" my shouts dwindle into a whisper. Light-headedness takes over as my thoughts scramble.

"Because you had enough to deal with. And Anabel, not trying to be harsh honey, but until recently, you weren't strong enough to deal. Since I've come back, I've seen the old Bellie back, the one who wouldn't take any shit. Back then, when this nightmare started for me. No, not even close, you couldn't have dealt with it, especially on your own." I close my eyes momentarily, hating that she's right, that I've been so wrapped up in my own failings, that I wasn't able to be there for my best friend. "It's okay, honestly. You're here now, and this is when I need you, Bel. Right now."

I look at my friend. "I'll be here. I promise." My words are pushed up past my raw throat and I ease the lock on my jaw as the dullness in my chest spreads.

"I know you will," she whispers. A tear, followed swiftly by another, flowing from her bright eyes. "So anyway, I had a mastectomy. I had chemo, lost all my hair and felt like shit for six months. They thought I was better, well, in remission at least. Turns out, it came back. This time, it's more aggressive. I found out about eight months ago. I've had a few treatments, but then I'd had enough, I decided to stop trying to fight when it was pretty much inevitable that I was going to die. So I chose instead, to concentrate on prolonging my life as much as possible." She closes her eyes and the silent tears keep spilling out. Apart from the tears you wouldn't know she was crying.

"Why did you give up?" I ask her softly, knowing I have to support her decision even if I don't want to, even though it's breaking my heart.

"Because I'd rather live fewer months, and have as much fun as possible only being really uncomfortable at the end, than have months more with all of them in pain or discomfort. You wouldn't do it to a sick animal, you'd put them out of their misery, I just wanted the same consideration."

"I get that," I tell her, with a sour taste in my mouth, and she smiles.

"I knew you would, my Bellie." Squeezing her hand, my heart is breaking, but as long as it's on the inside, as long as it's not touching her then I'm good, I can deal. Amanda bites her bottom lip then carries on. "My pop was so mad, Bel. So angry. He shouted at me, told me I couldn't give up, he couldn't lose another woman in his life. My compromise was trying this trial drug. I have for a while, but then I knew… I can't explain it, Bel…" She stops shaking her head and chuckles, but it's an empty, hollow, false laugh, "…I just know whatever it was doing to prolong had stopped working. I told Pop when I found out the cancer was back, and especially that it was worse this time, that I was coming back here. He wanted to argue, but I said I wanted to be buried next to Mom." She takes a breath in and so do I, remembering her mom. A grave in the same place as my parents, a grave I visit every month and lay flowers when I do my own parents—for Amanda. "Also, I told him I wanted to come back and spend time with you. Luckily, he never actually sold this house, only ever rented it out. I didn't realize, we all thought he'd sold it. But I can't say when he told me, it wasn't like music to my ears. He's coming back in about a week. He wanted to give us some time first. Pop's girlfriend, Simone, the one I've told you about… she's very sweet. They've been together for about eighteen months, so she's been on most of this journey with me. I'm glad he'll have her when I'm gone. I would've been so scared for him otherwise. And Bellie, I'm glad you'll have Danny. Lean on him, he'll be the strength you need. Let him in, honey, let him love you."

I signal the waitress and ask for more coffee, she brings over a pot and refills us.

"What about Pierre?" I ask gently.

Amanda's face pales and automatically my hand shoots out and grabs hers. "What? What is it you haven't yet told me, Mandie Moo?"

Her lip wobbles and I suck in air through my nose. I swear I may not have a passport or a gun, but if he has hurt my beautiful girl, I will hunt him down and rip him a new asshole, then I'll shoot him in the dick.

"He couldn't cope," she says in a low voice.

"He what? He couldn't cope? Him? What a fucking asshole!" I spit out, angry for Amanda and already planning how I can get a passport real quick so I can tie his balls together with angry snakes.

"It's okay," she tells me sweeping her hand down the side of my head.

"No. It is absolutely *not* okay. It's the exact fucking opposite of okay. You've been married for three years and together for five. What possible excuse could he have for not coping?" I bite out, my skin hot with anger.

"His mom died from cancer and his sister survived, but had to have a mastectomy," she tells me and I blink, taking in the news.

Then my senses are restored when I reply in a softer tone, "So then, he of all people, should know how hard it is. For better or worse, in sickness and in health. Those words are supposed to cover you. He should be treating you delicately like you're precious, healthy or unhealthy. Not turning tail the minute things become hard." I swallow my own feelings, quickly dismissing the guilt that threatens to choke me. Knowing, in the end, I ignored my own wedding vows easily enough.

I watch Amanda composing herself, she swallows and sighs, and I can see the pain in her eyes. Whatever has happened, she loved him back then and what he did scarred her on the inside.

"He was with me at the beginning. He held my hand when the doctor told me I had cancer. He held my body as I cried, and he cried with me. When I had chemo, he stayed by my bedside because I was too sick to go anywhere. He was truly amazing the first time around. When I got better things changed, I can't put my finger on it. He closed himself off, became distant. I thought he was cheating, but looking back I think it was more than that. I think he was closing himself off to me because he couldn't face losing me."

"But by doing that he was going to lose you anyway," I respond, amazed at how stupid someone could be.

Amanda nods sadly. "Yeah, I know. So stupid. Anyway, when the cancer came back there was already a divide in the relationship. When they said it was terminal, Pop was the one by my side, holding my hand." Amanda stops talking and I can almost feel the pressure in the air, the pain laced with sadness, hurt and betrayal swirling around us. Her face goes hard, and it shocks me. This isn't her, well, very rarely. I prepare myself for what she's going to say. "That day I got home and waited for Pierre to get back from work. I explained that he'd forgotten about my hospital appointment, and the lack of shock or remorse he showed for missing it told me that he'd not met me at home that day to take me to the appointment on purpose. I asked him what was going on. He told me that he couldn't go through it again. He'd never survive another round of chemo and seeing me so unwell. And that it had killed him not being able to do anything."

"What a fucking cop out," I growl, my body tensing as burning heat flushes through my body.

"Yep. You haven't heard the best bit." I feel my eyes go wide and screw my toes up inside my shoes, as Amanda smirks at me, but it's completely without humor. "He said that since I had my mastectomy, he didn't see me the same anymore. Said I reminded him of what he lost in his mom and also of his sister, who'd also had a mastectomy. He said part of the problem is that I didn't want to have reconstructive surgery done to have breasts again."

"That *fucking fucker, cock, jackass!"* I scream jumping up. Pounding in my ears takes over as my vision clouds.

"Bellie, calm down," Amanda tells me looking around the diner, luckily it's empty apart from the waitress. Furious I sit back down, only reining myself in for her. Adrenaline pumps through me as the cogs start turning, working out how I can inflict the most amount of pain on his sorry ass. "He cried. Told me he knew he was a jerk, that he shouldn't feel this way. That you always hear men say how they love their wives regardless, and even more so when they have survived something like this. Pierre said he knew he was in the minority and that it was a dick move what he was doing, but he also felt it best to be honest with me. So I could move on and find someone who would love me without my breasts." It's at this point that she breaks down, big gulping sobs erupt from her mouth and she doubles over, clutching her stomach. I quickly slide into the booth on her side and hold her, rubbing her back, letting her get it out, letting her put it on me. Knowing I need to do something in the future to break that man in two like he's done to her.

After she calms down, and the poor waitress worried about the crying women in her diner gives us free pie, I ask her, "Do you still love him?"

"No." Her reply is instant and I know she's not lying. "I lost any feelings I had for him the moment he left me to face cancer and possibly death on my own, basically because he was a coward. I never told him I was terminal, I didn't think he deserved to know. He left. Never came back, so to him I was dead anyway. I divorced him and now I don't think about him. It's like he's been erased. The only thing I get upset about is how horrible he made me feel. I've not thought about sex since he left. Oh, don't get me wrong, I'd like it. At least once before I die. Although not with just anyone. Pierre and I only had sex a handful of times between my mastectomy and him leaving. He always made sure it was doggy and now I know why. As much as I would like to find someone who I could spend a night with. I know as long as I have left, I'll be insecure about how I look. I don't feel beautiful anymore and he took that away from me. If anything, I hate him."

"Rubén's always a choice, right?" I wink at her, trying to make her laugh. It works when a bubble of laughter pops out of her throat. It calms the edgy, twitchy feeling sparking inside of me.

"Hmm, he was always a choice. He just never asked. I'm not sure I could show anyone my chest anymore…" she stops and bites her lower lip, then whispers, "I feel like half a woman." She grimaces and it makes me grind my teeth, anger spiking once again at the bastard she was married to.

"Come on. Let's get out of here, we'll start up a Nicolas Sparks movie marathon," I tell her standing up. She groans, but gets up and slips her arm through mine and I lead her back home.

Chapter FIFTEEN

Danny Quinn

"I don't believe this shit," Rubén says slamming the car door. I took him for a drive to share about Amanda. He's always had a thing for her. She was the one he never actually asked out. He never crossed that line with her, even though I know he desperately wanted to. He got with so many damn girls when we were younger, and yet he never had the balls to ask out Amanda Warren, when she was the only one he really wanted. I know what he's been thinking since I called him up the other day and he hauled his ass out here. She was alone, no husband in tow. He was hoping his shot might come up. It was a douche move, but a natural one, when he flirted with the waitress last night. We talked about them after we dropped them off.

"Never been anyone else who's made me see a possibility of a future. No joke." Were his exact words. Now I've had to break it to him, that she not only has cancer, but it's terminal. And fuck me, but if my heart isn't breaking because of this situation. I'm going to have to be strong for Bel, and also Rubén. That doesn't mean that I don't carry my own pain, I'm gonna lose Amanda too and I feel like a dick because I've left it so many years to connect, especially because she was one of my closest friends when we were younger.

Getting out of the car I follow Rubén up the path he's taken to the peak of Pikes Hill. I came up here because we needed to be away from people, then, if he had to scream he could—curse, no problem, kick something, fine—he can even punch me and we're guaranteed that no cops will be called.

When I reach him, he's sitting on the ground, looking over the town. I lower myself down next to him.

"Shit man. It hit me hard when Bel told me last night. She's off to the docs today. I expect it won't be good news. I figured I'd let you know so you can deal how you see fit."

He twists his head to face me. "How I see fit?" The words are growled at me.

"Yeah, didn't know how you'd handle it. So I thought, better you punch me than shout and scream if Amanda told you." His shoulders sag as the fight seeps out of him and the news sinks in.

"I don't know why I feel like this?"

"Of course you do. When you came back here, you wanted to make something happen between the two of you. You let your feelings back in. You've shut them off for years."

He nods his head. "Yeah, and now I can't switch the fuckers back off."

"That's how it happens." My cell buzzes in my pocket and I consider ignoring it. If it's Shannon, I may throw it. It buzzes again.

"You gonna get that?" Rubén says his tone flat.

Pulling it out of my pocket I'm relieved when I see it's Bel.

> **Bel:** *Just come back from the docs. It's as we expected. Not good news. They say two months. Tops.*

Her words are like a hot poker being stuck in my chest. "Fuck," I curse, closing my eyes, trying to bite back the sadness as a tightness spreads through my limbs.

"What?" Rubén snaps.

"It's Bel, they're back from the docs. She said they've given Amanda two months, at most." I push the words out through my clenched teeth.

"Fuck!" he screams into the empty space. I look down at my phone thinking about what I need to say to help Bel.

Me: Fuck. Honestly baby, I can't believe this shit. I'm here. You want me to pop over later?

Rubén's hanging his head between his knees and I give him the space he needs while I concentrate on Anabel.

Bel: *No. Thanks anyway.*

Her response is short. I'm not sure whether it's the best thing to do, but my fingers move across the screen dialing her before I can change my mind.

"Danny?" She answers, confusion in her tone.

"Sorry Bel, I wanted to hear your voice and texting is so impersonal. Can you talk?"

"Yeah. She's asleep again."

"Okay, so what exactly is going on?" I ask, my mouth dry.

"She was trialing this drug, it was helping prolong her life. It's stopped working."

"Shit," I mutter, which gets Rubén's attention.

"Her pop is coming back soon. He was giving her some time with me first."

"That's nice of him. He knows how much you mean to each other." I can feel Rubén's eyes burning into me.

"Danny… I don't know how to be strong this time… for her. I'm afraid I'll not be able to hold her up." My stomach drops through my shoes at hearing her pain.

"Hey, it's okay, as long as you're there that will be enough. You can cry, she will expect it. If you need to get your feelings out, then write them down. Get a notebook, put it in your purse so you can carry it around with you. Release the pain onto the paper, then you can stay strong for her. When she's gone baby…" I hear her catch a breath, "…when she's gone, you can revisit your words and let them out. I'll be there to hold *you* up."

She doesn't say anything for a few minutes and I give her the time she needs.

"I'm going to spend a couple of days with her. I'll call in sick at work, luckily I'm only in tomorrow then I have three days off anyway. We'll catch up with you and Rubes in a couple of days. If he's still about?" Her words are rushed out as she moves past the emotion she's trying to push down.

"I think he'll be staying in town," I say looking at Rubén.

"Fuck, yeah," he murmurs.

Anabel releases a relieved sigh into my ear. "Good," she says softly.

"Bel, I'm just wondering, you don't have to tell me if Amanda doesn't want us to know. But what's the deal with her husband? I thought she was married?" At my question, I swear Bel growls down the phone. "Bel?"

"He left her."

"What the fuck?" I ask, my pulse elevating.

"Said he couldn't cope with her going through chemo… said it *killed him* the last time, and he couldn't cope. His mom died from cancer and his sister had a mastectomy. And Danny, so has Amanda."

"Fuck me. What kind of a cold bastard is he? That should make him more compassionate," I answer, my voice spiking and now Rubén is frowning, even though he doesn't know what Bel's saying.

"I know, right? He said…" she trails off.

"What? What is it?"

"He said she was less of a woman to him because she wouldn't have reconstructive surgery."

"*The fuck!*" I shout jumping to my feet. A pounding has started in my ears and I curl my fists.

"Ow! That was right in my ear, Danny."

"Sorry, Bel," I snap like I'm not sorry at all. Luckily Bel gets me if her soft chuckle is anything to go by.

"That's pretty much how I reacted. I can't believe he was such a dick," she tells me.

"She still hung up on him?" I ask, my blood surging through me with purpose

"Nope. Not even a little bit. Only that he hurt her, made her feel ugly. Worthless."

"Good. A dick like that doesn't deserve anything from her," I say the words knowing I'm going to find out as much as I can about him. I'm going to make him bleed, one way or another.

"Yeah, he only deserves to be hung from a meat hook… by his testicles." I wince at her explanation, but can't disagree with the statement. "Where are you?" she asks.

"We're at Pikes Hill. I needed to bring Rubén somewhere, to explain." I hear her sharp intake of breath. "We'll be fine, Bel. You worry about Amanda and call when you're ready to meet up. Until then, we'll hang. Okay?" I say gulping in air and trying to calm myself down.

"Yeah," she whispers and I swear this woman makes my body do things without even trying. I bite my lip.

"I'll catch you later," I say.

"Yeah…" She breathes again, then the phone disconnects.

"Tell me everything," Rubén demands before I've even had a chance to put the cell in my pocket.

I sigh. "Sit down, man."

It isn't my phone that's busted by the time I'd finished.

Anabel Adams

I pace back and forth and the more I do, the angrier I get. Amanda is sleeping. She took some pretty strong sleeping pills and told me she'd be out for the night. I can't stop thinking about everything that has happened over the last twenty-four hours. My life has changed, in a way that I know without a shadow of a doubt, I'll never get it back, not to where it was before I found out. All I can focus on right now is that I'm going to lose my friend. The most important person in my world, the one who's helped me survive my life, a life that hasn't been easy. And she is going to lose hers before she's really even had a chance to start it.

Amanda is such a beautiful soul. Always trying to be the best kind of person, the one that the rest of us wish we were like. How is it fair that child molesters sit in prison, having three square meals a day and yet my generous, loving, inspiring friend, doesn't get to live for much longer?

I can't get all the emotions out, the thoughts and feelings running through me right now are a constant pounding on my skin, every nerve is on end and I want to punch something—repeatedly—until blood oozes through my fingers. Or maybe drive a car, I don't care whose, into a tree, over and over, until the numbness sets in. As I look across at her, my delicate and kind friend, all I can see is the disease on the inside, eating away, destroying her, trying to extinguish her life. The hardest part is knowing that cancer is winning.

More often these days people say they've beaten cancer, so why not her?

I pull my eyes from the tiny sleeping form and remember what Danny suggested. Pulling myself up, I walk to my room, grab an empty notebook, and settle on my knees by the window.

> ***Cancer.*** *I hate it. Why does it reside in my best friend? How do I cope? How can I be strong? She needs me and I'm falling apart. No. I need to put one foot in front of the other and do whatever it takes. Whatever she needs.*

I scribble my words in the notebook, hoping, somehow, they will relieve me of this pain. Because losing her, will tear my soul in two.

My thoughts wander back to Pierre. I can't understand how he could just desert her, leave her to fight on her own. I want to hurt him so bad. Sighing, I know I'm not in any position to do much about it. I think about Danny and Rubén, make a decision, grab my jacket and take Amanda's car.

By the time I stop at Pikes Hill, I'm surprised to see Danny's rental still here. I thought they might be gone by now. I've had time for the anger to bubble and I need someone to help me ease it.

Jumping out of the car and walking up the path, I spot them both sitting on the grass. I stomp up to them and they both look at me in surprise. Their eyes widen, they can obviously see the crazy bitch that's fighting to get out.

"Bel," Danny says standing.

"Babe?" Rubén says joining him.

I stare up at the two of them. "You two have money… I believe… I mean you both wear fancy clothes and have nice shoes," I snap looking down at their feet. "It's not a stretch to assume you have money when I compare you to the men of this town." I'm jabbering on so much that I miss the humor as they both try not to laugh. "I mean… if you have money, you can hire a hitman on Pierre, right? Not while Amanda's still around, I don't want to upset her, but after? Oh, yes…" I stop and look down at my hands, then my head snaps back up. "Oooh, we could totally get someone who will, like, play with him a bit. You know, like a few cuts here and there, maybe tie him to a chair and make him watch bad renditions of the national anthem while his dick is squeezed in a vise?" I stop and look at them when they both start flat out laughing.

"Babe, you have totally thought a lot about this, haven't you," Rubén states through his snickers.

"Not really," I dismiss, shaking my head. Then they both burst into rumbles of laughter, I watch Danny's throat as his head is thrown back. Taking in all that is him, and he's a sight to behold. Then he stops laughing abruptly and looks straight at me.

"What's his name, Bel?"

"Err… Pierre," I answer looking between the two deadly serious faces before me.

"Last name," he snaps and I swallow.

"Bellerose."

"You know anything else about him. Job? Location? Anything?"

"I know he lived in Paris. I'm assuming he still lives there. Other than that… no...." I trail off. "What are you going to do?" I ask, swallowing and suddenly wondering if I've bitten off more than I can chew.

"I'm going to make him bleed," Danny answers.

"What!" I shriek.

"Not with blood. Well, not unless there's a way to do that easily. But I'll find his weakness," Danny replies with a smirk.

"And if he doesn't, I will. Even if he does, we'll share in the fun of bringing that fucker to his knees," Rubén adds.

I nod and twiddle the car keys in my fingers, suddenly feeling slightly stupid at storming up here and ranting away.

"I'm gonna go for a walk," Rubén says, not waiting for a reply before leaving Danny and me alone.

My eyes get cut off from Rubén as Danny steps into my space. I'm starting to realize it's his thing. He gets close like he's claiming me. Grabbing my chin, he pulls my face up to meet his.

"Eyes babe," he demands and I look up to him.

"Trust me when I say, Pierre Bellerose *will pay*. I don't know how, and you may never find out. But just trust that between Rubén and me, no matter what he does, who he has at his back, we *will* make him pay for hurting her." I swallow and nod, feeling my nose sting. "I will be here, by your side, for as much or as little as you need me over the next couple of months. No pressure, this isn't me trying to be with you. We both get where we are, and right now, our relationship wherever it leads is secondary to Amanda and us being there for her. I'm gonna support you through this and I'll be here after, too. I'll be whatever you need me to be, and if that's just your friend, forever, then that's okay. If you want more. Then know, Bel, I'll love you forever. That I promise. You come to me broken inside or out. You have cancer, lose your breasts. Car accident, lose your legs. Alzheimer's, you can't remember me. I'll still fucking love you. I've loved you for this long. Nothing's gonna change that, baby. Not ever," he states and my knees weaken with not only his words but the pure emotion that has been within me over the last twenty-four hours. He catches me and pulls me up to him and I lay both palms on his chest, getting lost in his eyes. "Told you, I'll hold you up. Meant always, Bel."

I move my mouth forward without thinking and touch my lips to his. He stays still, giving me my play. Moving across his mouth, feeling it, tasting it. The softness is like velvet and I close my eyes groaning. That's all it takes for Danny to take over. He gently bites my lower lip and pulls it away from the top. Then he captures it in between his lips, before sweeping his tongue along and inside my mouth. My hands slide up his chest and wrap around his neck as he reaches down, grabbing me under my butt and lifting me. I cross my legs around his back as he pulls away from my mouth, bringing one hand up, off my butt and into my hair, gripping it at the nape and pulling my head back exposing my neck. He kisses under my jaw and moves up slowly, reaching my ear he bites the lobe and a moan escapes me. His fingers spread across my scalp and he wrenches my head back down finding purchase on my mouth again.

"Nice," I hear chuckled from behind, and it brings me back to my senses. Still Danny doesn't stop straight away, instead finishing the kiss I started. Then biting my lip before finally letting me down.

"You and me, Bel. We were always meant to be. You can't deny it. I'll wait, or I'll be here with you, as more than just your friend. The ball is in your court."

"I think…" I pant as my mind whirls trying to put the puzzle back together.

"Yeah," he whispers and everything inside me clenches.

"I think, I'd like to try just taking this slow. Kisses… okay. More than that… no. Not for a while," I tell him casting my eyes low.

"Eyes baby." I look back to him. "That sounds like a good call. Especially right now. And Bel, after kissing you twice, not sure I'd be good with seeing you but not kissing you, so it works out well for me." His lip twitches and I smile. My thoughts jump to Amanda and I frown. "She wouldn't want you to stop living life. Ask her, I bet she'll tell you that," he says knowing my thoughts.

"She already did," I answer, knowing he's right. She wants me to have someone, more than that. She wants me to have Danny, she of all people knows how long I've wanted him. "It's getting dark, I need to get back." He nods and kisses me softly on the lips then lets me go.

"See ya, Bellie," Rubén says with a wink and I salute him with two fingers.

As I drive away, my feelings are mixed and a sickness comes over me. I know what I want, Amanda has shown me how short life is and that you need to grab it, buckle down, and enjoy the ride. My other thoughts tell me I'm selfish for wanting my happiness when Amanda is losing her life, and knowing that she's part of my own happiness makes me wonder, what exactly my own future holds without her. That's a thought that I push from my mind, as I stop the car to hurl. Jolting to the side of the road, I only just manage to open the door before the lunch I had earlier makes a reappearance. As I wipe my mouth with the back of my hand and with my head hanging down, trying to catch my breath, I see a pair of feet come into view.

"Well, look at you, being sick in the street. Nice, Anabel." I close my eyes then look up to Declan, who stands in the way of me shutting my car door. "Now you've left Keith, maybe I can finally get a taste," he says and I can smell the full force of his whiskey stench now.

"Get out of the way," I demand, trying to pull the door. Declan clamps a hand on the frame to stop it moving.

"Now, now, that's not friendly." My stomach turns over and I hurl again all over his shoes. "*Shit!*" he shouts but, unfortunately, doesn't lift his hand from the door. "You fucking b—"

"Declan. What you doing, man?" Keith's voice rings out in the darkness, and I've never in my life been so happy to hear it. After the way he was when I left the other week, I'm hoping like hell his thoughts haven't changed.

"Just chatting," Declan growls as Keith reaches my door. A flicker of concern washes over Keith's face as he reaches the car and sees the vomit on the ground.

"Anabel, are you okay?" he asks me.

"Yeah, I'm not feeling too good, though. I want to go home." His eyes flash with pain on the word home. "Declan wants to talk, but I've been trying to tell him I'm not in the mood," I answer gesturing to the ground.

"Leave her be, Declan. She's not well. Come on, man," Keith says pulling him away from my door. I smile at Keith and he offers me a fake smile back. "Be well, Anabel," he whispers before dragging Declan away.

I shut my door, then close my eyes for a second, trying to pull strength from somewhere. Starting the car, I open the window and pull away, driving back to Amanda's before anything else can happen. When I get back, I check on her then crawl into bed. Knowing that whatever I feel right now, it's just a fraction of what she's suffered and still going through.

Chapter SIXTEEN

Anabel Adams

Snuggling up with Amanda has been my life for two days. The first day because I was still sick, after vomiting through the whole of the night. The second because Amanda wasn't feeling so hot. We decided there were enough films to keep us in bed for the foreseeable future. Anyway, if all else failed, we always had Chris Hemsworth as Thor. Him, we could watch on repeat. I must have fallen asleep tonight though, because the television screen is blue and Amanda has disappeared. Pulling back the covers, I throw on a robe over my PJ's and ease my feet into my slippers. Traipsing through the house, my eyes move to the kitchen door. The only visible light is coming from a crack at the bottom of its frame. Pushing through the swing door, the empty space throws me. Expecting to see Amanda, confusion stirs. I'm about to turn around when I spot a small light in the backyard. Trying the door handle leading to the outside space, it's unlocked, so I move out there. Immediately, I wrap my arms around my body. It's chilly tonight. I realize how cold it is as I walk through the garden and my breath dances in front of me, disguised as a white cloud of smoke.

"Amanda, what are you doing out here?" I ask upon reaching her. She's curled into a garden chair. Her small hunched frame leaning forward, almost reflectively, the heels of her feet sit on the edge of the chair, as her arms hold onto her knees.

She looks up at me and blinks like she's surprised to see me. "Oh, I was just watching the stars," she answers softly turning her face back up to the sky. "Do you think there's anything more? Anything after?" she asks quietly, introspectively.

"Yes," I answer, my tone absolute. "There has to be," I whisper, gazing up at the stars.

"I hope I end up there," she murmurs still staring up at the sky.

Turning to look at her again, my eyes take in her pale face, her usually pink lips have a tinge of blue. She only has her PJ's on. Slipping my robe off, I wrap it around her.

"What are you doing?" she asks, pulling her eyes away from the dark night.

"You're freezing."

"I'm okay. I'll go in soon."

"No. Wear the robe, warm up," I say moving to the front of her and pulling the cord tight around her waist.

She places her small cold hand on mine. "You'll freeze, honey," she says smiling.

I look up to her face from my crouching position. "That's okay, it's better this way, because it means I keep my soul warm," I reply smiling and running the back of my hand over her cheek.

The gasp she makes is muffled as her hands shoot up to cover her mouth. Slowly she pulls them away. "You remember that?"

"I remember everything we've shared, Moo. You have to know, although we've never been blood, you've always been my sister, my best friend, my soul, and I'll never forget anything. Not one single thing."

The tears she was controlling spill over and run down her nose. Watching them, I wonder how they don't freeze instantly, it feels cold enough tonight.

"I'm so scared, Bellie, so fucking scared," her voice is saturated with pain and my chest aches. Shooting my hands out, I grab both of hers. "What if everyone forgets… you'll have lives that grow… change. You'll move forward, I have no legacy. If I'm forgotten, it'll be like I never existed." Her face crumples and a little part of me dies inside as I beat back the tears stinging my eyes.

I throw myself around her. "You'll never be forgotten. *Fucking never*. Understand that now. You. Have. My. Soul." I breathe heavily, trying to calm my rapidly beating heart, stopping it from jumping into my throat, or breaking apart in a permanent way. "Since we sat out here after my mom died and I asked whether you believed in soul mates. You replied that they had to exist because you'd never seen another married couple, love each other, as much as my mom and pop. I asked if you thought your soul mate was the person you married. I remember it like it was an hour ago, Amanda. Your answer has kept me going for all these years." I stop speaking as she opens her mouth.

"I hope not, because I don't want to marry you, Bellie. But you sure as fuck have my soul." She repeats the words she first said all those years ago and lets slip a small, hollow laugh. The sorrow in her voice crushes me inside, but I know how she feels about the memory. I feel the exact same way. She has my soul. Always has, since we were kids. I remember her saying those words all those years ago, as we stared at the sky back then, just like now. Her saying them again is both happy and sad, and I feel the melancholy surrounding us both.

As we stare upward, me crouching next to her chair, not really feeling the cold anymore, but welcoming the numbness in my limbs.

She speaks so low that it's barely audible. "Knowing someone will remember me gives me peace, Bellie. Knowing it's you that's gonna be the one to remember me… gives me the strength to face what's coming." At her words, my silently breaking heart slams into my chest as I quietly slip my fingers through hers, saying nothing, knowing automatically that she just needs to watch the stars, to believe there's something more. Seeing the light amongst the dark. Trusting in the unknown.

Later that night, after taking her back to bed and watching her fall asleep, I pull out my notebook and sit on the window ledge. Cracking open the big window, I relish the breeze hitting my legs, it makes me feel like I'm closer to the stars as I scribble away.

> *She's so beautiful—inside and out. Her light should remain here. If she has to leave… knowing she's burning bright for everyone to see. Eternally watching over us all. It's all I have to cling on to. The good things about her are too many to list, the bad—there is no bad. She has so much more to give. Her heart is so big. No matter how long I think on this, think about my friend. I know, I'll never find a good*

enough reason for her to be taken. Not one single reason.

It's time to go back to work. A couple of weeks ago I would have found it hard enough, knowing Amanda was back here, and I couldn't spend time with her. Now it's like torture, being truly aware that every second counts.

"Hey, stop worrying! I'll have Danny and Rubén to keep me company, and you can't keep me to yourself," Amanda says winking. I warm inside, happy that she seems cheerful.

"Pfft." The sound pops out of my mouth and we both laugh. I calm myself first and watch as she wipes happy tears from her eyes. I so badly want them to be the only kind of tears she ever has. "So what's the plan for tonight?" My question is because Amanda wants to fit so much in.

She made a list yesterday. *A bucket list.* It's mostly silly things, like rowing a boat out to the middle of the lake. It's her way of feeling like she still has a say in her life, by choosing what to do with the time she has left. Until she tells me differently, every day is Amanda's way. Her wish, her wants, her dreams. *Whatever that entails.*

"Well, I've asked the boys to take me to play golf."

"Erm… what?" I reply scratching my head. Never in my life has Amanda talked about golf.

"I thought it might be a cool… new thing to do," she tells me smirking.

"You want to ride the golf buggy," I state, placing my hands on my hips.

"Wanted to since I was ten. I *cannot* freaking wait!" she says bouncing up and down on her tiptoes. I smile. *Huge.* This is what I want for her, every moment savored. It's selfish because I get to see most of these moments too, which means I get to keep them forever.

"'Kay, I'm going, before I get fired." Moving toward her, I lean down and clutch her to me. I know just how important every last hug is. Kissing her on the forehead before I make my way to work. Wishing I could just stay with my girl.

Danny Quinn

"So what do you want to do now?" I ask Amanda. We've spent the last two hours pretending to play golf. In reality, Rubén and I have tried to play a few holes, to make it look legit, but Amanda has pushed the golf cart to its limits, not only with speed but some of the terrain she's decided to test it on. Ending in both Rubén and me falling out of the cart more than once. We've laughed. *Huge.* It's been amazing. I hate knowing this wonderful person is being lost to the world. Lost to *our* world. And there's nothing we can do to stop it.

"There is something I'd like to do, but I'm not sure if it will be okay?" she speaks so softly, all feminine and kindness. She would have made a fantastic mother. My eyes move to Rubén, who watches her intently. If our paths had taken different routes, she could be here with Rubén now, maybe even have a child. Still, I expect it wouldn't have made any difference in the end. It hurts, thinking that if I'd been honest with Bel all those years ago, if Bel and I had gotten together and stayed together, Amanda and Rubén may have stood a chance. Being that I would have always kept in contact with Rubén, likewise with Bel and Amanda. Spending time together as adults has shown that their flirting hasn't waned over the years, in fact, it only seems to have become stronger. If Rubén had been given those few extra years to grow up, man up, make his move, they may have been together now. Shaking the thoughts from my head, knowing they won't make any difference now, I smile at Amanda.

"Whatever you want, babe," I say. The smiles she gives back, lights up her whole face.

Rubén slings his arm around her shoulder. "Tell us what you want, your wish is our command." He winks and she blushes slightly. *Maybe it's not too late for them.*

"Well, I'd really like to go and have lunch where Bellie works." She looks between Rubén and me and when neither of us says anything, she carries on speaking quickly, "I mean, not to annoy her, or get her in trouble. I just… I miss her, and want to spend as much time with her as possible." Amanda stops talking, looking down at her hands and fiddling with her fingers, lacing them together and unlacing them, back and forth and back again. Rubén grabs her hands in his and pulls them to his lips, kissing them three times. It's intimate and I feel slightly out of place watching, so I avert my eyes but I'm glad they're having a moment.

"We're going to see her, have lunch, and then I'm going to speak to the manager. See if I can ask him to put her on hold for a while, let you two spend some time together," Ruben tells her.

"She can't… I mean, she needs to work." Amanda's cheeks pink again.

"It's okay, I'll cover Anabel," he replies, realizing what Amanda means is that Bel needs the money.

"No." The word pops out of my mouth before my brain engages. Once it's out there, though, I know with one hundred percent certainty, that I meant it.

"What the fuck, dude?" Rubén hisses at me. His body tenses.

"You will not cover, Anabel. I will talk with her. She's mine, Rubén. *Mine.* Remember that," I say glancing over to Amanda then back at him. He gets my point when the annoyance seeps out of him and his lips tip up. He wouldn't want me taking care of Amanda in that way, and they haven't even kissed yet. *I don't think.*

"Come on, let's get our asses some food," Rubén demands, dragging Amanda with him, his arm around her once again, possessing her. It's a deliberate move, and I smile, knowing all too well where this is headed.

"How many, sir?" the hostess pulls me back into the room with her question.

"Three," answering robotically, my attention sways back to the location where I just saw Anabel. With some sleazy little prick fawning all over her. I could see how uncomfortable she was, even from this distance. Stretching my neck from side to side, I follow the others.

"Can I take your coat, sir?" The hostess asks as Rubén cocks his eyebrow at me. Only then do I realize that the woman asking for my coat has been paying extra attention to me. But I don't see her or them. It's Anabel, it's only ever been her.

"No." My dismissal causes her shoulders to stiffen, as she walks away.

"Harsh, dude," Rubén says before I sit opposite the two of them.

"Amanda, do you know who Bel works with? I mean, does she speak about the other members of staff here?" I question, stretching my neck to try and spot her again, pushing down the rumbling that's trying to come out as a growl.

"No. She hasn't really said much about it here. Just that it's pretty boring, but it's a job, and her choices were to work here or to continue living with Keith."

Amanda's words clog my throat, knowing my girl only had those two choices. I have enough money to give her the life she deserves. Bel won't take it, though. I'll have to find a way to make her. Get her to see it's not a handout. Just as I'm thinking of how to get her away from this place she comes into view, with the prick hot on her heels. Without thinking, I stand up and move, stopping at her front. She comes to a halt and looks up at me, staring as I hear him behind her saying, "Dude?" like I'm some little prick friend of his. I switch off the part of my brain that wants to punch him, and instead merely concentrate on Bel.

"You're here?" she whispers.

"I'm wherever you are," I tell her. "I never left."

She just stares up at me, biting her bottom lip. Making me want to drag her away. Now.

"Errr… dude, we're working here. Bella, come on, we've got work to do."

Him calling her Bella grates on me, especially because she winces when he says it. She never liked being called Bella. Trying to be diplomatic, knowing that's what Bel needs right now, I level my gaze on him.

"She's dealing with me. Last time I checked, I'm a paying customer. Seems it's her job to talk to me. Why don't you collect the dishes and stow them in the kitchen, like a good little boy." I know my words are rude, but I give not one shit. His eyes narrow on me, but I drop my gaze to Bel, watching her biting the inside of her mouth, trying not to giggle. Her eyes twinkle as she moves them to me, then widens them in a '*you're so bad'* kind of look. Dickweasel goes red in the face and opens his mouth until some older guy calls his name. His eyes cut to the guy and narrow before he stomps away with all the grace of a small child.

"That's Malcolm," Bel says glancing over her shoulder at a now angry looking Malcolm, being talked at by the older guy. "He's Mr. Cumberland's nephew." My eyebrows pull into a questioning look. "Mr. Cumberland is the manager," she clarifies and I release my eyebrows on a nod.

"Is he decent?" I ask her, annoyance still sizzling under the surface.

She bites her lip and her eyes move sideways to the ground. *Not good.* They come back to meet mine. "Mr. Cumberland…. yes, absolutely. He's a good guy through and through. Malcolm, I'm not sure about. He's not a bad guy, but he's a bit of a creeper. Apparently, he likes me, Esther, one of the other waitresses told me. I don't think she's right, but he asked me about Keith and I explained that I'm still married." Those words scorch like acid in my stomach. "He talks to me a lot, even when we're busy, especially since I came back after those few days off with Amanda. I don't have any reason to be annoyed, he's not done anything. He's just chatty."

I hate this for her. I want her to be divorced now, to be in my arms, to let me look after her. "I want to talk to you later. Can we carve out some time?" I ask.

She glances over to Amanda and Rubén, who are seated but fully engaged in conversation. "Yeah, as long as Amanda is happy and entertained then I can spare some time. Not too much, though, I want to spend as much time with her as possible." She swallows a couple of times. She must be thinking about the short timeframe we all have left with Amanda.

"Okay, when she's asleep? That way you're not losing any time with her," I propose.

She smiles up at me. "Sounds perfect. Anyway, go, sit, I have work to do." I nod, running my thumb down her cheek, then turn and make my way to the table.

Chapter SEVENTEEN

Anabel Adams

“I can’t believe you did that. I never expected to see you lot at work,” I say looking over my shoulder to Amanda. She sits at the kitchen table, while I wash that morning’s dishes.

“I missed you, Bellie, I wanted to come see you.” Although she’s smiling, her words cut me inside, and the sadness covers me, knowing my best friend just wants to spend time with me, and I can’t give her everything she wants. It’s not like she’s being unreasonable. It’s a week since we went to the doctors, he told us she had a couple of months at best. We’ve used a week of that time already. Why, when you’re somewhere crappy, like at work, or in a dental appointment, does time go so slowly, but when all you’re wishing for is more time it whizzes by?

"What do you want to do tonight?" I ask, washing the last plate and placing it to drain. I pull up a cloth and dry my hands.

"Well, I asked the guys if they would go pick up some fast food. You do realize, the worse it is for your waistline, the better it will taste and the happier I will be. So they're out right now, doing just that," she says grinning and I mirror her grin. "I think they're going to the drive thru over on South Street. I figured after food, it would be nice to settle on the big sofas with popcorn and movies. They picked the *Die Hard Trilogy*," she says rolling her eyes, but I know she doesn't mind in the slightest.

Sitting on the chair next to her, I bring my feet up resting my heels on the edge of the seat and wrapping my arms around my knees. "So, tell me. What is going on with you and Rubén? I saw the whispers over lunch, I may have been working and Danny might have been sitting at your table—"

She cuts me off. "Danny, didn't know what day of the week it was. He was more interested in you. That guy made you feel uncomfortable. It was obvious to us all, he wasn't happy, but he reined it in for you."

I sigh. "Yeah, that guy's a creep. I didn't lay it out completely to Danny earlier, there's no point. I need the job, it's good money, and dealing with Malcolm is just an annoyance, one I *can* deal with."

"What do you mean, you didn't lay it all out? Tell me," Amanda demands and I roll my eyes.

"He's asked me out, every day since I started working there. I have no idea why? I'm an over the hill housewife, with badly dyed hair and, as Keith always pointed out, I'm at least thirty pounds overweight. Still, I've told him no, explained why, he just doesn't grasp it. I think he's just playing with me. That last shift, though, I think Mr. Cumberland saw him, I think he's finally clicked onto the situation. Seriously, that man is lovely, but he's an old coot, he has no real idea of what goes on in that place. Anyway, I don't know what he said to Malcolm, but it pissed him off. He went from creepy but nice, to nasty." I shake my head and sigh again. I don't need another thing to deal with.

"How has he been nasty?" Amanda's tone is gentle as she reaches over and grabs my hand.

"He told me I shouldn't set my sights up for the likes of Danny. I mean, he doesn't even know who Danny is. Malcolm only moved into the town five years ago to work with his uncle, so he has no idea who you, Danny, and Rubén are. But he knows of Keith and me, everyone does." I bite my lip and pull my hand away from hers, tapping my fingers against the table.

"And? What happened?" Amanda prompts.

"He said that Danny is out of my league. When he realizes who I'm married to, he won't want to touch a ho like me. Then, after dishing out those snipes, he turned around and said, he'd be willing to take me on." I shudder. "I swear he creeps me out more than Declan, and he's a nasty piece of work. But the truth is, he's right, Danny could totally be with someone so much better. What if it's just history pulling him to me?" There's a thickness in my throat as nausea sweeps across me, when I utter the words out loud.

"Firstly, shut the fuck up. Whatever you think of yourself, it's because Keith pulled you low. And incidentally, you are not, nor have you ever been even close to thirty pounds overweight. You know Danny, you know how he's always felt about you, and on top of that, he's not the type of man that plays with someone's emotions. *He is not that man.*" I nod, knowing she's right. If Danny says he loves me, then he does, even if I don't understand why. "Getting back to the subject at hand. You've told me about Declan. If this guy is worse than that piece of trash, you'll have to be careful."

"I don't get why Declan keeps on at me either? I mean when we were younger, yeah, he would try and attach himself to anything that moved. But still, after all these years? Why doesn't he go and annoy someone else?"

"He just wants a piece of you," Amanda says, curling her lip in disgust.

"Why would he want me? Why would anyone want me? I'm no prize," I groan with annoyance, feeling my cheeks tingle.

"Yes, you are, Bellie. You're beautiful inside and out. You have a heart of gold and the figure of a stripper—no matter what Keith ever told you. Why wouldn't anyone want you?" Amanda tells me with a snort as she shakes her head.

"Whatever. Anyway, now I have to figure out what to do with Malcolm," I complain wrapping my arms back around my legs and tucking my face into my knees.

"Maybe one of the guys should take you and pick you up from work, make sure you're safe?"

"No. I can't ask that of them," I mumble into my knees then pull my face out to look at her. Seeing how strong she is, knowing I need to be just as strong. "I'll work something out. Anyway, you're getting off point. What's going on with you and Rubén?" I question again, bringing the conversation back to her.

She grins. "We've gotten closer."

Sitting up straight, I cross my arms at her answer. "And?" I ask eagerly.

"He told me that he's always liked me."

"We all knew that. He was just too chicken shit to do anything about it back then," I snort.

"Yeah, he said I was so focused on getting away, moving abroad, he couldn't see how we'd have a future," Amanda explains.

"Cop out," I answer with a smirk but a feeling of warmth bursts inside.

"I thought so… but then, he said, that he knew even back then if he started something with me and it ended, it would have broken him." She blows out a harsh breath. "So he didn't even try. Instead, he bedded every girl, having them all hanging off his arm, but never me."

She stares down at her feet. "Hey," I murmur, letting my feet drop from the chair and leaning forward to grab her shoulders. "What's wrong?"

Amanda pulls her lips in-between her teeth as her eyes gather moisture. "If I get close to him Bellie, and honestly I really want to and he does too, he told me, but if I allow it to happen… he's going to lose me. It's not a question that doesn't have an answer, not like the possibility of breaking up with someone. He's *going to lose me*, and I can't leave him broken, Bellie. I can't, he means too much to me." I watch as Amanda loses yet another tear.

"Listen to me," I say, shaking her slightly, waiting until her eyes come to me and fighting the hot tears burning the backs of my eyes. "He's a grown man now. He knows the situation. It's not like he's a teenager, unable to control his emotions, confusion constantly raging within him. No. He knows what he wants, don't take his choice away from him. That's not fair." Amanda opens her mouth to speak, but I get in there first. "Moo, listen, if it were the other way around. You knew you were going to lose him." I watch her swallow. "Would you appreciate him saying no to you, based on the fact that he's worried how you're gonna feel after he dies? Or would you want those memories to forever cherish, knowing you may have loved and lost, but it was the best experience you ever had? Or would you rather not know... but live with the fact that you would *never* get the chance to find out? Knowing you'll be leaving him with regrets that nobody can ever fix?" Amanda hangs her head and I feel bad. "I'm sorry, honey. You need to do what you think is best."

"No. I'm glad you put it like that. You're right. I mean, I need to talk to him some more, make sure he really is ready to have me, even though he's going to lose me. But it's true, he's a grown man, he should know what he wants from his life… and if that's me… then I'll be so lucky to *finally* have the one that got away." She lightens the mood with a wink.

"You *will* be lucky… but so will *he*. To have someone you love, even for a short time is always a blessing. Just make as many memories as you can," I whisper.

"Hmm, maybe you should take some of your own advice?" she says it in a question, arching her eyebrow.

"I am, although it's going slow because that's how I feel it needs to go."

"Bullshit," her pissed off tone takes me back and my mouth hangs open. "You're taking it slow for one reason. You're scared." She blows out a frustrated breath and her tone softens. "You're so scared of him hurting you again. I get that, honestly, I do. But can't you look at me and see time is precious honey. If there is one thing… just one, that I want you to take from me, it's to savor every moment, good and bad. They all help make us who we are, they shape us, but they don't define us. We do." She looks away thoughtfully, before continuing, "We can let shit that's hard make us give up, or we can let it light a fire under our butts. We can let the good stuff make us think we're entitled, or we can be grateful. We define the kind of people we are and how we deal with things. You can't let the past taint your future, Bel. Danny wants his future with you. All of it. *Every. Single. Moment*. You have the power to give that to him… *to you*. If it were me, I'd be running toward that as fast as I could." Amanda blows out a harsh breath. "He's always loved you, it's not like that's in question. I know how you've always felt, so what else is holding you back?"

Looking down at my feet, I weigh up how honest I want to be with her until she slaps her hand on the table. "Tell me!" she demands and it makes me chuckle. Amanda rarely gets annoyed so it can be comical when she does.

"Okay, I'll be honest, but I already know you're not going to like it," I say in warning.

"What?" she asks confusion washing across her face.

"I'm scared of losing time with you," I answer quietly.

"Huh? I don't understand," she replies.

"I want to devote all my time to you, not feel like I have to give half of myself to someone else," I explain, grimacing, knowing she's not going to be happy with my admission.

Amanda closes her eyes and shakes her head. "Jesus, he really did a number on you, didn't he?"

"Who?"

"Keith! Oh my God woman. Any real, loving relationships make allowances, no matter how new they are. The fact that Danny is the guy makes it even easier. We spend nearly all our time with him and Rubén anyway. When it needs to be just you and me time, do you really think that he won't give that to you?"

"I know he will. I just wanted to keep my mind clear. Amanda, I love you. You're the most important person in my life, honey. I don't want to fail you," I tell her, my hands trembling.

"Bellie, you could never fail me. Never. You've been there through everything in my life. The only thing I ever kept from you was the cancer. I admit, I did keep Pierre and me splitting up from you too, but that was only because it was related to the cancer. I know this illness was a huge thing not to tell you, but I didn't want to know you couldn't do anything, you couldn't be there for me. You think I don't know what lengths you would've gone to, just to get to Paris to be with me? I know Anabel. *I know*. Trust me. Explore this thing with Danny, properly, wholeheartedly. Do that. For me. I want to see you two settled before my time comes. It will make me happier to know someone is looking after you. My pa, he would look out for you, but I already know once I'm gone…" her voice cracks and I reach my still trembling hand over to squeeze hers, holding tightly, "…when I'm gone, there are too many sad memories here for him. I already know he's gonna move back to France. So you'll be alone. Honestly, it's one of the things I've had on my mind for a while now. Danny being here, with you, and knowing how he feels. It's the light I needed to see." She reaches across and wipes the two stray tears that I couldn't contain from my cheeks.

"I love you, Moo. Truly. With all my soul," I tell her, catching my words as my lungs constrict.

"Me too, Bellie. Always," she replies. "That's why I want you to be happy. Danny is that for you. He's your slice of happiness, and I want you to take it all, everything he offers you. Don't let it slip through your fingers." I nod and hug her as the rattle of the door indicates the guys are back with food.

"So you have me alone, now what?" I ask, feeling the wine kicking in as I laze back on the sofa.

Danny smirks, just one corner of his mouth, my eyes move between his lips and the cute little dimple in his chin.

"Babe, eyes," he demands. "I'm not sure tonight is the night to have this discussion," he continues, humor in his voice.

"Why?" I ask.

"Because you've been drinking, and I want to talk about something important."

"It's okay… I mean, I'm okay." I giggle.

"Hmm…"

"Oh, just tell me," I say putting my wine glass down and crossing my arms for emphasis.

"All right," he answers, still smirking. "I want you to leave your job." I open and close my mouth, but no words come out. "I've been thinking on this a lot, Bel. It's not a great job, and you're capable of so much more. Also, I don't like that douche you work with."

"I don't like that douche I work with either," I mumble almost forgetting who I'm with. When my brain kicks in I widen my eyes and look to Danny, he's staring at me with his eyebrow arched.

"Is there something you need to share, Bel?" he asks and I shake my head. "Listen, you want to spend more time with Amanda, I know she wants to spend as much time with you as possible, she told us that today. There's something else… I was thinking on the possibility of reviving your parents shop."

I feel my lips part as my mouth gapes at his words. "You were?" I whisper, as happiness and nostalgia bursts inside me.

Danny nods. "It makes smart business sense. I'll never sell it for any decent money. It's already set up as an ice cream store, it just needs a refurb, and I have contacts as I own a few restaurants. Plus Bel, who would be better to run that shop than you?" he asks with a smile.

"Me?" I breathe out, now feeling completely sober. It feels as if Danny is laying the world at my feet, if he could only offer a miracle cure for Amanda, my life would be complete.

"There would be no one better, Bel. You've worked it before, okay many years ago, but you know the layout, you know most of the people who live here and you know how to manage this kind of venture. I'm aware you were running things before your pop passing, so I'm pretty sure you can cover the ordering and accounts too—"

I cut him off, "Yes."

His head tilts, it's very slight, but I notice. He's surprised. "Yes?"

"Well… yes," I answer again.

"I thought I was going to have more resistance from you. Glad I don't." He stops and rubs his chin, then his eyes flare when he continues, "Although, I would have enjoyed putting you over my knee." Heat infuses every part of me and I bite my lip. Danny's eyes drop to my mouth. "Fuck it," he growls before grabbing the back of my head and crashing his lips down onto mine. He kisses me—no, he possesses me—as he works wonders with his tongue, all the while guiding me low until I'm laying back on the sofa and Danny is covering me like he owns me. He pulls back and looks at me. "Fuck… what you do to me. It's hard to keep control," he says biting his lip and it's enough to make me lose any indecision that was still swimming in my mind.

"So don't," I whisper, pulling his head back down to me, once again crashing our lips together. He takes over again, making this kiss slower, allowing me to savor the feeling of his soft lips and hot tongue caressing me. I tingle as one of his hands slides up the inside of my pajama top, running against my ribs and gliding over my bra cupping my breast. I groan in his mouth and he rips the cup down, exposing me to his hand. Danny's thumb rubs over my hard nipple and I'm vaguely aware that I haven't been touched like this for years. Suddenly, he pulls away from my mouth, leaving me dazed, then before I realize what's happening, he pulls up my PJ top and his mouth descends quickly capturing my nipple, his other hand slips into my pajama bottoms and runs straight through my folds. It doesn't take much, just a couple of minutes later, I'm experiencing my first orgasm—

not from my own hand—in years. What's even better, is this is the first orgasm Danny Quinn has ever given me, and it's better than all my previous orgasms rolled together. I open my eyes while panting and find Danny smiling down at me.

"If I lost my sight right now, I'd deal with it, by replaying the way you look when I give you that pleasure over and over in my mind, babe," he tells me. Then before I can react, he leans back down and kisses me again. Gentle, soft, loving. I feel the emotion clogging my throat before the tears come, trailing down my cheek. He leans down and kisses them away.

Not really sure what to do, having been so long for me since I've done this, but feeling like it's my turn to give Danny something. I sit up, staring at him. "I should—"

Danny cuts me off before I can really say anything. "You should just sit here in my arms and watch the film, I'm pretty sure that Rubén will be up there all night," he says pointing up to where Rubén and Amanda disappeared to earlier before sitting back on the sofa, his attention back to the television. "Just chill, Bel. I'm gonna stay. You want me on the sofa, that's fine. I'll tell you now, though, I want to be in your bed beside you," he continues.

My mouth opens and closes a couple of times, then I pull myself together and whisper, "You can sleep in my bed with me."

"Right. Don't worry, babe, there's nothing more than some making out happening for a while. Slow. I'm good with that. Anyway, we missed out on this part all those years ago." He turns to me smiling and it warms me.

"You're wooing me?" I ask, as my cheeks heat.

"You want to look at it like that Bel, have at it. For me, you're mine. It doesn't matter whether we're dating, living together, married, it's all going to happen anyway. All you need to know is through it all, you're mine." My heart picks up speed, in a great way, thinking about all our future possibilities as I snuggle under his arm. Then my stomach hollows, thinking on all the same things Amanda is going to miss out on. My eyes move to the ceiling. Whatever Amanda might miss out on, it's not going to stop her making the most of the time she has now, and neither should we.

Chapter EIGHTEEN

Anabel Adams

Waking the next morning, warmth envelops me. Danny. Strangely I don't feel suffocated like I always did when Keith's arms were draped over me in those early years. I smile and allow myself these few moments of quiet, as I bask in his love. His powerful but gentle arms, holding me, even in sleep, like I'm precious. Delicate. Loved.

My ears pick up noise in the kitchen, so carefully I slip from his body. I stand and stare down at him. His face is gentle, soft, while in sleep. Not that I don't see that side of him generally. It's just his face always seems to be doing something. It's like, even if I see him standing, looking relaxed, his mind is constantly going and his face portrays that. It shows he's always aware. Right now, it's like I'm looking back at that seventeen-year-old, the one I first fell in love with. The one I never stopped loving. My battered heart constricts from the pain, then just like that, like a rubber band snapping, I exhale letting everything out. Knowing this right here—this is my future.

Happier than I've felt in a long while, knowing that's what Amanda wants for me too, I feel as though I'm walking on clouds as I make my way to the kitchen. Putting my hand to the door, Amanda's giggles make me stop. I second guess my decision to enter the room, knowing they need time.

"Make me toast then stable boy."

"Yes, milady." I take a tentative step back, scared of what I might find if I open the door. "You want jelly, babe?" Rubén asks and hearing his voice back to normal, my feet automatically move forward. My palm going to the wood I push through.

"Morning, Bellie."

"Morning, babe."

They both chorus together and all the wariness leaves my body.

"Morning," I chirp back.

"Danny?" Amanda asks nodding toward the living room.

"Still sleeping," I reply.

"Toast?" Rubén asks me, waving Amanda's freshly cooked, jam covered breakfast at me.

"No thanks. I can only stomach coffee when I've first woken up," I tell him, dragging my feet until I reach the coffee pot, pouring myself a fresh cup and adding creamer. I inhale the scent before slugging back a few gulps. Moving to the table, I watch as they eat their breakfast. Throwing each other meaningful glances, while consuming their food, my brain starts working and a realization kicks in.

"You two did the nasty, didn't you?" I wink at them both sitting opposite me as Rubén encourages Amanda to eat some toast.

Rubén shakes his head smiling, gets up, takes his cup to the basin, walks back to Amanda, then crouches down to her height. Leaning in, he kisses her mouth softly and says, "I'm going to take a shower, come join me soon?" Amanda nods, biting her lip. "No one more beautiful, babe," he whispers then walks out.

I feel the emotions get clogged in my throat as I watch him walk away.

"So?" I say smiling.

"He… he…." She stops and takes a breath, reining in the emotion. "We made love, Bellie. He was gentle, caressing me, touching me, holding me. He kissed every scar on my chest, telling me it meant I survived, that I was a fighter, and nothing should make a man prouder than to see battle scars on his woman. He said he knew I was beautiful when we were younger, that he was a douche not pinning me down then. But now, I wasn't just beautiful… I was perfect. He wouldn't change a thing." She smiles through the tears that stream down her cheeks and I mirror her as my own tears threaten to erupt.

"He's everything I could have ever wished for… for you, Moo," my voice trembles as I try to convey to her just how much I believe what I'm saying.

"This is… it's what," Amanda sighs, twisting her fingers around each other.

"What is it?" I cough out, as a happy sob finally escapes me.

"This is what I've always wanted, someone to love me for me. My faults, my attributes. All the things that make me exactly who I was always meant to be. I… I just f-feel cheated. After all these years, I find the one for me at the end… when I can't live the life I wanted with him." She shakes her head and stands. The wooden chair scrapes against the floor, but she doesn't notice, seemingly completely lost in her own head.

"Amanda, the way you feel. I don't know… not for sure, but it sounds like a natural reaction to me." The explanation spills out of me, but my head and heart don't match with my reasoning. Everything still screams that this is unfair. My whole being wants to lay on the floor and scream like a toddler.

"It's not that my understanding of the feelings I'm having are completely blurred. I'm sure they're natural. It's just, I feel selfish." Losing the grip I had on my coffee, it drops to the table and I watch, in what seems like slow motion, as the handle breaks off and the remaining dregs of coffee that were swirling in the bottom of the cup ooze out onto the table.

"I'll just—"

"No. Stop!" I cut Amanda off as she's about to clean up the mess. Standing and making my way around the table, I step up to her until we're face to face. Close enough for our eyes to bore into each other. "Tell me why? Right now, explain what you mean?" I whisper, as my stomach cramps from the uneasy pain slithering through me.

"I… it's… o-oh, Bellie. I know okay? I know that I don't have long left. I feel it in me. Every day I wake a little weaker, every day I'm a little more tired." She stops and swallows, bringing her hand up between us, she clenches her fist biting down on it. I remain still and quiet, waiting for her to explain what she's feeling, while trying not to let my legs buckle with the weakness I feel in them at every word she speaks. "Every day a little more of my fight goes, every day I'm a little more resigned to the fact that I'm going to die," her voice breaks and I tremble with fear, anger and frustration as my eyes trace yet another of her tears escaping the pain. "I feel selfish because some people don't have a warning. They can't say goodbye, or write a bucket list. They don't get to spend time with their loved ones… Bellie, they don't get to *fall in love.* Here I am complaining, whining that I've finally found the person I was always meant to be with. And now, I'm going to lose him. Worse, he's going to lose me. He's the one who has to live with that. He's the one who has to carry on. He's the one who has to survive. When I think of what this might do to him, it just about breaks whatever fight I have left. I love him Bellie and I know, down to my bones, that life is too short. I've been in pain for a while, he could be in pain for the rest of his life. I don't want to destroy him." My head throbs with a buzzing in my ears and I realize, right there is what all this anguish has been about. Watching her face crumble, I wonder what I can do, how I'm supposed to make it better for her. Then the weight crashes down on me when I realize there's nothing that can make things better for her. All I can do is be with her, show her just how much I love her. How much I'll always love her.

"Amanda, I promise… swear, I'll look out for him. Danny and me will. Everything we can do, even if he tells us to get lost. We won't. We'll be there when he needs us. I swear, honey." I grab her hands in mine and catch her eyes. "*Swear.*" I show her the conviction in my eyes. She smiles and nods through the tears. "Remember what I said. *Every. Single. Moment*. Now go," I say pointing upstairs. "He'll be waiting in that shower." Placing my palm on her cheek, my thumb rubs away the tears. "Give him everything you have baby. Give him it all," I whisper. Her eyes light up as she bites her bottom lip, then turns walking to the stairs. Just at the last minute, she spins around and rushes to me, throwing her frail body into mine and wrapping her arms around my neck. I feel her nuzzle into my hair.

"Love you, Bellie," she whispers and I close my eyes, drinking her in, her smell, her feel, her heartbeat.

"Love you, Moo."

After Amanda goes upstairs, I spend my time staring vacantly into the backyard. I'm brought out of my trance when two warm, strong arms wrap around my waist. Danny's chin rests on my shoulder. "You made her feel better, baby," he whispers.

"I just told her the truth," I reply.

"I know. We both know. It doesn't matter what she does or doesn't do, or say, Rubén won't be leaving her. He's all about Amanda. But you gave her the peace that she needed. You took a load off, and with everything else she deserves that." Unable to reply I work my throat, holding in the emotion. "Proud of you, baby," Danny finishes and the tears I kept in check while talking to Amanda fall. And I know they can, I know the man standing behind me, the one who came from the boy I loved. He'll always look after me. He'll always protect me. He'll always make me feel loved, safe… *wanted.* That's when I decide he needs to know, just how things lay for me.

"Danny," I breathe out slowly and quietly. He squeezes me silently, letting me know he's all here for me. “I know we haven’t… that my thoughts are filled with Amanda right now. But I need you to know, no matter what happens, I still love you. I never stopped, and more… I want us to be forever Danny. I never want to lose you.” Closing my eyes, I let all my secrets out.

“Best thing I’ve heard in forever, sweetheart,” he says softly into my ear. I melt back into him, knowing he’ll hold me, support me, love me. Forever.

Chapter NINETEEN

Anabel Adams

"Seriously, you need to stop," Amanda gasps, doubled over, clutching her stomach with laughter.

"You think?" I ask, looking between her and the oar in my hand.

"Yes! For the love of God, yes! We're just going around and around," she says wiping her eyes, the laughter forming as tears.

Shrugging my shoulders, I sit back smiling. Letting my hand hang over the side of the boat, my fingers dip in the water as I study Amanda through my sunglasses. It's been three weeks of amazing fun. We've completed a lot of the bucket list Amanda made. Thinking about it causes instant pain, but knowing I'm helping her do all the things she wanted takes the edge off. She's getting worse, though. Her frame is getting frailer and it's harder getting her to eat now. The tiredness is seeping in quickly and her eyes dull slightly more every day. Her pop is coming tomorrow. She told him he needs to come. He wanted to let her have "one last hurrah!" That's what she tells me. But I heard her on the phone yesterday, telling him she could feel her time closing in. It hurts, all of it. So again, I found myself in my room, staring at the stars with my little notebook.

> *No matter what time is shared between us, it will never be enough. She is, and always will be, my best friend. Her pain is crippling me, but I never show her anything other than strength. I wonder if I give her my strength, will it help her hold on, just a little while longer. I know my thoughts are selfish, but I'm not ready to say goodbye. I'll never be ready. The problem is mine, when her body needs to rest, when she can't fight anymore, I will let her go. It will be the single hardest thing I've ever done in my life, but as long as she knows I'll always love her, I'll miss her every second, minute, hour. Every. Single. Moment. That I'll never stop thinking of her…*

"I can see you watching me from behind your glasses, Bellie." She smirks at me.

"Okay lazy, have you had enough? Shall we call the guys to come rescue us?" I ask with a wink.

Amanda nods. Glancing over to the guys, they're sitting on the lakeside, clutching their beers and chatting. I noticed that all through their conversation they always had one eye on us. Danny looks up and catches me looking, he raises his beer in an *'are you okay?'* salute.

Cupping my hands around my mouth, I shout, "Help us… we need strong men to rescue us." He shakes his head with a smile and looks towards his feet. Moments later they've grabbed the motorboat and are headed our way.

"What seems to be the problem, ladies? Can we give you a jump?" Rubén asks looking at Amanda with a smirk and we all laugh.

"How did you end up with only one oar?" Danny asks and his lips twitch.

"Look, those things are heavy and hard to maneuver," I say blowing a strand of hair off my face.

"Okay baby," he coos at me with a smirk. So I flip him the bird, after which Danny and Rubén burst into laughter.

"Are you going to save us? Or do we need to find some new heroes?" Amanda butts into their mirth.

Rubén chokes on his laughter as Danny's eyes narrow on me. "Wouldn't happen babe, 'cause then we'd have to give your new heroes a beat down." Rubén winks and Amanda rolls her eyes.

I blow a kiss to Danny and he cocks his finger at me then points to the boat. "Well, I guess that's my cue to get over there with my man," I tell Amanda raising my eyebrows and she giggles. I stand, Rubén and Danny take a hand each and help me across. Danny tugs me down, twisting my body around until I land in his lap. Rubén gets up and steps over to the other boat, securing a rope between the two crafts, he nods at Danny, who starts the motor. We drag the boat I was just in, behind the one where I'm now nestled in Danny's lap, back to the dock. He ties our motorboat up as I watch Rubén doing the same with the other one.

"Stand up," Danny says and my eyes move back to him. I nod, standing and immediately he places both hands around my waist, lifting me onto the wooden dock like I'm as light as a feather. I watch mesmerized, my mouth hanging open, as he places his palms to the dock and jumps up like it's nothing. I'm glued to his arms, the movement captures my attention, and now I can't seem to tear myself away from the flexing muscle. "Baby, eyes," he demands as his chest stops in front of me. I look up to him, but he doesn't say anything, just leans down claiming my mouth. One of his hands slips into my hair at the back of my head, the other travels down until it's firmly placed under my butt cheek. Then with a little jolt, he lifts me up. Automatically I cross my legs around his waist, moaning into his mouth, as I wrap my arms behind his neck and pull back slightly so I can nip his lip.

"Get a room, dude," Rubén shouts behind us and I hear Amanda chuckle, but it's drowned out when Danny groans down my throat, rubs my butt, and I feel his arousal pressing into my heat. Detaching my lips I pant, looking at Danny.

"Come on, we better get going, it'll be dark soon," he says, brushing my hair off my face lovingly. Easing my legs down, I look back to the lake. "What's wrong?" he asks.

Sighing I try to explain. "It's another thing done. Something else ticked off her bucket list. I'm worried when all the items are done, will she give up? I…" Breaking off, I rub my chest. "Sometimes… when I think of what's coming, what's going to happen and that we're going to lose her, I can't breathe. It feels like I have a Cadillac sitting on my chest."

"Hey. It's not going to be easy. Just remember, you're giving her everything she wants before it's too late. You're being strong for her. She knows how much you love her. That's all you can do. Make each moment count, baby," he tells me.

Every. Single. Moment. The words float through my brain, giving me strength.

"Come on," he says, grabbing me and once again picking me up, until I cross my legs around his waist. With my position set, my head on his shoulder, he carries me back to the car. "I'll be your strength when you feel like giving up. Just keep holding on baby."

Danny Quinn

"How is she?" I question Rubén as he walks out the back to join me.

"Asleep. They both are. I'm glad, she needs the rest," he replies.

As he stands next to me, I reach across to the table and pass him the beer I had waiting. Running my hand down my face, I sigh, feeling drained. Getting back from the lake a couple of hours ago, we were all on a high. It had been a great day, until tonight. Almost as soon as we got home Amanda had some kind of breathing attack, she was struggling and there was nothing we could do. I thought she was going to die. I called the doc and he came straight away. By the time he got here she had calmed. He checked her over, of course, but said she was okay now. That this wasn't uncommon in the later stages… at the end of life. *Fuck.* Those words hit us all like a fucking train. Bel wouldn't leave her side when they propped Amanda into a sitting position in her bed. Now it seems they've fallen asleep together.

"Hate to bring this up, but she doesn't have a nurse at home. I thought you needed one. Unless she was going into a hospice?" I ask Rubén.

"I don't know. Her pop is coming tomorrow. I'll find out. I need to have a chat with him. There are a few things I want to get clear. Mr. Warren was always a decent guy. Hopefully, he'll be happy to know I'm with her."

"He will. After that dick, Pierre, I bet he'll be over the fucking moon," I can hear the growl in my own voice. Amanda isn't mine, I care about her, of course. The four of us were close when we were younger, even with the extended group, we always gravitated toward each other. I'm hurting that she's dying. It's fucking ridiculous that in this day and age cancer still kills so many of us. She hasn't even really lived yet. Still, the pain I feel is mainly for Bel. I'm sad for her, I hate seeing her hurting so much, but it's more than that. I can't help watching her sometimes and feeling sick in the pit of my stomach. If that were her dying from cancer, watching her go through this would just about kill me too. I kind of get where Pierre was coming from, it would be soul destroying to watch her die. But I'd never leave her. I'd be by her side for every appointment, every bad and good day, every time she was sick, every little bit of chemo. *Fuck!* I'd be there when each and every fucking hair dropped from her beautiful head. I don't understand how that douche just walked away from her. Just left her when she needed him most. If you love someone, there isn't a single thing you can do about it. You can't just stop, turn away, and pretend they don't exist. Not if you truly love them. I know that I love Bel. The reason I know is because she's ingrained onto my soul. I tried to forget her, every day after I let her walk away. Every damn day. I never won that battle. There was no way I'd ever get her out from under my skin. My love for her would always exist, beyond the scope of life or death. When there was nothing else, there would still be her. It's just the way it would always be.

"He's someone else I need to deal with," Rubén mumbles.

"Let me know what you need from me. I'm there, with fucking bells on," I tell him.

"I will. For now, it's all about Amanda. I want her last few weeks…" he stops and swallows a couple of times. I place my hand on his shoulder and squeeze. Letting him know I'm here. I pull my hand away, taking a gulp of my beer until Rubén speaks again, "Anyway, I want to know what's going on with Shannon. And that realtor you had working for you. That crazy bitch still stalking you?" He chuckles and I let him have that, knowing it's his way of covering up, his way of composing himself.

"Shannon and I are officially divorced as of ten days ago," I reply. Finally, I feel like the weight of that disaster has been lifted.

"Did you fold and give her anything?"

I nod and he rolls his eyes, but he doesn't get it. "I gave her a quarter million."

"The fuck is wrong with you? She should have walked away with nothing, you didn't have to give her dick," he chastises me.

"Yeah, I know. If I'd have done that she would have never left me alone. This way it's small change to get rid of her forever," I explain.

"How do you figure that?" He raises an eyebrow in question.

"I had it written into the divorce. Not a phone call, visit, letter, text, not a fucking telegram. No contact. If she does then the money is gone, she pays it all back or goes to jail. *Simple.* I figured it was more than worth it. Hell, I would have paid double that to get rid of her," I answer him with a smirk which he mirrors. It's a half truth, I know that even as it leaves my lips. After everything that Shannon put me through, the phone calls, the bitching, the cheating, in the end, I couldn't blame her. She knew I was never really with her. I never chose her. I just stayed, when I should have let her go, probably fucking up her life while I blindly traveled through my own. I knew my life would never be blessed because Bel wasn't a part of it, not even as a friend. Anabel was my home. Since I forced her out of my life all those years ago, I've been homeless.

"And the other crazy one?" Rubén asks bringing me back into the conversation.

"Layla got rid of her. She was getting clingy, then she became unprofessional. She stopped being able to do her job, which was the only reason I kept her ass on the company list of contractors. We've got a new guy. He seems pretty legit, although I leave that all to Layla now." I stop talking and rub my chin. There was a time, up until recently, that I wouldn't have even considered handing the reins over to anyone else. I control everything, like to know what's going on at all times. I don't have a board of directors or any shit like that, I manage it all myself. It's never been an issue as I've never needed to answer to anyone. Even when I was married to Shannon, I was never worried about getting home by a certain time. She just wasn't a priority. Now things have changed in my life. Everything has done a one-eighty. My priority is Bel. There isn't a doubt in my mind about whether to put her first or not. She just is. I've handed a lot of my work over to Layla. I trust her, it's about time I gave her more responsibility. Other CEOs would think I was crazy. She's a PA, but I know that she's way more than that. She's been there through the last five years. Working day and night if needed. She's earned her dues, but more than that, she's damn good at whatever work I have her do. I need to take a step back, especially at the moment. I've put enough into the company, so I'm comfortable in the knowledge that it's running smoothly, even if it's not me at the helm.

"You can trust her to do good. She's a fucking bulldog when it comes to work. I remember when she helped me out for a month, back when Heath worked for me. Sheesh." He shakes his head with a grin. "She was better than most of the men who sit on my board," Rubén says. I think back to that time, it was the only occasion I was worried about losing her to someone else. I knew, as loyal as she's always been, the chance to work with her long-term boyfriend, someone she doesn't get to see very often, was a definite pull. Rubén's marketing company is big and as such manages to haul in some widely headhunted employees. He can pretty much hand pick his management. Thankfully, she stayed with me. We've both been lucky with our work. I believe that's because we got away from this fucking place. The fact that two people from the same year in our town, both went off and made something of themselves, is big news. I know the guys that we used to hang with don't like it, they can't deal with the jealousy. Still we both did it, but in the process we left our hearts behind. If I could go back in time and change things, this time I'd tell her I love her too. Ask her to be with me, and beg her not to marry Keith, I would, without question. Even if it meant that I never played football, never had my company and never made my money. She's worth everything to me. I'd give it all up in a heartbeat, I'm pretty sure Rubén would answer the same way as me about Amanda. Hopefully, in Bel, I'll have my future. The one I've always wanted. I know one thing. Now she's here with me, I finally have my home back.

•

Chapter TWENTY

Danny Quinn

"Mr Warren," Rubén says holding out his hand. Amanda's dad has aged. His once dark hair is now white all over and the lines on his face show both age and worry. This illness has been hard on him too. His eyes are sad and tired, and once again my stomach turns thinking about what's coming.

"Rubén, Danny, I think we're passed the formalities now, you're both men. Please call me Mike." He smiles but it doesn't even come close to reaching his eyes. Nobody questions the lack of warmth. We know what he's going through.

"Mike," I say once he's shaken Rubén's hand, offering him my own.

"Danny, how's your mom and pop?" His smile seems genuine this time.

"They're good, thanks. Loving the Florida weather," I return and he nods. "We're this way," I tell him, leading the way back to my rental.

Once we're all in the car, Mike in the front with me, while Rubén squashes his big frame in the back. We make idle conversation until Rubén turns things a totally different way.

"Mr… Mike. I know this isn't the time nor the place, in the back of a car from the airport to see your sick daughter, but when you get to the house obviously you'll want to be with Amanda and I need to get this clear before we get there," Rubén mumbles.

"Spit it out son," Mike tells him with a smirk.

"I'm in love with her." Rubén's words make me think of Bel. I have nobody to share that with from her side, because apart from Amanda, she has no one. I did share with my parents the night we became more than friends. My pop said about time, my mom just sighed happily down the phone line.

"S'pect you are son," Mike replies and I can see Rubén's surprise when his head jolts, just slightly, at the words.

"You knew," Rubén says but it's not a question.

"Probably get this Rubén, but I'll lay it out anyway. My daughter and me, we're close. We have been since her momma died, but more so when we moved to France together. She had Pierre for a while." Mike stops and grinds his teeth. "You know that didn't end well. Always thought he was a bit weak. Didn't realize my daughter would be walking down the aisle to a man that would abandon her when she needed him the most." He stops again, I can feel the emotion rolling off him, it's choking. When I look in the rear view mirror at Rubén, his face is hard, angry and I know it's because he's thinking of Amanda being left to deal with all her shit alone. "Still, I know she had a thing for you when she was younger. Nothing seemed to develop between you, unless I missed it?" He turns to Rubén, who shakes his head once in the negative. "So that was that. A bit like you and Anabel," he says looking over at me. "She was smitten with you. After you left she was closed off for a while. Never seen a girl of that age, manage to convince herself so fiercely, that she was doing the right thing by marrying someone she didn't really love." He shakes his head sadly, and I grip the steering wheel harder turning my knuckles white while clenching my jaw. In that moment it dawns on me that I'm no better than Pierre, I abandoned her. Granted, I thought I was doing the right thing, but still, there's no way to pretty it up. "Mandy has told me she's happy with you. I figure she's told you she loves you. Not sure if she has, and normally I wouldn't be the one to say it but obviously she hasn't got time. You make her happy. Continue doing that and we'll be solid. She could do with a bit of beautiful before…" He stops talking and we all go quiet. Everyone seems lost in their own thoughts for the rest of the journey until we turn into Amanda's road. Then Rubén breaks the silence.

"Mike, when things aren't all about Amanda anymore…" he stops and grinds his teeth before continuing, "…I'll be coming to you, asking for a favor."

"And what might that be, son?" Mike asks turning in the passenger seat to look at Rubén.

"Everything you know about Pierre Bellerose," Rubén answers. A tinge of anger in his tone.

Mike turns back around, looking ahead at the road. He nods. "Consider it done." Then the car, once again, falls silent.

Anabel Adams

"Anabel," Mike breathes out as he clasps the top of my arms and just looks at me. "I've missed you, darlin'." He crushes me into his chest and I take in his scent of Old Spice and ginger, even after all these years, he still smells the same.

"I missed you, too," I whisper back.

"We need to talk later sweetheart, after I reconnect with my little girl. How is she?" The worry in his voice makes it wobble. I glance down to my clenched fists, before looking back at him.

"She's gone downhill… since yesterday." I bite my bottom lip and look at him. His eyes have a faraway look, and I know that my words are causing him pain.

"It's okay, darlin', not like this is a surprise. Got her call the other day, knew it was time to get my ass in the air." He hugs me again.

"She's downstairs," I tell him and watch as he nods, giving me a small smile, making his way to Amanda. I don't need to explain where the room is, this is his old house. It must be hard for him being back here. I know it's not somewhere he ever wanted to revisit. On top of all the pain that he's feeling right now, he has to walk into the room that Katherine, Amanda's mom, spent her last hours in. Now he's going to watch his daughter, in the next few weeks, lose her life there too.

"Hey baby," Danny whispers pulling me into his arms, only leaning back slightly to wipe away the tears I was ignoring.

I cling to him for a few minutes as I hear Rubén leave the room, heading out back. Then I pull away from him. "Danny, I'm going to go and jot down some thoughts."

"You know, although I suggested that notebook and I still think it's a good idea, you can come and talk to me. I'll always be here to listen if you need me. I'm here for whatever you might want. Always," he says, wiping away yet another tear.

"I know. Thank you. I just need to purge everything, so my mind is as clear and as focused as possible for her. I'll return to look at my thoughts after..." I don't finish my sentence. He knows what I mean. Danny leans down gently kissing my mouth then letting me go, he walks off in the direction that Rubén just went. As I walk up the stairs to my room, the house is quiet and I hear Amanda and her pop chatting.

"No. It's fine, Pop. I'll be fine," Amanda's voice is muffled, but I can still hear the sadness.

"I'll figure something out," Mike tells her.

"You can't. You don't have the money to get a nurse," she replies and I want to walk down there and butt into their conversation. Now isn't the right time. I will bring it up later, though.

Their voices become quieter as I continue to my room. Sitting on the windowsill, I grab my notebook and open up a new page.

> *I watch people with Amanda since she's been back. Of those people who know about the cancer—mainly people we've known for years, that inevitably, we have bumped into around town and she's shared her illness with—they all look upon her with pity. I hate that for her. It's not what she wants, needs or deserves. I*

want to shout at them, tell them if they want to do something then smile or chat with her like they would if they didn't know she was dying. Give her the last few weeks of normal that she so desperately craves.

Still, I can't be mad, I get it. I do. It's just that I've had time to work out what she needs from me. I can't say I've gotten used to it because I don't think that's possible. I can't even say I've come to terms with it, I'm not sure that will ever happen. But, I do feel like I've learnt how to deal with her. I say deal with her because, although I have no experience, I would imagine everyone is different. Every single person that is facing imminent death will, no doubt, want or need something different than what the next person does.

Knowing Amanda, and more than that, asking her honestly what it is that she'd like from the time she has left, has determined how I deal with her. Giving her strength, showing her normal, helping to fulfill her wishes and just being with her as much as I possibly can... that's what I do for her. That's what she wants.

Holding myself together is getting harder. When she's spending time out with us, doing fun things, I can somewhat overlook that tiredness creeping in. Dismiss the weight she's losing. As she starts becoming more unwell, bedridden, weaker, and starts wasting away, I'm scared. Scared of my reactions to her. Scared that I won't be able to control what she sees in my eyes. Scared that the fight in me, the fight I have... for her... that fight might be overpowered by the sadness I constantly feel. The pain that I'm always battling with.

I won't give up fighting. Every. Single. Moment.

I'll pull out everything within me and wring myself dry for her.

As long as I'm fighting, I hope she will too.

I wander around the grocery store, grabbing things without really thinking about it and throwing them in the cart. Over the last couple of weeks, I've managed to pick up some cleaning jobs in the evening, specifically after Amanda's in bed. Unfortunately, there were no night shifts at the Hatfield Club. The money I'd saved from working there, though, has been keeping me afloat. I need to find another job soon. I know that Danny mentioned the possibility of reopening my pop's ice cream store, but he hasn't said anything more and I don't want to ask him. He wanted to come with me to the store, to help, more likely to make sure I was okay, but I asked him to stay at the house with Rubén.

It's strange, for all of us, it's like real life has been put on hold. Not one of us cares what's happening in the rest of the world. It seems Rubén and Danny are not in the slightest bit interested in their businesses either. Danny argued that I shouldn't be on my own, even visiting the store. I explained that being on my own was exactly what I needed right now. Mike was with Amanda when I left, they hadn't seen each other for weeks and need that time together. The cupboards need restocking and Rubén is wandering around like a lost sheep. Now, though, I seem to be in a trance, aimlessly in search of nothing and something all at the same time.

"Anabel…" the soft voice startles me and I spin on my heel. Finding myself looking straight into the eyes of Ashley Summers.

"Ashley?" I choke out. It's not like I haven't seen her around here and there over the years. But we've never spoken.

"Is it true?" she asks softly.

"Is what true?" I ask, my stomach dropping, hoping she's not asking about Amanda. Ashley Summers is the last person I want to talk to about Amanda.

"You've left Keith? It's just that the town is all talking about it. Since I moved just outside of town,

I don't hear the news real quick, so I only heard two days ago."

I stare at her, shaking my head. *I can't believe this is what she's asking.* After everything that has happened to me in the last few weeks, Keith is the furthest thing from my mind.

"I take it that's a no then?" she asks looking back at me and I realize I'm still shaking my head.

"Sorry, yes, no. I mean, yes, I've left Keith." Her eyes widen and I let myself think about Keith for a moment. I started the divorce, but it's kind of stalled since I left my job. I plan on picking up where I left off, though, as soon as I can. The last few times I've seen him, he's been polite, nodding a hello to me or smiling. He hasn't approached me, apart from that one time with Declan. He seems to be letting me live my life. This is the first time in all the years that I finally feel some peace between us. Ashley shatters that with her next few sentences.

"Oh good, I hoped so. I mean, he told me you were, but I really wanted to confirm with you. I'm just glad he's finally spending time with Bobby. They've now got as much time as they need to get to really know each other. Not that I'm saying you were stopping him," she tells me, placing her hand on my arm and I'm thrown. The first thing that comes to mind is that I can see the sincerity in her eyes. Now, I haven't seen this woman in years, but whenever I have, her eyes have always sliced through me. She was nasty to me back at school as she always wanted to be with Keith. *Now, suddenly, she's being nice?* Confusion swirls around my head. The next thing that hits me, I realize probably should have been the first thing I thought about, was her talking about a Bobby? And Keith getting to know him?

"Sorry… what?" I manage to push out through the complete jumble that is now my brain.

"Oh… s-sorry, is this too hard for you to talk about? I was hoping I'd left it long enough," she mumbles back nervously, looking everywhere but at me.

"Okay. Let's just clear this up, Ashley. Otherwise, I can see us going 'round the houses, and I for one, don't have time for that." She nods in response so I can carry on. "I have no idea what you're talking about. Who Bobby is or when I was ever capable of stopping Keith doing anything? I'm sorry, but you lost me after you asked if I was still with him."

Her eyes widen as my words sink in. She takes in my face, and I allow her time to assess me. When she nods, it's with an understanding that I'm not lying. "Can we… do you… have time to talk?" she asks.

I glance at my watch and reply, "Yeah, but let me grab this stuff. I don't have long. Meet me at the coffee house across the street in ten, yeah?" I ask and once again she nods with a sadness in her eyes. She moves away, her shoulders sinking and I can feel the dread in my stomach. I know this isn't going to be good. I'm just not sure how bad it's going to be, and whether I'm ready for it.

Ten minutes later and after loading the bags into the car, I make my way to the coffee house. After ordering a coffee, I join Ashley.

"So, do you want to tell me everything?" I ask, smiling at the waitress as she places my coffee in front of me.

Ashley looks at me. "I have a son. You know this because everyone in the town knows this. I got pregnant at eighteen. A little while before you got married, I was sleeping with Keith."

There it is.

Ashley doesn't mess around as she stomps on my whole life.

One that wasn't really real.

She pauses to take a sip of coffee and I can feel my heartbeat picking up. Blood whooshing in my ears. "I'm sorry. Back then, I thought you knew. There was a lot of talk. People said that you and Keith weren't together, or that one or the other of you was going to call everything off. Some people said you were in love with Danny Quinn. I didn't talk to you directly, so I only had one side of the story… Keith's. We were sleeping together, but you have to know, I was in love with him. I still am," she tells me softly, looking up tentatively from under her eyelashes.

Her words fill the air, and I think back to that time. I didn't even know where our relationship stood, so it stands to reason that nobody else would. Still, we were very clearly not broken up as far as Keith and I were concerned, and so he was definitely cheating on me. The idea that Keith was cheating doesn't bother me like it should. Although, I never really did anything with Danny… except that one kiss which I still felt guilty for all these years later. Just knowing I've always loved him, knowing I never gave my all to Keith. The cause of my racing heartbeat though, is the knowledge that has just clicked into place in my brain.

"Bobby's his? Keith's?" I push out.

She nods sadly. "I'm sorry, he said you knew. I never thought to question it. He always used you as an excuse not to see him. To miss all his birthdays and Christmases. I loved him, so I let it go. When you split he told me, and I stupidly welcomed him back with open arms. He seems different, changed somehow. I can't quite work it out. Either way, I thought this was it for us, our time. Bobby is so happy. Of course, he knows all about Keith and has spent time with him, whenever Keith has graced Bobby with his presence. I want that for him," she says the last sentence staring down at the table and I watch tears slipping out of her eyes.

I can't lie and tell myself this isn't painful. Not because he cheated on me, not because he lied. No, it's because he has a child. Something at one point we wanted together, something I can't have. Obviously, it must be me. That's why he always blamed me because he already had a kid.

Now I know it will only ever be me.

There's a crack in my heart for my own loss.

I can't concentrate on that right now. It's something else to lock away until another time.

"Ashley," I whisper her name, taking her hand in mine across the table. "Thank you for telling me. I think you need to talk with Keith, I'm happy you're happy and that Bobby can have his dad around more. I'm truly over Keith, and we're going through a divorce. He's all yours," I say with a smile. I hold no malice for her though. With everything that has happened to me in the last while, I know life is too short to hold a grudge. "I have to go. Take care of yourself." She nods in reply, a sad smile gracing her lips as I get up, leave money for the coffee and walk away.

When I reach my car I feel something strange in my stomach, it feels a lot like relief. I knew that Keith and I were done, but I still worried that his new easy-going persona would change, once the divorce was in full swing. As he has someone else in his life, I'm thinking his attention will be now taken up, with the family he should have had all along. Plus, as a bonus, he won't be able to contest the divorce, on the grounds that if he does, I'll bring to the attention of the court the fact that he's had a secret family, and had one for all of our married life. Reaching into my bag to get the car keys, happy thoughts dancing through my mind, suddenly I'm knocked back, spun around and pinned against the car.

"Anabel," Declan's whiskey breath accosts my nose. I try to pull my face back.

"Declan, leave me alone. Seriously," I snap.

"So, you've gotten a bite since you left him. I wouldn't mind feeling that particular bite," he tells me, leaning so far into my personal space that he's almost kissing me. Something snaps in my mind and my heart. All the years I let this creepy, lowlife, predator, get away with anything he threw my way. So scared of the repercussions that standing against him would bring. Knowing my husband would take his side. Always feeling so alone. And that, somehow bled into my subconscious, making me think I was incapable of being who I wanted to be. Of having strength, like without Keith standing behind me, I was nothing. I know better now, I'm stronger, I have more important things to worry about than a drunken slob, who shouldn't bother women out on their own. Seeing red and before I really know what I'm doing, I raise my knee quickly, forcefully, and connect with Declan's balls. It's the second time I've done it in as many months and his eyes widen in shock before he drops to the ground. His hands automatically move between his legs as he clutches his balls while lying on his side in the fetal position.

I bend down and smile at the pain contorting his face, then whisper, "You stay *the fuck away* from me. That's a friendly warning. I will tell people how you've behaved over the last few years. I'll make sure to visit the sheriff, to inform him about all your recent behavior. But more than that, Declan. We grew up together, you've grown into a complete douche. Yet, I still know where your momma lives. I've never wanted to upset her, tell her about the kind of boy she raised, but I will Declan, I will. And I know your momma, she'd be disgusted with you. Hand on heart, I won't do that. You just need to clean up this drunken bum thing you have going on." I don't say anymore, ignoring the frightened look on his face, knowing that upsetting his mom is not something he wants. *What with him being a momma's boy.* I get in the car and head for home. Back to the real fear, the fear that sits in my heart at the moment, right next to the love.

Chapter TWENTY ONE

Anabel Adams

"Hey," I whisper sitting down next to Amanda. When I got back, Mike said she was in the backyard, watching the sunset with Rubén. I gave her time. Rubén came inside five minutes ago, telling me she missed me. It's dark now so I grabbed a blanket on my way out and have it placed around her shoulders.

"Thanks." She smiles over to me.

"Watching the stars again," I say. It's not really a question.

"Yeah. I was thinking about being up there. It's the only way I can face what's coming. Knowing I'll be in the sky looking down. Up there with my mom, and with your parents."

I swallow and bite the inside of my mouth, trying to keep my emotion under control. "Okay, well, as you'll be up there I need you to do me a favor," I tell her and she turns to me, her eyes sparkle with fun. "Tell my mom and pop that I'm putting in a complaint. Every damn time I ask them a question, they never answer." What I said was supposed to be funny, but it ends up being sad and I know it's because I wish, just once, they could answer me.

"I bet they do," she tells me interrupting my sad thoughts.

"Huh?"

"You probably have to look out for signs. You know that's the way it works on television, right?" I raise my eyebrow skeptically. "Oh, ye of little faith," she chides. "You probably haven't been looking hard enough. Tell you what, you ask me something, or just need me, I'll give you a sign. Now we just have to think of what." She winks at me.

"Okay, how about a feather?" I say.

Amanda scrunches up her face. "Really? That's the best you can do? Pfft!" she answers and I chuckle.

"Okay, what about you send me flowers?" I offer.

"What do you think I am… FedEx? She snorts and I chuckle again. "How about this…" she stops and grabs my hand. "If you talk to me and it's important, if you ask a question and want to know I've heard you, I'll try to make it rain. To let you know I'm still here," she whispers and I pull her in for a hug.

"You'll always be here. You'll forever be in my heart, Moo. You know that." She nods and I can feel her tears running down my cheek as I hold her tight.

A couple of hours later and Amanda is tucked into bed, sleeping like an angel, and I'm still out here staring at the stars. I don't move or look away from the sky, as I feel a presence take the vacant seat next to me. Nothing changes, all seems still and calm, just like the night.

"You know, she's scared. So scared," Mike's voice makes me jump slightly. It had been so quiet that I'd forgotten someone joined me.

I turn to look at him, immediately seeing the sadness and pain in his eyes. His age is now undeniable, his lines and wrinkles are obvious when I really take my time to roam over his face. I know he's older, but it's more than that. Cancer destroys more than one person's life. Turning away, my answer comes out in a squeak, "I know."

"It's not right," Mike continues and I look back to him but, this time, he's the one staring at the sky. He doesn't look at me, just stares at the stars. I can't stop the sudden drop I feel in my stomach as goosebumps break out across my skin. "Children shouldn't die first," he chokes the words out and I watch, as someone who I always thought of as a big strong man, crumbles before me. He leans forward, crossing his arms over his knees. His shoulders shake with the big sobs that break out of him, splintering his strength right before my eyes. I move over to him and place my arm across his shoulder. I feel cold, hollow and I'm hanging on by my fingertips.

There's nothing I can say to make this any easier for him. My chin trembles as renewed pain shoots through me. "I remember holding her when she was born," he whispers bringing his head back up to look at me. He smiles through the tears that still run down his face. I blink, trying to hold back my tears. "She was so little. Her skin was all wrinkly and I wondered… wondered what I'd do with this delicate little thing that the doctor had handed me. Then she t-turned her h-head into my chest and closed her eyes." He stops talking, looking away and taking a deep breath. The tears that were pooling in my own eyes spill over. I don't have the energy to control them anymore.

"I never understood what unconditional love was Anabel… until that moment. People had explained it, I thought I had it with Katherine. I wasn't even close, not until that very moment." His breath hitches and my chest burns as my lungs tighten and I struggle to breathe. He pulls out tissues, wiping his nose, handing me one and trying to pull himself together. His voice is more controlled when he speaks again,

"I'm not sure how I'm going to carry on. She's my whole world, sweetheart. When I look into her eyes, I still see that little bundle laying in my arms. It's my job to protect her. It's always been my job, but I'm having to watch her waste away. I'm helpless, utterly useless. I had the honor of seeing her grow, watching her develop and now it should be her best time. I should be watching her fall in love, get married, and have children. She's been cheated out of that, and instead of getting to watch these things happen to her, I'm having to watch my child die, slowly. She's disappearing before my eyes. I'm losing my little girl…" He stops speaking, his control lost again, and I wipe my face with my sleeve having wet through my tissue. My breath hitches and catches as I try to pull myself together, try to be strong again, even though it feels like acid is swimming through my veins, dissolving me from the inside out.

"I have no words, Mike," I whisper, feeling hopeless. I can't even give him anything more than a hug.

"Didn't s'pect you would darlin'. I know this is ripping you up inside, too. 'Bout as close as any two sisters could ever be, you and Mandy. I know she's scared of leaving you. She doesn't want you to be alone. I want you to know that I'll always be there for you. If you ever need family, sweetheart. I won't be staying here. This house belongs to Mandy, I know what she's gonna do with it and I'm fine with that. It's nothing to do with me anymore, and I never intend to come back here. Simone will be arriving in a few days. I asked her to let me have time with Mandy first. Once she's g-gone." He shakes his head and takes a breath. "Once I can leave this place, I'll be moving on. Not sure where yet. You're always welcome to come and live with me. If you ever need me. Just wanted you to know that. Also, I wanted to say thank you. Amanda had been so low before she came back here, never seen her like it. That ass she was married to had a big hand in that. Since she's come back here, it's like my real baby girl has returned. She's been happy, swear to you girl. Not heard her laugh so much, in so long, as I have over the phone these last few weeks. That's your doing." He smiles at me and grabs my hand giving it a squeeze.

"Rubén and Danny, too," I wheeze out through the still bubbling emotion.

"Yep. S'pect they both had a hand in it, too. But when I've talked to my girl, she's all about you. Bellie took me here, Bellie made me laugh about this. Pop you should have seen Bellie over at the indoor ice skating rink, she couldn't stand up, grabbed onto some poor boy's coat and dragged him down with her. The poor boy could've only been fourteen and was trying to hold onto the side for dear life," he says mimicking her voice and I laugh through my tears. "Mandy had to say it three times before she could finally get it out through her laughter. You did that, darlin'. You gave my girl happiness right here at the end when she desperately needs it. I'll never forget that. I'll always love you because of it. Proud of you. Know your mom and pop would be too, sweetheart." His words are the end of me. This time, it's me who leans forward, on my knees, my chest painful as I can't breathe through the sobs. Mike says something and walks off, the next thing I know, I'm being lifted into strong arms. I turn my head into Danny's chest as we walk through the house. My tears haven't dried up, but thankfully my body isn't heaving anymore. We get to my bed and Danny places me under the covers, pulling off my shoes, socks and sweatshirt, leaving me in my yoga pants and a wife-beater. Then stripping his clothes off he slides in next to me, pulling me onto his chest. He strokes my hair silently for a few minutes as my eyes droop.

"I'm broken," I whisper to him.

"Shhh baby, I'll fix you." His reply is the last thing I hear before I fall to sleep.

Chapter TWENTY TWO

Danny Quinn

Holding Bel in my arms last night as she broke was one of the hardest things I've ever had to watch. I love this woman with everything I have, and there was nothing I could do except hold her. The dawn is breaking and I watch her sleeping still in my arms. Bel has a connection to the stars, I've always known that. But being away when she lost her parents, meant I didn't realize how much stronger her fascination with the stars had become. I listened to her and Amanda talking last night after she grabbed a blanket and walked outside. I watched her through the kitchen window, but when she got to the chair, she covered Amanda with it. It warmed me inside, my beautiful, selfless girl. Still, I wanted her to be warm too. So I found another blanket and went out to give it to her. As I got closer, I heard Amanda telling Bel that her way of dealing with dying was imagining she's going to be up in the sky and that she was going to be one of the stars. It made my heart hurt when Bel said she talked to her mom and pop, but felt like they never responded to her when she needed them. I wanted to give Bel and Amanda something. There's nothing I can do to make life better, but I want to give them something to hold on to. Something that is more of a statement, a thing to believe in, a sign of hope in the darkness, not necessarily something tangible.

"Morning." Bel's voice is raspy with sleep and I smile down at her.

"Morning beautiful," I whisper back and lean down kissing her mouth. She quickly pulls back into the pillow. I stare down at her, confused.

"Morning breath," she tells me, holding her hand over her mouth. I smile down at her then move her hand, lean down and take her mouth again. This time biting her lip, so she opens up for me allowing my tongue to slip in. She moans into my mouth which I take as a sign of encouragement. I push my hands up under her top and pull up the bra I didn't remove last night. I'm just about to put my mouth over her when there's noise from downstairs followed by Rubén shouting.

"Anabel! Call… nine one one, *NOW!*" his roar makes me jump off the bed and throw my cell at Bel.

"Call quick, baby. I'll go see what's happening," I tell Bel while pulling on my sweatpants. She nods biting her lip as a frown passes over her face. I want to kiss the worry away, but right now, we have to focus our attention on other things. As I move out of the room, I can already hear Bel talking to the operator. Making my way down the stairs two at a time and jumping from about six steps up to the floor, I run through to Amanda's room. Once there I can see what Rubén is worried about. Amanda is doubled over in obvious pain. She's clutching her chest, struggling to breathe and is so pale. Her eyes are closing like she's losing consciousness.

"Fuck this, I need to get her to the ER now!" Rubén shouts. "Give me the keys to that piece of shit car," he demands but I shake my head.

"Listen, the ambulance is about two minutes out, you won't get to the hospital quicker than an EMT will get to her if we just wait."

He runs his palm down his face. "Fuck!" he shouts again as Bel comes around the corner.

"Oh God!" she says, panic threaded through her words. "Amanda," she says rushing forward and getting on the bed. She grabs hold of Amanda, bringing her into her chest. "Just hold on baby girl, hold on Moo. The ambulance is coming, they'll take the pain away. Come on, baby."

I look back to Rubén and his face gives everything away. All the pain he's been holding in, the torment he's currently feeling, having to watch the woman he loves fade away and more, suffer pain like she is right now. The tell-tale sirens indicating the ambulance can suddenly be heard, so I move to the front of the house opening the door for them.

When they get here, everything moves so quickly. Before I really know what's happening Amanda has been rushed off and Bel has gone with her. I walk back into the bedroom to find Rubén still standing in the same place. Unmoving and staring at the bed which is now empty. I walk over to him and place my hand on his shoulder. He jerks at the movement. "Come on man. This isn't going to help her. We should get to the hospital, and we need to call Mike. You have his number, right?" He nods and swallows before pulling his cell out of his back pocket and dialing as we move through the house. I snatch up the house keys which always hang on the wall next to the front door, before stepping outside and locking up. Rubén stands at the car waiting for me and saying goodbye to Mike on the phone. I can't help but look at the sky, thinking if there were ever a time to answer a call of despair then this would be it. I hope like hell that this isn't the end. Not yet. It's too soon.

Anabel Adams

I pace back and forth as the doctor is in with Amanda, her pop by her side.

"Bel, come sit with me, baby." I sigh and look at Danny. He sits next to a scared, sick looking Rubén, who right now seems like a little boy. I move to Danny and he pulls me onto his lap, burying his head in my chest he places a hand on each shoulder and pulls me into him like he's trying to mold himself to me. We sit, unmoving, not talking, hardly breathing, for what feels like forever. When Mike appears in front of our seats, it takes all three of us a few extended moments to grasp that he's there.

"Is she…" my voice cracks and breaks off.

Mike nods. "She's okay, sweetheart." His words cause my chest to deflate and I feel the blood filter back into my fingers, from where I was cutting off the circulation with my grip. "Can I see her?"

"Yeah, darlin', but she wants to talk to Rubén first." His words cause a spike of pain until I mentally slap myself and think about how I'd feel if it were me. Who would I want to see first, and I'm honestly not sure at this point, but I have a feeling if I were faced with the possibility of dying, then Danny would be my first thought. Rubén stands and Mike looks at him. "She's fragile, son."

Rubén nods. "I assumed she would be."

"No, not just physically. She had a turn, she needed pain relief and she didn't have any," Mike replies.

"Why not?" Rubén asks.

"Well, that's why she's fragile. The meds she needs at this late stage can only be administered at the hospice or by a registered nurse at home," Mike sighs.

"I don't get what the issue is? What am I missing?" Rubén snaps, his patience obviously thinning.

"Look, son, I'm a proud man, but I'm a father first. My pride can take a hike when it comes to my girl, so I'm gonna be honest. She should be in a hospice now. They can give her the drugs she needs as and when she requires them. She doesn't want to go to a hospice. She's being stubborn, but I can't say I don't get why. You know you've got a few weeks to live, you want to live them how you want." He stops and shakes his head. Rubén goes to open his mouth, clearly sick of waiting to get to Amanda. Mike speaks before Rubén can say anything, "Money son. Money is the problem. I'm able to cover a hospice, but Mandy doesn't want to go into a hospice she wants to stay at home. We've lived in France for so long, I don't have medical insurance to cover her anymore. I do have money saved though, enough to cover her treatment at a hospice. What I don't have is enough to cover her care and pay for a nurse twenty-four-seven, so she can stay at home." Mike hangs his head, admitting that he can't take care of his daughter is obviously hard. Showing that his daughter comes first is all I saw from what he said.

Rubén turns to Danny. "Do me a favor?" Danny nods in reply. "Call Stanford. Tell him I need money transferred to Mike… whatever amount is needed." He then turns to Mike. "Can you set up whatever she requires then?" Mike swallows and pulls a hand down his face nodding. "Great. Now please tell me where my girl is?" Rubén demands.

"Along the corridor. Room 73," Mike says, emotion in his voice. I watch Rubén stride in that direction as Danny pulls his phone out to make a call. I slide off his lap and go sit next to Mike.

"I know how hard that was for you. It would've been hard for my pop." He doesn't say anything. "To me, what you just did, shows just how much you love Amanda. That makes you the best kind of person there is in my book," I tell him, placing my hand on top of his. Mike turns his hand around and closes it around mine, giving me a squeeze. "So, she had pain and needed drugs which we didn't have? That was why she was so sick?" I whisper.

"Anabel. She's dying, you know that. In a nutshell, you're right. But the truth is, the chances of her completing anything else on her bucket list is small, darlin'. The doctor thinks she might not last the week." His words hit me and I feel like they've come from nowhere. I thought this was a hiccup. A bump in the road. I figured we had another month, at least. I struggle to breathe, gasping and clutching my chest.

"Breathe, baby." Suddenly Danny is next to me and pushes me forward so my head is between my knees. He rubs circles on my back as I concentrate on taking air in, then out, in, then out. I feel the panic receding as I let his warm hand calm me.

"I want to go, I can't wait anymore," I tell Danny and he nods.

We get to Amanda's room and push the door ajar. Rubén sits next to her bed, his head laying on the mattress as he holds her hand in his.

"Rubén?" his name comes out as a question.

"When I got here she was asleep. So I just held her hand. She looks so peaceful." I nod, walk over and kiss her head. Moving to the end of the bed I back up nearer to the door, trying to give Amanda and Rubén space, while not actually leaving.

"I'm going to go and see Mike, baby," Danny whispers in my ear and I nod. "I'll be back."

I don't take my eyes from Amanda. She looks peaceful, calm, and I let a stray tear slip down my cheek while no one can see.

About an hour later, a nurse came in and tried to get us to leave. We ignored her, there was no way she was waking up alone and scared. Amanda starts stirring. It takes a few minutes for her to wake up completely and take in her surroundings. Her eyes widen as she glances to her left, straight into a mirror which sits above a lowered basin, obviously set up for wheelchairs. She turns back to Rubén and her eyes water. Now she's awake she looks different—sick.

"Don't look at me!" Amanda's words are raw, pained and raspy as she tries to shout at Rubén. The bed swamps her now. She's tiny and frail, her eyes are sunken, but the fear is there on the surface for all to see.

"Just looking at my girl," Rubén whispers back and I hear his voice hitch, which makes me swallow down emotion. My back warms as Danny steps into me and wraps me in his arms, offering me his strength.

"You can't want me. Look at me, I'm hideous." The unrestrained terror in Amanda's voice causes a violent reaction in me as my stomach lurches and brings tears to my eyes as I battle to keep myself still.

"That's just not possible," he says sitting on the bed beside her. He tucks a stray strand of hair behind her ear and rubs his thumb over her hollowed cheek. "I wouldn't want to marry you if I didn't see your beauty inside and out," he whispers. Amanda's face is a picture of shock and disbelief. The internal struggle she's been fighting with her emotions breaks and the tears overflow. For once, those salty drops of water, have been born from happiness.

"You knew?" I softly ask Danny, not tearing my eyes from Amanda and Rubén.

"Yeah," he replies on a squeeze.

"He's making her so happy," I tell him something he already knows.

"She says yes, he'll be the one feeling like his dreams came true." Danny's words warm me. To know Rubén feels, about my best friend, exactly like I thought he did. I look up at Danny and he tilts his head down, grazing my lips with his. He pulls away slightly, but I can still feel his hot breath against my mouth when he whispers, "Know what it's like to want something so bad. When you finally get it, nothing will ever compare. Nothing."

Chapter TWENTY THREE

Anabel Adams

"Come on, Bellie, hurry up. I'm ready to go!" Amanda complains as I sit by her bed. She's sick of the hospital, even after only twenty-four hours and is more than ready to leave.

"The doctor should be around to discharge you soon, Moo. Stop complaining," I tell her wagging my finger.

"Where's Rubén? I thought he'd be here to take me home." Her voice is quiet, forlorn.

"Sorting out wedding stuff." Her eyes alight at my words.

"Oh," she answers with a grin. It's the first smile I've seen on her face this morning. "Tell me what he's doing," she pleads.

"No," I answer simply. Amanda frowns at me then pouts. I can't help the giggle that bubbles up.

"You wanted to have it on Saturday, so that's when it is, leave the rest up to Rubén," I say teasing her.

"I wanted Saturday because it's Momma's birthday," she whispers and I lift out of the chair moving myself to sit beside her on the hospital bed.

Stroking her face, I smile. "I know, Moo, and you know your momma she'd be so proud of you honey. So proud of how brave you are," I tell her, my chest swelling with my own pride in her.

"I don't feel brave, Bellie. I'm so scared. I'll be l-lucky if I live another week. I know it, even if p-people aren't saying it to me. My breathing is going downhill fast and I c-can't eat… I just can't face it. I want to live, but I'm letting myself die." She stops and closes her eyes, just trying to catch her breath and I grin through the pain that's like a red hot poker in my heart. "What the hell is wrong with my body? I've lost my f-fight Anabel… I don't have the energy to battle on anymore. I can feel my will slipping away." She scowls and thumps her closed fist on her thigh, although it's weak that's how I know she's still fighting.

"I think you *are* brave, but remember, when you aren't feeling it then tell me, I'll give you my strength. I'll be strong enough for you." I smile down at her, biting back the fresh swirl of emotions, as the door behind me opens and the doctor greets us with a good morning.

Taking a step back, I allow him to look her over. At one point he tries to talk to me about Amanda. I'm not sure that I'm in his good graces when I point out that she might be ill, but her hearing, speech, and brain function is still all in good working order. So maybe he should try talking to her about the illness rather than me. This results in him turning his nose up and ignoring me for the rest of the appointment. Only at the end, when he's about to walk out does he talk to me.

"These are for you. Well for a family member, but as none of them are around—"

I cut him off. "I am her family." His eyes slide back to Amanda, then to me, before he walks away. I shove the paperwork in my pocket and a nurse comes in to help me put Amanda into a wheelchair. I rush down to bring the car around before someone else appears in the entrance with Amanda sitting waiting for me. Her foot tapping, like an impatient child. "Come on then happy," I say with a smirk and she smiles back.

When we're about five miles down the freeway and the car is on cruise, Amanda grabs my hand. I glance over at her but she's like a statue, facing forward. "T-Thank you, Bellie. Thank you for everything you've done for me. I l-love you. Always have. Always will. You're the s-sister I was gifted with. The person who knows me more than anyone in t-the world. I've been blessed to have h-had you as a part of my life and I'm so sorry…" She stops talking and once again I glance over to her. She's still facing forward, but now a trail of tears run down her face. She ignores them, like they don't matter because they don't. Not anymore. They're just a release now. "I'm sorry I'm going to leave you," Amanda says, and the pressure on my chest suddenly gets heavier. She's silent and I allow my own tears to fall, I can't stop them. I rub my thumb across the back of her hand. That's all I have to give her, so I don't want to let her down.

I realize that it's time for me to whisper the words that I don't want to say, the words I know she needs to hear. The words that will break the last thread holding me together. I have to say them. For her. "Listen Moo, I know you're fighting. I love that you're brave and you're trying to hang on, I know you're doing that for your pop, for Danny, Rubén… for me. I need you to know, it's okay. If you feel like you can't fight anymore. If your body is too tired, too worn, if you are desperate to let go then don't worry about us we'll be fine. Just remember one thing," I tell her, but I have no idea how I'm managing to push the words out as my heart is shattering, piercing my insides with their sharp edges.

"What?" she says on a wobble.

"Bring the rain, Moo…. just remember to bring the rain," I tell her and she squeezes my hand tighter.

"You look to the stars, talk to me. I'll bring the rain," she tells me.

The rest of the journey we sit in silence. Still holding hands.

"Bel," Danny calls my name, catching my hand in his. I look away from the stars and into his eyes. "I did something for you. Well, for you and Amanda. It's something small. It's meant to be a symbol of hope."

"What is it?" I ask, curious as to what this beautiful, kind hearted, strong man has done for Amanda and for me.

"Come with me," he says, turning and dragging me through the house. We pass Mike in the living room, looking sad with a glass of whiskey in his hand. Then Danny drags me into Amanda's room. Rubén is standing in the corner next to the window with a telescope behind his back.

"What's going on?" I ask glancing around at everyone.

"I have no idea, Rubén won't tell me anything!" Amanda complains sitting up in bed and I laugh in reply. Since we came home from the hospital yesterday, she's been trying to find out all the information about the wedding. Nobody is giving her any details. But I will… tomorrow. Rubén agreed that she should know what's happening, just in case there was anything she wanted to change before the day, so she'd still have time. Tomorrow is Friday, so when I tell her in the morning, we will have the rest of that day to change things before her wedding at noon on Saturday.

Rubén chuckles. "This," he says moving to one side and pointing to the telescope. "You're going to find out about now. It was Danny's idea, so we set it up for the both of you." I raise my eyebrows at Amanda, and she shakes her head back at me with a shrug of her shoulders.

Danny tugs on my hand, placing me on Amanda's bed, close to her. I wrap my arms around her skinny body and Danny looks between the two of us. "You always loved the stars," he starts and I catch my breath. "I heard you the other day talking about what the stars mean to you both. Amanda turns her face into my chest and I rub her back. "Amanda…" Danny speaks softly and she looks back to him, "…I had a star named after you." My heart stops at his words and hot tears hit my cheeks. Amanda's breath hitches, but it starts her coughing. Her breathing is labored and we have to call the in-house nurse, the one that has been set up to come help her. She places breathing equipment over Amanda's face and my chest compresses. Watching my best friend, who's the same age as me struggling to breathe, one of the most basic of human functions, is hard, devastating. Forty minutes later we manage to continue with our earlier conversation.

Amanda wheezes, telling Danny to carry on. Even though I can see the concern and reluctance to continue in his eyes, I nod, telling him to continue. It's what she wants. Regular. Normal… as normal as is possible.

"There is a star out there called Amanda Katherine Warren. So you see, there's already a home for you. You're already a star." Amanda smiles through the tears, and I look at this man that I love with butterflies in my belly, knowing I love him more. Just for giving her, *us*, that extra special connection. "When Bel needs to talk to you, she can speak to the stars, knowing you'll be there listening. When she needs to see you, she can look through this telescope and stare at you brightening up the sky for her." His words are sentimental and loving. It takes everything in me not to shatter, my bones feel weak and both sadness and gratitude sweep over me.

"Thank you, Danny. Thank you for g-giving us this connection," she whispers, unable to talk any louder. Holding out her hand for him, he immediately moves to her. Once there, she grabs his fingers weakly. Seeing her struggle he turns his hand clutching her fingers instead, and holds on waiting for Amanda to tell him what it is she needs to say. "Please l-look after her, I need to know she's not alone. I need to know… you h-have her," she tells him, biting her bottom lip. I cough out my pain, before it chokes me.

He leans down and kisses her cheek whispering in her ear. She smiles at him and weakly tugs his hand again until he leans into her, then she clumsily throws her arm around his shoulder giving him a hug. I can just hear her saying another thank you before they pull away from each other.

Danny shows me the star through the telescope. I'm surprised that he knows about this stuff, but apparently he took Astronomy at college. Rubén sits next to Amanda as I explain how beautiful the star is. I want her to see. Rubén lifts her out of the bed and holds her until Danny points the telescope and shows her where the star is located in the sky. She gasps and throws her hand over her mouth. "I'm beautiful," she tells us all with a smile. I wipe across my eyes with the heels of my palms, as my chest shudders while I try to calm myself.

"Always babe," Rubén replies, gazing into her eyes and I know it's time to leave them alone. Danny obviously feels the same as he kisses the back of my hand.

"We're going to bed. See you guys in the morning," he tells them with a smile and goodnights are said all around. When we walk back past the living room to the stairs, Mike is asleep on the sofa, so I walk over grabbing a blanket and covering him before joining Danny at the bottom of the stairs. "Let's go get some rest, baby," he tells me and I nod.

Sleep eludes me as I lay in Danny's arms. I think about how easily I've come to this point, where I'm sleeping, even without sex, next to Danny every night. I wanted to take things slowly. With sex I have, but my heart has raced ahead at a million miles an hour and I have no control over it.

"Love you, Danny," I whisper to him.

"Every day, Bel," Danny replies and I feel myself pulled under by exhaustion.

"Right, now we're here I w-want you to tell me everything," Amanda says as I sit in the chair by her bed.

"Okay. So firstly, as you probably suspected, Pastor Wilson will be marrying you. We're going to set it up outside, but if you can't manage going out there, then we'll just do it with us, here, in the bedroom."

A frown passes over her face. "Errrm… do you think that m-maybe Danny would carry me outside, you know, if I'm too s-sick to walk?" she asks biting the inside of her mouth, her eyes are wide making her look like a little girl.

"Of course, honey," I reply with a smile, warmth fluttering in my belly, knowing Danny would be happy to play that role. She claps her hands together, a small smile playing on her lips, but says nothing so I take that as my cue to continue, "Like you asked, I have your momma's wedding dress. I found it in the attic just like you said it would be. It's been dry cleaned and is ready for you."

She grabs my hand and jerks her head asking me non-verbally to come closer. I lean in and she whispers in my ear, "I want to be b-buried in that dress, Bellie. Please make sure that happens." I swallow the boulder in my throat but nod in agreement. Whatever she needs, I'll drain myself trying to achieve it for her.

"Okay," I continue with happier thoughts. "Mrs. Archibald from the church is doing some flowers and Simone will be here today. Your pop has gone to get her from the airport. He's going to show her around, then they're getting an early night at the hotel just like you told them to." A frown passes over her face at my comment. She knows that everyone disagreed with her insistence on Mike spending some alone time with Simone. They have all the time in the world, she doesn't. But it was Amanda's request, so her pop agreed. "Anyway, they'll be over early in the morning about eight. Then Simone will start making the French food you love so much." She smiles but it's a lie. We asked Simone to make some food because we know how much Amanda loves it. The truth that we're all avoiding is that she won't be able to eat anything. She hasn't eaten since she went into the hospital, everyone is worried including the nurse. "So, Rubén and Danny are out now, choosing their suits," I tell her with a grin.

"Bellie, I want you to d-do something for me," Amanda tells me. "You remember that dress I bought you?" I nod, remembering it clearly. It was our senior prom. Keith was supposed to take me, but it was when my feelings were at their strongest for Danny. Amanda had seen this dress while we were out shopping. It was floor-length, navy satin, it had spaghetti straps and it naturally clung to every part of my body. Keith didn't pick me up for prom that night, and the following week I heard that Danny had hooked up with one of the girls. I put the dress in my closet and never took it back out.

"I'm not sure it will still fit me," I reply.

"T-try it, for me. I'm pretty sure with all the w-worrying you've been doing, you've lost at least t-ten pounds in the last few weeks. I love that dress on you Bellie. I'd love to know that you've f-finally worn it, whatever the occasion."

"Okay, Moo," I agree.

"Now, I've w-written this," Amanda says. Hands shaking, she pulls some paper out from the drawer in her bedside cabinet. "This is for tomorrow. What do you t-think?" she asks me passing the note over. I pull it from her hands, unfolding it I stare down at the shaky handwriting, mixed emotions surge through me.

If I knew this was how my life would have turned out, would I have done things differently?

If I'd have known that I would be dying so young, would my desires, wants or needs have changed?

If I was aware that my time would be limited, would my choices have been different?

The answer to every question is no. I would not change one thing about my life. This time was a gift, and I have used it in the best way I know how. Making one change could mean I'd lose myself, the person I've become and I like me. Making one change could mean I lose the people that I love, the people that have filled my life to the fullest, with nothing but love and happiness. But more than anything, making one change could mean I'd lose this moment.

This one right now.

The one where I get to say 'I do.'

The one where I get to devote myself to you. I choose this. And if I had my time again I'd still choose you. If I were to be told right now that I'll have another fifty years to live, I'd still choose you. You're my choice. You're the one

> *I've been running toward. If I had to have cancer to bring me to you. Then when my time comes, I'll lay down happily, knowing I got to have the best few weeks of my life because of you. Because you loved me.*

I can't control the weeping this time. I hate that I'm crying, it's not what I want to give her, she has enough to deal with. But the floodgates have opened. All I can do is whisper I'm sorry, over and over as we hold each other.

Chapter TWENTY FOUR

Anabel Adams

I can't stop fidgeting in bed. Huffing and glancing over at the clock, it's two a.m. I throw the pillow over my face and growl. Rubén and Danny are having a bachelor party. Well, when I say that what I mean is they've gone to the hotel bar, had about three drinks then got in bed for eleven. All right, I know that's not exactly the story. However, it isn't far off the truth. Amanda—being the Amanda we all know and love—insisted on Rubén having a bachelor party. Something he really didn't want, but she got her way. He was also banished to a hotel, on the grounds that he shouldn't see the bride before the wedding. I tried to convince her that she was being silly, but she wouldn't have it. She said that she didn't want to tempt fate, with her run of luck she needed to do everything by the book. I rolled my eyes and Rubén growled, but yet again Amanda got her way. So they left this evening—Rubén making sure he didn't go until the last possible minute—and went straight to the hotel, the same one as Mike and Simone. Just the two of them. They drank a couple of beers at the bar. Had something to eat, then just after eleven Danny called me and said he was back in his room. Rubén was next door. He said that it was killing him watching Rubén suffer, and knowing he couldn't do anything to help. Danny told me that he'd never seen his friend so twisted up about anything before, and he was worried about how Rubén was going to cope afterward. We changed the subject after that, both of us knowing there's little we can do for him right now. He finished by telling me he loved me and that he was going to get some sleep. He said Rubén wanted to be up at six so he could be back at the house as soon as possible even if he couldn't see Amanda until noon. He also added that he told Danny to be careful when he carried her up the aisle to him, and if he harmed her then Rubén would kick him in his ball sack. That made me laugh and our conversation ended on a high, which was much better than how it started.

I fell asleep quickly, but woke up about an hour ago, now I'm struggling to drift off again. Deciding to pull out my notebook, I arrange the pillows behind me propping myself up. Bending my knees, I place the notebook against them and grab my pen. The moon shines in through the window and the light bounces off the empty lines waiting for my ink to fill them.

Amanda's getting married today. It's two a.m. now, so we're officially less than twenty-four hours away. My emotions are so mixed. I thought about her wedding when I was a child. It may seem strange thinking about your friend's wedding day. But we used to dress up, put on old pieces of lace or cloth our parents had. Plastic tiaras and Momma's old lipstick. Knowing one day our princes would come. We had it all arranged. Amanda would get married first—it was only fair as she was a whole two months older—and then I would be her bridesmaid. A year later I would get married and she'd be my bridesmaid. Then I'd have a child first because I'd always wanted children and she was never sure about them.

I'm not sure when my dreams became irrelevant or when my desires died off. Knowing Keith has a child cements the fact that I'll probably never be able to have one. I got married first. Unhappily. I missed my best friend's first marriage, to a douche who didn't deserve her. Now I get to see her truly happy, truly in love. Then I get to watch as it's all ripped away. I'll look around after, at the scattered pieces of everyone's hearts. The devastation she'll leave behind will be huge. You can't love someone that much, never imagining a time without them, to then survive this pain.

Hearing a noise I stop writing. Clutching the notebook to my chest, I keep listening out, not sure if it was my imagination or not. Suddenly something smashes and my heart pounds as I jump out of bed racing down the stairs. I see Sandra, Amanda's nurse, rushing into her room. Moving through the doorway, my eyes immediately snap to Amanda. She's laying perfectly still. I watch her chest rise and fall with achingly slow breaths and feel myself exhale a relieved sigh. Her breathing is noisy, gurgling and rattling loudly. I look to Sandra, who's hooking up a heartbeat monitor.

"I just want to measure her stats for a while," she says with a sad smile. I nod but say nothing. I feel like my legs are stuck to the floor and I'm scared that if I move something will change. Maybe if I stay right here, at the door, I can keep our world the same. I can feel it, see it in the nurses eyes. Amanda's giving up. "She hasn't got long sweetie," the nurse announces my inner monolog to the room. Molding myself to the doorframe and feeling my legs give way, I try to block out the truth.

"But the noise, the crash I heard," I mutter.

She shakes her head. "Sorry Anabel, she wasn't conscious for that. It can be common at the end of life, sometimes patients make sudden movements, jerking or jolting. I think her hand must have hit this," she says pointing to the medical table. The one that's been set up for Amanda just slightly higher than her bed making it easy for her to reach things. I can see glass on the floor which has obviously been knocked off.

"Will she…" I swallow a couple of times trying to compose myself. "Will she wake up?"

I can already see the pity in her eyes and I want to scream and throw something at her. My insides are burning and I clutch my stomach, waiting for her answer.

"I don't know." Her reply is weak, vague. I can't help but think about Amanda being so strong, she deserves the same from everyone else.

"But you don't think so, do you?" I challenge her on a hiss, twisting my hand into my stomach, trying to ease the pain.

She doesn't get angry at my tone. Her face doesn't even change to impassive. She just keeps throwing out pity from her eyes as her head moves from left to right, giving me the *'no'* I already knew was coming. "Sit with her. Hold her hand," Sandra tells me then moves out of the room.

Still not moving from the doorframe, I attempt to collect my scattered thoughts. I need to roll all my feelings up and lock them away for a while. If I can give Amanda that strength I told her about, maybe she can hang on at least for her wedding. She wants this so badly. Forcing my legs to relax so I'm able to move, and releasing the skin on my stomach from the painful grip my fingers hold, I slowly move into the room sitting next to Amanda's bed. I place my notebook and pen—which is still clutched to my chest—on the bed next to her. I reach over to her bedside table, opening the drawer and pulling out her cell. Without realizing, I pull a piece of paper with it. It falls away and flutters down onto the bed. I recognize it straight away. The vows for Rubén. My hands shake as I claim the piece of paper, slipping it into my notebook, scared that it's going to be lost and knowing she would want Rubén to have it. I sit back and look at the cell, then back to Amanda's face. Apart from her noisy breathing, she's also very pale and obviously weak. Suddenly, everything seems so surreal and I'm convinced that I'm imagining it all. I pinch my cheek, which hurts and also, unfortunately, confirms that this *is very real*. I slip my left hand over Amanda's right and clutch her gently, willing her to hold on. With my right hand, I shakily dial Mike.

"Sweetheart?" Mike's voice is raspy and laced with sleep.

"No, Mike, it's Anabel."

"Oh, my good God, please tell me you're not calling to shatter my world?" I understand his words, they're not said with malice or to upset. Still, it's hard being the bearer of bad news. I hate seeing people I love in pain, and more than that I still have to try and manage my own. Right now, I know I've locked up the emotions, but the box is shaking and I'm attempting to keep a hold of it. Loosely.

"She's not gone. But you need to get back to the house," I tell him.

"I'm leaving now." He rushes out before hanging up.

I decide to try Rubén next. His phone rings, but there's no answer.

"For fuck's sake!" I growl and dial Danny.

"Amanda?" he answers sleepily, he must have seen the caller ID.

"Danny," I whisper as the emotion snaps, the loose hold I had now non-existent.

"Babe?" Oh, fuck. Shit. Is she—"

"She's still with us. *Barely.* Please, come as quick as you can." I cry now, my chest compressing.

"Be there as quick as we can baby."

"Hurry," I sob out and hang up the phone.

I watch her for what feels like forever, tears continuously roll down my face. Amanda is struggling with every breath. It sounds like she has something loose in her chest and liquid at the back of her throat. I want to sit her up, help her breathe. The nurse comes in and we adjust her position, but it makes no difference. In the end, we lay her back down as that's where she seems to struggle the least. Sandra tells me this is very normal and that she's in no pain. Giving her a dirty look, I wonder how many times she's died and, therefore, can say for certain how much pain Amanda is in. Looking back at the clock when she exits the room again, I realize it's only been ten minutes since I made the phone calls. It feels like hours. All I have in me now is sadness that runs throughout my body. I want to punch the wall, throw things, cuss and scream.

I want to make everything okay.

There's an ache in my throat that matches the one in my heart, and I feel like every part of my body hurts, like the pain inside has managed to attach to my skin. I lean over and stroke Amanda's cheek. Her face is so cold. The noise from her breathing and the heart rate monitor create a sad melody. Glancing at my notebook, I pick it up. Hoping I can expel some of the emotions.

> *I've never really thought much about our heartbeat. It's just a pulse of the heart. I've also never given much thought to the length of a heartbeat, the time it takes for each pulse.*
>
> *I decided to Google it a couple of weeks ago.*
>
> *Google knows everything, right?*
>
> *I'm not sure why I was wasting time, maybe it was a distraction. My findings said that the*

average heartbeat—I mean what is average about anyone these days—is seventy-two beats per minute. Seventy-two. That's less than a second for every beat. Less than a second. Yet, even with that small timeframe, I'd still need even less time than that to answer yes, if someone could offer me the choice of taking her place.

Taking a deep breath as I watch my tears hit the notebook paper, just touching a corner of the ink causing it to blur.

"Mandie Moo," I sob out, zero control over my own feelings now. "Please don't leave us. I k-know I said when you needed to go, I'd... that I'd let you go, that I'd be strong for you, but Mandie Moo I lied. I'm sorry, but I need you here. We all do. I'm not sure how to function without you," I bawl as I lay my head on her legs, my shoulders jerking up and down with each snotty wail.

I try to calm myself and turn my head to watch her face as her breathing starts quieting down. Feeling hope pulsing through me, I check the time again praying everyone will get here soon. My own heartbeat picks up speed quick when Amanda stops breathing altogether for a few seconds. She does it again and I count the time—five seconds. I can feel the fear creeping up my throat and when it happens a third time, I call the nurse who comes rushing in.

Explaining what happened, she just shakes her head sadly, telling me once again that it's normal. I pick up a book that sits on the bedside table and throw it at the door when she leaves. I know logically this isn't her fault. But right now my logic, reason, and understanding has vanished and I'm just left with sadness, anger and confusion.

"Amanda, please come back to me!" I screech as her breathing slows right down. I squeeze her hand as fresh tears assault my eyes. Then it's like everything stops in my head. All the sounds. All the air is sucked out of the room. Time stands still as I watch a tear roll down her cheek. Before a sigh seems to escape her lips and the machine brings me back to my senses with one long continuous beep. The nurse quickly runs back in, she then turns off the monitor as I scream, unable to control the anguish coursing through me.

Feeling like my lungs have seized, I gulp down as much air as I can. My stomach twists and I jolt back from the bed, throwing up on the rug. Finally sinking down into my own vomit. A commotion erupts behind me, and I'm jostled and hoisted back into the strong arms that I know will keep me safe, keep me warm, and give me a home.

With those thoughts, my body feels limp, the room blurs and I finally let myself go, let myself drown as my whole world is submerged in darkness.

Chapter TWENTY FIVE

Danny Quinn

My muscles ache. I haven't physically hurt this much for at least two months. An intensive training session in the gym always makes me feel like this. I know the reason my body groans with every moment. Standing, I allow my neck to drop back, easing it slowly from side to side trying to help my muscles. When Bel called me at two a.m. I knew… how could I not know? What other reason is there for a two a.m. phone call. But shit… I hoped like hell, in the first few seconds, that it was a butt dial or maybe she was calling to tell me she missed me. When her sobs echoed through my cell, I knew I needed to get my shit together. I'm not sure I've ever woken up so quickly.

Having to knock and tell Rubén what was happening—watching his face—that sent a burn through me. He quickly recovered, re-arranging his features to keep his feelings inside. The journey back here was silent. The tension rolling off him was suffocating, I really could have cut the air with a knife. I'd barely brought the car to a stop when Rubén had the door swung open and he was pounding the lawn running to the front door. Lights shone in my mirror as I switched off the car and angled out. Automatically glancing that way, I saw Mike copying Rubén and running to the front door. I gave a sad smile to Simone as I pushed forward eager to get to Bel.

I'll never forget walking into that room. I've loved Bel every day since I first started crushing on girls. I've always wanted to protect her, to look after her. Never, have I ever, felt that feeling more fiercely than when I saw her sitting on the floor, completely desolate and empty. Every thread of my essence fell deeper in love with her in that second. I didn't think I could adore this woman more than I already did, but seeing her in so much pain made me want to be her balm and soothe her. I felt a tenderness for her that I'd never felt for anyone, *ever*.

Ignoring the noise around me and gently lifting her into my arms, whispering soft words that I don't think penetrated, I brought her to the bedroom. Held her through the tears, the pain, sadness and sorrow. Ignoring my own pain spiking inside me. At some point, we must have both fallen asleep. I was uncomfortable when we laid down, not that I cared. She cried into my chest as I kept her on my lap. Sleeping half sitting up caused me to acquire this literal pain in my neck. And somewhere along the line we lost nineteen hours. It's way past nine p.m. now and I have no idea what's happened with everyone else in the house, but looking at Bel somehow she's still managing to sleep. The past few weeks have drained her, and the past few days have taken their toll.

I stretch a bit more, then quietly creep out of the door making my way downstairs. The whole house is silent. Reaching the living room, I see Simone sitting watching the television. An empty glass is in her hands and her eyes aren't really taking in the program on screen. She seems lost in thought.

"Simone?" I call her, questioningly, gently.

Her body jerks, surprised by my arrival. "Oh, hello Danny," she says, her French accent coats her words.

I hold out my hand. "This seems a bit formal in the circumstances, but as we've not officially met I thought I should say hello." She takes my hand with a sad smile. Mike took Simone straight off to the hotel as per Amanda's wishes, which means Simone didn't get to see her. "You didn't get to say goodbye?" I ask, but I already know the answer.

She shakes her head sadly. "I-I went through this with them both. I was already with Mike when

Amanda was diagnosed, and when Pierre ran…" she stops and shakes her head looking down, "I missed my chance. But she knew I loved her, I told her before she left for America. Still, my pain is nothing compared with Mike's. I need to be strong for him, to focus on him," she says it all then her eyes widen like she's worried that she's said too much.

"It's okay. I'll not say anything to anyone. You can talk to me if you need someone to lean on while you're here," I tell her, thinking that's what Amanda would want for her.

"Okay, chéri, but who are you going to lean on?" She smiles sadly at me.

"Don't worry about me. As long as I can look after Bel, and be everything that Amanda wanted me to be for her, then I figure I'm following Amanda's wishes and that she'd be happy with me." I believe one hundred percent in what I say, but I also know there's a searing pain in my heart. It will dull with time, but it'll never go away. Amanda's loss will forever affect us all. "Where's Mike?" I ask.

"He's sleeping. After last night… well, he didn't go back to sleep. He's been organizing the funeral all day today, it's keeping him busy, something to focus on. I don't think he wants to stay here any longer than he has to. Some may say it's wrong, but all around here," Simone gestures to the house, "it has ghosts for him. Katherine and now Amanda. It's hard. I know. I lost my first husband and still, every day, I miss his smile. Understand me, I love Mike as he does me, but he also feels the same pain I still feel. So I understand his need to get free and clear of this town."

I nod, knowing we all deal with things differently. This is just his way, what he needs. "So when is the funeral?" I ask.

She looks at me and winces. "Monday."

"Monday," I repeat her word slightly shocked. "It's now—" I break off looking at my watch, "ten past ten on Saturday night. Monday doesn't give us much time," I tell her, working through things in my head.

"Oui, I know. Mike wanted it tomorrow, but Pastor Wilson refused, being a Sunday and having service in the morning. He tried to talk Mike into late next week, but he was stubborn. Monday at noon. Not much time at all."

I shake my head in disbelief. "Has he sorted anything other than the funeral? Like a wake?"

"No, he doesn't want anything after, he just wants to leave. I called some people today explaining there was no wedding. Rubén also called some, then he disappeared for a while."

"You know where he is now?"

"Oui, outside," she replies pointing to the back yard.

Figures.

"Okay, thanks, Simone."

As I walk out of the back door, it's hard to see anything. The only sound is the rustle of the wind through the trees. I glance up at the stars and they give me some comfort. Striding the length of the yard and back again, until I finally sit on the wall in the corner. I can't see Rubén anywhere. "Well, Amanda, you've left me with a mess to clear up. You asked me to look after her, to love her always. That's something I can promise you. It's Rubén I'm worried about. How do I help him? I keep thinking what if it were me… I don't imagine I'd ever get past losing Bel because I never did. So how do I help him get past you?" Sighing to myself I know there are no answers to be had.

Standing up ready to go back into the house, I see a shadow emerge from the doorway. *Rubén.* He doesn't see me there as he walks to the furthest point of the garden. I'm about to walk over to him when I jump, as he stares up at the sky roaring into the night. It's a full on release of pain. Raw and uncontrolled. I stare at him before jogging over, he startles when I appear but says nothing as I grab him pulling him into me and holding him with my hand on the back of his head. He slips his hands under my armpits and up, clutching my shoulders with his fingertips. Suddenly, he buries his face in my neck and his back heaves up and down as he completely unravels.

"I-I d-don't know how to… just… w-what am I supposed to do now? We should be m-married now."

He cries like this for a couple of minutes then stops, pulls himself back suddenly and wipes his face with the back of his hand. "Doesn't matter anyway. It's done. I'll cope."

"Rubén, brother, don't dismiss—"

"No Danny. It's fine. I just need a few days, sort my head out. When the funeral's over, I'll head back out to San Francisco or New York. Wherever. I just need to get back to reality. This shit…" he waves his arms around, "…this isn't my reality," he says and before I can say anything more he spins on his heel and walks away.

"Rubén," I call and he stops. He stands still but doesn't look back. "Love you man," I say and he nods once, then walks around the side of the house. My legs root me to the ground until I hear my rental car start up and the tires squeal as Rubén leaves.

Anabel Adams

I'm blessed really. To have those few dreamily peaceful minutes after waking from sleep. A time when everything is as it should be. But everyone knows… for every action, there's a reaction, for every positive a negative exists. To have those few peaceful moments, I also have to suffer the almost intolerable pain… pain that surges through me when the memories fall back into my consciousness.

This morning, after my breath is taken away by the agony, I look around the room. I'm alone. Waking up around midnight that was the first time I experienced the pogo stick of emotions. Danny was awake next to me, he told me I'd been asleep for nearly twenty-four hours. I wanted to get up, but I must have fallen back to sleep, as the next time I woke up, it was a little after three a.m. This time, I didn't move, I just breathed through the pain. Counting every time I inhaled and exhaled.

Danny sleeping at my side helped keep me calm. I stared at him, sleeping, peaceful. His face is so soft, so unassuming while he sleeps. It's open and almost joyous. It makes me feel special, that I get to see that. I laid awake for a while, the last time I checked the clock, it was a little after five a.m. and the light was starting to break through the dark. Now it's nine forty-three a.m. and I have to face the day. I haven't spoken to anyone since Amanda left us. I jolt up in bed, as my heart slams into my ribs like it's trying to break through. Jumping out of the bed, I frantically search around the room pulling clothes out of drawers and tearing books from the shelves.

I hear a door click but don't really take it in until Danny's arms calm me, as they always do, by wrapping around my chest and holding me gently while giving me his strength. I slump forward but he supports me as I cry again.

"I'm so sick of crying. I don't want to be this sad… will I be like this forever?" I sob.

"No, baby. You'll learn to live with the hurt. She'll always be there, but when this isn't so raw, you'll remember that she wants you to live for her… live for you."

I turn around so I'm tucked into his chest. "I can't find my notebook, I have something in there I need to give to Rubén," I explain my crazy behavior, looking for my book.

"It's okay, baby, I'll help you look. Where did you last have it?" he asks.

I swallow. "In Amanda's room, when I was with her."

Nodding he kisses my head. "Stay here, I'll go look."

"Thank you," I whisper out, sinking back into the bed. Once Danny walks out, I bring my legs up to my chest wrapping my arms around my shins and laying my head on my knees. Facing the window, I look out to the fields. "What would you say to me, Mandie Moo? What would you have me do? I'm in so much pain. You left and I'm angry with you Moo… I'm so angry with you." I keep staring outside, waiting for her to show me she's heard me, willing the rain to fall.

I have no idea how long it is until Danny comes back into the room, telling me he found my notebook. I'm stuck in position watching the sun mock me.

Chapter TWENTY SIX

Anabel Adams

I sit on the floor, in the corner of the cloakroom at church. I came here early, wanting to be by myself. Danny wasn't happy, but he gave me the space I needed. Now I'm sitting here, stuck in a loop. Wave after wave of nausea lashes my insides. My knees pulled up to my chest, protectively, once again. I'm trying to hide myself from the world. It's time for me to say my final goodbye, the funeral has come around too quickly. Burying my head and trying to pretend this is all some dark dream, some nightmare where everything can be fixed, is my new way forward.

People filter into the waiting area, and I can hear their chatter from my hiding spot. Voice's I recognize float into my hidey hole, and I wish I had the strength to hurt someone right now. I wish I felt stronger.

"It's awful, something like that happening to someone our age. Imagine! It could have been any of us."

"Well, I think it's strange that she came back here. Why? To die? I mean she hasn't graced us with her presence for years."

"Jenny! You shouldn't speak ill of the dead. I mean what if… she could have a ghost here or something."

"Stop talking rubbish woman. Ghost! Pfft! Next y'all will be telling me that Ashley Summers had an immaculate conception and that boy isn't Keith's. Even though he looks the spittin' image, let me tell you."

"Jenny, Samantha. Nice to see nothing's changed, you're still talking trash about everyone. Don't have enough to fill your lives, I see?" Ashley's voice shuts them both up momentarily and confirms who I thought it was. Ashley must walk away because they start right back up.

"Bitch, thinking her shit don't stink since she's hooked Keith back." I can place Jenny's voice now.

"Uh-huh, not like he ever wanted her anyways," Samantha answers with a snort.

"True, but then he never wanted Anabel either, not after realizing she was barren."

They giggle at their own comedy show and I feel tears spring into my eyes.

"You two still letting your acid tongues loose?" My stomach dips as I hear Danny's voice.

"Danny Quinn… well, aren't you a sight," Samantha purrs.

"Mmhmm, you grew well, you always were a looker. I'm surprised to see you're back for Amanda's funeral," Jenny adds.

"Nuh-uh, I heard he's been spending time with Anabel."

"So that's why she kicked Keith out. I gotta give it to the girl, she traded up."

"Yeah, but Danny, you know she can't get knocked up, right?"

"Enough!" Danny roars. I startle and it snaps me out of my self-pity party. Standing, I move to the door cracking it open. Danny's face is a sight to behold. He's furious, and I wouldn't want to be Jenny and Samantha right now. The ten or so people in the room all stand still staring at what's happening in front of them. A flutter takes root in my stomach, pushing down the nausea. "You two cannot help but put others down. Are you that insecure that you have to try and make yourselves feel better by bringing others low? You know that shit doesn't work, right? You can talk trash all day, you still got to go home and look at your own faces in the mirror. Every. Damn. Day. You see the ugly, right? It seeps from inside of you, making its mark all over. Everyone in this town knows what you two are. Bitchy schoolgirls still stuck in a time which worked better for you, a time when you were on top. Listen, and listen good… that time is gone. People rarely think anything of you, and when they do, do you know what they feel?"

Both of the women shake their heads automatically.

"Pity." Their heads jerk back at Danny's word. "They don't envy you, they don't want to be like you, hell, most of the town can't *stand* you. All you get from people is pity. They feel *sorry* for you. The reason I'm laying it out is because I *don't* feel pity. I think you're both pathetic, and what you've turned out to be is your own doing. But hear this ladies. I will *not*, hear you speaking badly of Bel. That woman has more class, more beauty, and more grit than you two will ever know. She's better than you, both her and Amanda, they always were. Now. Amanda wouldn't have wanted you here. I know that, she told me. If you had come to pay your respects, then I would have let you be. Seeing as you can't keep your big mouths shut, I suggest you use the door. Don't worry, no one will miss you," Danny snarls the last bit and Jenny opens and closes her mouth like she doesn't know what to say until Samantha pulls her away disappearing out the doors.

I take a step back, pushing myself against the wall. My breathing has picked up, matching my rapid heartbeat. I hear people approaching Danny, to congratulate him on a job well done with the bitch twins. Closing my eyes, I think of how he described me. He said I have more grit than them. I'm embarrassed. I used to be that girl. When he knew me all those years ago. I lost myself for a long time. I'm aware that I have found pieces of me since Amanda came back and since I left Keith. But these last few days, I'm breaking and my fight has slipped out between the cracks. I need to start building myself back up. My first step is facing today.

I breathe deeply. "You can do this," I chant, before swinging the door open and stepping into the waiting area. It's empty. I don't spend time looking for everyone, I make my way to the graveside. Once I reach the huddle of people I see Danny, he walks forward grabbing my hand in his.

"I thought you'd run off," he states, concern in his voice.

"No, I just needed some breathing space."

Nodding he says nothing, instead pulling me through the crowd until we reach the side of the grave. Mike stands next to me, Danny at my side with Rubén at his. I don't look at the other mourners. I don't see the point. They didn't really know her, and I have no interest in chatting, this isn't a social function. I feel only slightly guilty that I don't really listen to a word Pastor Wilson says, being lost in my own thoughts. I ignore the casket, sitting opposite the big hole in front of me.

I'm brought back to the here and now when the coffin is lowered into the ground. There's a sharp pain coursing through my heart, and I clutch my throat wondering if I'll stop breathing at any moment. Danny rubs my back gently and calms my body. But my mind is totally in its own world, not quite believing what my eyes are seeing.

Mike moves from my side, I immediately feel the cold. He holds a white rose between his fingers throwing it in the hole. Mumbling a few words, then taking a step back, his shoulders shake and I know he's silently sobbing. Simone walks to his side, wrapping her arms around him.

"Here," Danny says passing me a white rose. I look between the flower and him. Almost robotically, I pull the rose from his hand and stiffly walk to the hole. Looking down, I see the shiny brown box. I wonder why they make it so pretty. It's going to be buried in the dirt. What's the point? My ribs feel like they're cracking under the pressure on my chest. Feeling cold and hollow, I drop the rose but say nothing. I'm not sure what I'm supposed to say in front of a bunch of mourners, who are probably just here for a day out.

I edge backward while Rubén moves in for his turn. Dragging my feet more and more, I only realize how far away from the grave I am when I can't hear Pastor Wilson anymore. I can see Danny's eyes on me, he wants to come to me, but he's stuck in between Rubén and Mike and it would be very obvious if he left now, right at the end.

A few people glance over to me, but I don't know them so I don't care. I edge backward a bit more. If I can't see it, then it doesn't exist, right? It's as I stumble, I realize I'm on the road. My heart thumps faster and faster. Looking around, I spot Amanda's car. The one Mike used after… I know Mike always leaves the keys under the visor. So quickly, I run and jump in the car. As I start and reverse out of the parking space, I see Danny running toward me. I just have time to mouth *'I'm sorry,'* before I drive away.

Amanda and I used to go to the park when we were younger, but there was another place we escaped to. Somewhere that was quiet, peaceful. And when we needed space, time to think or just to watch a wicked beautiful sunset, we would come here. This is where my subconscious has brought me. I drove for an hour just mindlessly moving from street to street, then back again. I ended up at old creek bridge. I'm not sure if that's what it's called. It's a small bridge, only big enough for one small car to drive over, right next to an old creek, with a rundown shack which sits in a big field. We used to run through the field, holding our arms out and letting the sun beat down on our faces. I'm not sure anyone has been here for years. It looks the same as it did when we were kids. I remember asking my pop if he knew the story behind this place. He didn't even know this place existed. And he lived in our town his whole life.

I abandoned the car across the field and walked here. It's the only way I know how to get to the creek. Sitting on the wall of the bridge, looking down into the shallow river about thirty feet below, the ebb and flow of the water mesmerize me. I feel cold, like I'm a shell, numb and empty. Amanda and me used to say we'd buy this cottage one day. Do it up and make it look pretty. Then we'd always have a hideaway, one that only the two of us knew about.

I'm not sure how long I sit, but I do so until it gets dark. The stars in the sky are always welcome. Especially when they're this bright, because there's no light pollution. I feel inside the pocket of the black jacket I'm wearing, and exhale as I pull out my small wallet. Instantly opening it, I ease out the dog-eared photos I always keep in there. Pushing the others back in, I keep the one of Amanda and me firmly grasped between my fingers as I allow my eyes to scan every morsel of her face. I gasp for air as I heave. It's like my body is trying to expel the agony.

"I miss you," I whisper. "When you lived in Paris I missed you, but this is different. I'm never going to be able to speak to you again. You're never coming back. I'm sorry I was mad at you. I'm not anymore.

There's just a hole in me, and I don't know if it will ever close." I look up to the stars. "You're my North Star, Amanda. You always were. I want to let Danny in, but I'm scared. I know he loves me, and he knows I feel the same. But I can't… I'm not sure I could survive it if I lost someone else I love. I need some of your strength. I love you, Mandie Moo. Who am I without you?"

I sit still, the cold whipping around me, just allowing myself to work through things in my head, while my body only seems to get weaker, my limbs tingling either from the cold or the pain.

"Bel," my name is whispered from his lips and for a second I think I'm dreaming his voice. That is, until his signature move. His arms wrap around me, and he pulls me down from the bridge wall. "What are you doing, baby? You can't sit up there. You might fall in." The tone he uses is soft, but he's angry and I'm not used to dealing with an angry Danny. Not these days. He pulls back and turns me to face him. But he doesn't touch me, not this time. He takes a step away from me. "I didn't know where you were, everyone's been worried. It's not fair Bel, you didn't give a second thought to anyone. Mike's been worried sick. He's just buried his daughter and you're the closest thing he has to family. Not only do you leave him swinging in the wind at the funeral, but then you disappear. We've been looking for you for hours. It was selfish, you think you're the only one hurting?"

His words are sharp and they cut me. He's right of course, but nothing I did was out of spite and I didn't run away to be the center of attention. I step away from him. "Why are you here? Because you need to reassure everyone? Well, you've seen me, I'm fine. You can go back and tell everyone I'm fine, that I'm just being melodramatic. Although, just FYI. I might be overly emotional right now, but I wasn't sent the memo on how to act when your best friend dies. Sorry, maybe I should be stronger. I'm not. I don't have *grit*."

His eyes widen and he realizes I heard the conversation earlier. "Bel." My name is warm on his lips now. But I'm not interested, my stomach twists as I bite back the sobs trying to escape.

"It's fine. Go. I'll be fine on my own. I've survived this long," I tell him. The pain is evident in my voice, even I can hear it. I walk away from him, moving across the gray-stoned floor of the bridge and the tears that had dried up, that I was keeping in check, free-fall now. Danny grabs my hand, hauling me back to him.

"Baby," he whispers and I turn to face him.

"What!" I shout. "What do you want from me?"

"Nothing!" he shouts back. That's when the heavens open and the rainstorm starts.

My tears mix with the rain and every part of me is soaked and numb. "Nothing? Then why are you still here," I ask.

He lets his head fall back and stares at the dark sky. I follow his lead and look up too. Some of the stars are covered by the clouds that carry the rain, but others shine bright white, almost blinding against the pitch black. I wonder if Amanda is looking down on me. Finally sending the rain, telling me I'm being stupid. I can almost see her face. The thought twists something in my gut and my knees give out. I only realize what's happening as my body jolts on impact with the ground. Within seconds, Danny is there crouching down and patting my body checking I'm okay. But I can't think past the fact that I didn't even realize I was falling. Not until it was too late and then there was nothing I could do to stop it.

"Are you hurt?" Danny asks grabbing my chin and turning my head toward him.

I have no choice but to focus and answer, "I'm fine." My voice sounds robotic and cold, even to my own ears, but I just can't seem to add any warmth when my insides feel like they're hollow.

"Here, have my jacket," he says shrugging it off his body and wrapping it around mine.

I look up at him. "What do you want, Danny?" And he knows my question holds weight. He opens his mouth to speak, but I quickly talk over him. "Don't say nothing, we both know that's not the truth." His eyes search mine then drop down to my lips momentarily before he returns back to my eyes and I can see the resignation in them.

"Just you, Bel. You're all I need." At his words my very fragile dam breaks and I tuck my face into his chest, as he wraps me in his arms and lets me grieve.

The next morning I wake alone again. Hearing movement downstairs, I throw on a robe and wander to the kitchen. Mike is sitting at the table, a coffee in his hand and the paper in front of him.

"Mike," I whisper, taking a seat.

"Anabel," he says, looking up from the paper with a sad smile.

"I'm so…" I sigh and shift so my chair is next to his. Throwing my arms around him, I close my eyes and breathe in his scent. "I'm so sorry about yesterday."

"Don't apologize, sweetheart. We all deal with things differently. I've had a while to come to terms with this, and I have to say girl, I don't think you ever really come to terms with it. Still, you did your thing. Feel better now?" he asks and I think for a few minutes, letting the different emotions flow through me.

"Yeah, actually I think I do." I'm surprised by the revelation. It's completely honest. I know I'm not past losing Amanda, but I also know I never will be. "I'm not fixed Mike. I still wake up, and for those few seconds until I remember, life's good. But I'm not crying every five minutes anymore either."

"You remember how you felt when your pop, then your momma died?" he asks and I nod my head. "You feel that badly now?" My stomach dips at his words. I don't feel as bad now as I did when they died, but maybe I should? My face must give me away because Mike chuckles and places his hand on mine.

"It's okay darlin', it's supposed to get easier, there's nothing wrong with that. We'd never move on if it didn't. You're good, you have the support of a good man. Hold onto him."

I nod in response, not having any idea where Danny is today.

"He about went crazy when he couldn't find you yesterday. Never seen a man so shook up with worry. Go easy on him. He loves you. Seems like he's loved you forever. You deserve that. Amanda thought so. I think so. Hell, even Pastor Wilson thinks so, and that man is all about the sanctity of marriage. I'm heading out today. Can't be here in this town much longer. Do me a favor, okay?" I nod again. "Remember, life is short. We have but one, that we know of. The good Lord may grace us with more, but while we don't know, we have to live this one like there's no other. You've known Danny for a long time. I know you hadn't seen him for a while, but take a leaf out of Amanda and Rubén's book… don't waste a second. 'Cause you just don't know, baby girl."

I smile and squeeze his hand. "Where's Rubén?" I ask him.

"Not sure. Danny said he didn't come back here last night. Simone and I crashed here last night, though. I was in no state to drive, Rubén was AWOL, Danny was with you and Simone can't drive here."

"Sorry," I whisper.

"Nothing to be sorry for Anabel. Anyway, we need our stuff from the hotel and to check out. I asked Danny if he'd take Simone so I could talk to you."

"Oh?"

"Part of it was that what I've already said. Wanting you to know I love you, that I want you to grab a hold of life, and to tell you I'm leaving. The offer I gave you before still stands. You want to get away, you'll always have a room in my house, wherever I am." I smile and bite the inside of my cheek so I don't get emotional. *Again.* "The other part is this house." I draw in my eyebrows confused. "It was Amanda's. She put it in her will for you."

"What?" I shriek.

Mike chuckles. "She said that you didn't have anywhere to live, that she wanted to be able to still look after you." The emotion I was keeping a check on flows out of me as I bite my lip. "The other thing was this, she wanted you to have it." He pushes a big book my way. I look between him and the book. "Well, open it, sweetheart."

I carefully pull it open and gasp, my stomach twists as tingles run over the whole of my body. It's a scrapbook of sorts.

"Amanda started that when we moved to Paris. She firstly put photos of this town, you and your friends, then she started adding little notes underneath. I asked her what she was doing and she said it was a memory book, *and* a wishes book. Baffled me then, but now I get it. As the years went on she added to it. I didn't see it again until a few days ago when she told me I needed to give it to you. I had a flick through. It's pictures she took from then until now. I'll leave you with this. I'm gonna go wait in the front yard for Danny and Simone."

"You don't have to do that."

"Know that darlin', just want some fresh air." I nod and he gets up, then leans down to kiss my cheek. "Love you, Bellie," he whispers, using Amanda's nickname for me. The pain crushes me when I register that I'll never hear it from her lips again.

As soon as the front door clicks shut, I finger through the pages, occasionally stopping to sigh at us or our history, then to laugh at a picture with a thought attached. Like the Eiffel Tower, with *'We better be sitting on blankets, on the grass, with a glass of champagne one day Bellie. You, me, and two hot dudes.'* My heart jumps into my throat when I reach a picture of Danny and me, a photo that could only have been taken two or three weeks ago. Danny is sitting on a chair and I'm on his lap. I've fallen asleep and Danny has his eyes closed as he kisses my head. Amanda has written underneath. *'Marry him. He loves you. Nobody will ever love you more than this man. Don't waste precious time.'* My stomach clenches, but with happiness and warmth this time.

"Wow," I murmur. "I think you were right honey, I need to marry that man," I say the words out loud and they make me smile. A noise catches my attention and, still smiling, I look to the window just as the rain starts pouring. "Okay Mandie Moo, you've made your point."

Chapter TWENTY SEVEN

Anabel Adams

"Rubén." I'm almost shocked when he walks through the door. I waited for him all day yesterday. Saying goodbye to Mike was even harder without him here. It was evident Mike wanted to speak to Rubén before he left, but he just couldn't bear to wait any longer. I stayed in the house, my head swimming with a thousand thoughts. Danny tried to take me away, out to the lake or the beach. My mind was set, I needed to wait for Rubén. I still have the note with Amanda's vows on them. I haven't really seen him since she left us. So I haven't had a chance to pass them onto him. I know he told Danny that he was heading out ASAP. I'm surprised and happy he's still here.

As yesterday floated into last night then the early hours of this morning, Danny fell asleep on the sofa. I think the fact that over the last few days, I've slept more than I've been awake, helped me to wait up for him. I'd just about given up hope that he was coming back at all. It's nearly six a.m. now and his creeping in makes me think he wanted it like this, he wants to avoid everyone. Especially if his startled look, when I called his name, is anything to go by.

"Anabel," he whispers looking over to Danny. I glance across at him too. His face soft in what I hope is a beautiful dream. I move my head, signaling for us to go into the kitchen. We both walk that way and take opposite seats at the table.

"Talk to me," I say, reaching across to grab his hand, but he pulls it away sharply.

"Nothing to say," his reply is hard and cold.

"She wouldn't want you to go through this alone," I tell him softly.

"Well, she's not here to kick my ass is she? She fucking left."

Ouch. He's so angry, I can see the fire in his eyes, but it's not warm or inviting. It's like looking into the pits of hell.

"Rubén…"

"Stop fucking saying my name and tell me what you wanted to say, so I can get out of this shithole town." I nod, but pull on my strength, the strength I'm determined to build back up.

Reaching into my pocket, I grasp the note she gave me. "Here," I say, passing it to him.

He takes it from my hands. "What is it?"

"It's Amanda's vows." At my words, he drops the paper like it's a hot potato. "What's wrong?"

"I-I c-can't… it's… my… the…" His words die in his throat as he stares at the paper.

"You want me to?" I ask. Rubén looks between the paper and me, then back again. Finally, his eyes meet mine and he nods. I clutch the paper and will myself to stay calm, control my emotions because Rubén needs me to. I unfold the creased note, smoothing it out between my fingers and staring at the words, the ones I haven't read since the day Amanda showed them to me.

Taking a deep breath and exhaling slowly I begin, "If I knew this was how my life would have turned out, would I have done things differently?" After the first line I look back to Rubén, all I see is a pained expression covering his face and it hurts to look at him. I tilt my head back to the paper in my hand and continue.

"If I'd have known that I would be dying so young, would my desires, wants or needs have changed?" I take a breath, but don't look back up at Rubén, scared of what I'll see on his face. If he's breaking apart, I might not be able to read the rest of this note, and he needs to know this. Amanda wanted him to know.

"If I was aware that my time would be limited, would my choices have been different? The answer to every question is no. I would not change one thing about my life. This time was a gift, and I have used it in the best way I know how. Making one change could mean I'd lose myself, the person I've become and I like me. Making one change could mean I lose the people that I love, the people that have filled my life to the fullest, with nothing but love and happiness. But more than anything, making one change could mean I'd lose this moment. This one right now. The one where I get to say *'I do.'* The one where I get to devote myself to you." I steel myself, bag up my emotions and look up at Rubén. His eyes are closed and I can see he's clinging to his control. "I choose this." His eyes open and he stares at me, not really seeing me. "And if I had my time again I'd still choose you. If I were to be told right now that I'll have another fifty years to live, I'd still choose you. You're my choice. You're the one I've been running toward. If I had to have cancer to bring me to you. Then when my time comes, I'll lay down happily, knowing I got to have the best few weeks of my life because of you." I bite my lip, as a lone tear escapes my tight control and finish. "Because you loved me." I carefully fold the paper back up and watch Rubén.

His face has no emotion, no tears, no fury, no sadness. It's just blank. Lifeless almost. "She…" He swallows but doesn't say anymore as his fingers reach for the paper and he picks it up, slipping it into his pocket.

"She loved you so much. Only time will make things easier," I tell him softly.

"Time? Are you fucking high? This was my one shot. *She* was my one shot. Now I have nothing," he snaps.

"You'll always have us. One day you'll find love again like Mike did."

"You don't get it! I don't want any fucking one else. She was it." He stands up and so do I. It's a good job too because the next second he roars, "Fuck!" Then grabs the table flipping it over, it hits the side and smashes all the plates that were piled up ready to be put away, knocking them to the floor and I watch as everything shatters. I've never seen anyone so angry. Danny comes barreling into the kitchen as Rubén reaches for a chair, throwing it toward the window. Luckily it falls short, but the legs splinter on impact with the floor. I try to melt into the corner. Danny takes in Rubén, then looks to me, a dark shadow passes over his face before he grips Rubén's arms.

"Out, *now!* You need to walk it off."

"Fuck you, Danny, fuck you all," Rubén screams and tries to pull away, but he can't shake Danny. The next moment, Rubén's being pulled out of the house while I look at the damage in the kitchen.

"What a mess," I whisper, my mouth dry, but I'm not talking about the room.

"Bye, babe. Sorry, about before." Rubén holds me in his arms and I close my eyes as I rest my head on his shoulder.

He's leaving. It's too much for him being here, especially in this house. His outburst this morning just made him realize how much he needs to get away. After calming down and spending a couple of hours talking to Danny, he came back and apologized, telling me he'd booked his flight back to Seattle. We've spent the rest of today, trying to remember all the good times with Amanda. We had dinner, he packed and now it's time to leave. He's taking Danny's rental and dropping it back.

"It's okay," I tell him. "We all have to have a breakdown or two." I smile and he offers me a sad one in return.

"I better go," he whispers and kisses the top of my head. Stepping back, I watch, unable to tear my eyes away as he walks to Danny, who's standing next to the car. They do a manly pat hug thing, until Danny pulls Rubén in for a proper hug and Rubén clings to Danny, almost as if his life depends on it. It chokes me and I look back at the house, giving them and myself a moment. Once Rubén's in the car, Danny walks back pulling me into his side, he slips his arm around my shoulder and I rest my head against his chest.

"Will he be okay?" I ask looking up at him.

"Eventually," he replies not looking from the location where the car disappeared.

It's been three weeks since Rubén left. Danny and I have spent some of that time just getting to know each other again. Without all the outside struggles. I've not slept with him yet, although it's been on my mind, and we've definitely gone to the point that there's nowhere else to go now except sex. I'm scared, if I'm honest. I haven't had sex with anyone in years. It was never what I would consider good with Keith, not that I'm entirely sure because I have nothing to compare it to. He never made me feel good, and although I know Danny wouldn't be the same, what if sex is just not something I'll ever enjoy? My stomach twists at the thought, and the fact that I'm going to have to try it soon.

We've also spent some time at the ice cream parlor. Every plan we've talked about is up in the air. We can't decide on a single thing even though Danny is letting me make the decisions. He's not rushing me, *on anything.*

"Hey," I say walking toward Danny, admiring his strong, broad shoulders as he turns and smiles. I'm not only caught on how beautiful it is, but also how amazing his eyes are. And they're aimed at me. Full of love.

"Baby." He returns as I make it to his side. Pulling me into him, he rests his mouth on my head. We stand like that for a moment, and I think about the shop. "What's wrong?" he asks.

Sighing I pull back, out of his arms and look up to him. "I'm scared." His eyebrows pull in. "What if we set the shop back up again and it fails? That's almost as bad as it never being opened again after my pop and then my momma," I whisper my fears to him.

"Baby. I own this shop. You have no mortgage, and I'm going to facilitate everything. Even if it all fails, the costs will be covered by me." I look at him confused. "If I throw money into getting this place up and running, which let's be clear, it's not going to need a lot. You've kept the shop clean and in working order. All we need is some new equipment, fridges, etc. If we do that and after six months it's not making money, so what? You want to keep it going, we'll feed more money into it. This place won't cost much to keep running, it's a drop compared to my restaurants. You want to give it up, that's fine too. I'm here, with you, we're in this together. Don't panic."

"But, your money—" I start to say, but he cuts me off with a growl.

"Is yours too."

"Danny, how is that even possible?" I snap, aggravation whizzes through my body.

"You see a future without me?" he asks, the muscle in his jaw works while he waits for my answer.

"Well… no," I reply.

"Question answered. That's fucking how," he tells me crossing his arms over his chest.

"So… y-you're saying…. what exactly?" I huff out.

"Our future is together. You're gonna marry me right." He doesn't ask me, he tells me.

"Is that a proposal?" I question, folding my arms with a smirk, waiting for him to squirm.

He stares at me, I return his stare, slowly a smile creeps over his face, and I can hear my heartbeat thumping in my ears. "You'd be happy with me proposing like this, in the house, without a ring? Not a big fancy dinner? None of those big romantic gestures that all women love?" he replies, still smiling.

My hands move to my hips and I tap my foot. "Danny Quinn! You should know me by now! Since when have I ever needed big fancy anything?" I'm on a rant now that I just can't stop. "You really think if you proposed to me now, in this house, without a ring, that would make a difference to my answer? You think that anything would stop me marrying you? That anything would make me say no?" I'm suddenly aware of what I've said and I slap my hand across my mouth, like the words could be trapped even though they're already out in the wild.

Danny takes a step toward me and grabs my hips, leaning his face into me until our noses touch. "So that's a yes? You'll be my Mrs. Quinn… forever?"

I swallow at his question and feel my hands shaking. This is a big deal, a huge deal. I've only been back in Danny's life for a couple of months. Then my mind wanders to Amanda and Mike, to the things they said about how life is too short. I know I love Danny, I've never questioned that. Since just before Amanda passed, he's been basically living in Amanda's house—well, my house now—so I know even though it's only been for a short time that we can live together.

"I'm not sure if I can have children," I blurt something that he already knows.

Danny places his hand on my face, cupping my cheek. "You know what would have happened if I hadn't have come back here if I hadn't have found you again?" he whispers and I watch his lips move, thinking how whispered words sound so sexy coming from his mouth. I shake my head. "Nothing. That's what would have happened. If it wasn't you, it wasn't anyone. That means I would have never had kids. If we can, then we can, we can't then it's you and me and I'm over the fucking moon about that. So what do you say, Bel? You want forever with me?"

I go up on my tiptoes and place my lips against his. "Forever and ever. You and me. The way it should have always been," I tell him.

"Is that a… yes, I'll marry you, Danny?" I feel his lips twitch against mine and I let my tongue slide out to lick them. He groans.

"That's a, fuck yes, I'll marry you, Danny." He groans again, kissing me deeply, sliding his tongue in, and pushing his hand up the back of my neck until he cups my head. His other hand wrapped around my lower back. I pull back from the kiss slightly and look at his face, his eyes open and I'm captured in the deep blues. "I love you," I whisper.

"Every day, Bel," he whispers back, and his eyes crinkle as I smile at my fiancé.

Twenty minutes later and we've been sitting in the living room talking about a wedding. Well, I've been talking, Danny's just been smiling. He pulls out his cell and calls Layla.

"Layla, I need you to book time tomorrow at two of the top jewelers in the city. I want to get an engagement ring for Bel. Yes. Okay." He hangs up the phone.

"You're so short and rude." He looks down at himself with a smirk.

"I'm not short." I blush and realize he's probably talking about his six-foot height, not his other parts. But it draws my attention to the fact that I need to speak to him about the sex issue before it becomes a real problem. If I want to marry this man, then I need to be able to talk to him, to trust him. I have to explain.

"Danny," I say, looking into my lap.

"Hey, what's wrong?" he asks placing his finger under my chin and pulling my head up. "Eyes babe," he demands and I look at him.

I shake my head. "Nothing really… well, something. It's embarrassing," I admit.

"Nothing to be embarrassed about, not between us baby."

"Okay. Well, here it is." I swallow a couple of times and avert my eyes, Danny clears his throat and I look back up to him. He smiles and I feel myself warm a little. "I've only ever slept with Keith," my words are blurted out.

Danny's jaw ticks. "Kind of guessed that, babe. I don't really need a blow by blow or a reminder that you could've given that to only me."

I register what he's saying, if he hadn't pushed me away, I would have only ever slept with him.

"Danny…." I say and bite my lip. "You don't understand. I'm not telling you because I'm worried about how I'll perform, although that is a concern. I'm scared, terrified in fact. It was never… um, good with Keith." I keep my eyes on Danny as his jaw ticks. "It was uncomfortable, even painful sometimes. I've never enjoyed it. Never. I'm afraid—"

He cuts me off by grabbing my face, his eyes burning into me. "I've got you. I'll make sure you're good baby. With everything. *Everything*. You come first, and that's the way it will always be," he tells me. "You trust me?" I nod immediately. "Then trust me with this. Still, I'm glad you shared, even if it was painful to hear." He strokes across my bottom lip with his thumb. "You want to try, soon? Or wait?" he questions.

I take my time looking back into his eyes. I'm not sure what I'm trying to see, but anything other than love just doesn't exist there, not for me.

"Soon," I whisper and blink, amazed I admitted that to him. "Danny, it's been… years and years."

"Then it will be like starting fresh. You and me baby, you and me," he says and kisses my lips, closed mouth, but oh so tenderly.

Chapter TWENTY EIGHT

Anabel Adams

Sitting in the café the next morning, I'm reminded of the last time I was here with Amanda. The pain is still there. It still hurts, but it's bearable now. I've learnt to manage it, to control it. Coming here today was something that I could have done without, though. Keith contacted me through Pastor Wilson of all people. Said he needed to talk to me. Danny wasn't happy, but I agreed. It's something I need too if I'm ever going to move on with my life. To truly start afresh. It's something I need to face. This will give me the last of my strength back. As well as the closure that I need.

"Anabel." His voice grates on my very last nerve now, how I stayed married to this man for so long, I'll never know. Standing next to the table I take him in. He's lost some weight. Had a shower and a shave, he looks cleaner, fresher and much more like his old self. I can see his eyes again and they sparkle like they used to. Keith leans down and kisses my cheek. I tense and can almost hear Danny growl in my mind. The thought makes me smile as Keith sits in the booth opposite me.

"Happiness looks good on you, Anabel. I forgot how you were, how we both were actually. But let's talk about that in a minute," he says before gesturing to the waitress. "Coffee for both of us, please." I can't help my eyebrow arching at the fact that, not only is he ordering our drinks, but seems to be implying that he's going to be paying. That shocks the shit out of me. Keith glances at me but doesn't comment on my look of shock. Although I'm not entirely sure he's ever really been able to read me.

"So, you want to tell me about Ashley?" I start as I mean to go on. This isn't about pleasantries, I'm not trying to pass the time or shoot the shit with him. I came here for answers, then I fully intend to never see this man again. If I do in town, then I'll say hello, but that's as much as it will ever be. I don't hate him anymore, you have to care about someone to hate them, and I feel nothing for him—not anymore.

He swallows and looks everywhere but at me. "Keith, you had your reasons for asking me here. I had my reasons for agreeing. Ashley and your son, that's my reason for being here. Tell me," I demand. My voice is showing a strength that I'm not entirely sure I have just yet. But I need answers and that divorce.

He rubs the back of his neck, looking down. The waitress comes back, placing a coffee in front of each of us. I wait, silently, allowing him to get his words in order. He's never really answered to me about anything, at least not in the last ten years. Now I'm asking questions that I wouldn't have dared ask before, but I don't think that's why his words are caught in his throat. I think it's more than that, I'm just not sure what.

"I didn't love her. I never did, not like you Anabel." I sigh, looking at him disbelievingly. "Don't worry, I'm not here to win you back, I'm well aware *that* ship has sailed." His reply is a snap as he glances out of the window.

"Danny?" I reply.

"Yeah," he snorts. "Good old Danny, never could keep away from you." He grinds his teeth and my palm itches to slap him.

"So Ashley," I remind him and he nods, breathing out a wheeze through his nose.

"You and me split for a few weeks, I don't know if you remember? We were young, probably only seventeen. It was some stupid fight, although looking back, maybe it wasn't. If I recall, it was about Danny," he says rubbing his chin. "Anyway, I was out with the boys and we ran into those lot, Ashley,

Samantha and Jenny. It was the same as usual, flirting, you know the standard stuff."

I say nothing in response, years ago I would have ground my teeth or shouted at him. After a few years, I learnt not to care. Now… now I honestly don't care.

"Ashley and I hooked up. It started something. Not something I was ever going to pursue. I mean, we were broken up and I wasn't doing anything wrong."

"Keith, you don't have to justify yourself. You're right, we were broken up, but even if we weren't none of it bothers me anymore. Honestly," I mutter.

"Then why the fuck ask me?" he snaps and I see the real Keith again.

"Because I wanted to know why." My smile is saccharine sweet.

"Why what?" he replies, confusion and annoyance in his eyes.

"Why you made us stay together all those years? You knew I didn't want to be there, I always made that clear. Yet, you wouldn't leave and never gave me a way out. I was weak back then, but I'm not anymore," I tell him and he jerks back at my words.

Keith shrugs his shoulders. "I didn't want to be with Ashley. It's true, that night we hooked up was the beginning of the on-off fling we had. That carried on into our marriage," he says pointing between the two of us. "That was wrong. But there's no changing the past, so I might as well be honest." I nod in reply.

"I always wanted to be with you, Anabel. You have to believe me."

"I don't have to do anything," I reply and I can hear the edge in my voice.

Keith shakes his head and smirks. "One of the times we hooked up, she got pregnant. My feelings were mixed. I wanted a kid, but I wanted one with you. Then I got angry that you weren't getting pregnant, I figured it wasn't me and so I blamed you. I know that was wrong, but at the time, I couldn't see past my anger. I figure that was the beginning of the end."

"I think it was over before that. The love was anyway… well for me," I tell him in all honesty. His face shuts down, I'm not sure what he expected. I didn't come here to play nice or nasty. I came here for honesty, to give and receive.

"So I have only seen my son on and off over the years. When you left…" he shrugs, "…I had nothing to lose, not anymore. Ashley and me, I'm not sure whether we're forever, but while it's good, I'm there."

"What about when it's not?" I ask raising my eyebrows.

"Then I'll leave," he answers like it's a stupid question I've asked.

"So you'll just dump your son. *Again*?" I reply incredulously.

"Shut the fuck up, Anabel. You haven't been there and you don't know what you're talking about. You haven't even got kids." I feel a stabbing pain in my chest but nod in reply.

"This is true," I say nothing else. Not seeing the point in having a slanging match.

"Sorry. That was unfair. I know what you're saying, but I have no answers and the only person I really need to answer to now is Ashley… and my son."

"Fair point," I concede.

"So tell me about you and Danny Quinn." Danny's name is said in a sneer and I have to stop myself from kicking him between his legs under the table.

"We're together. It's permanent. That's all you need to know."

Keith works his jaw but doesn't say anything else. I look around the diner, thinking about how to leave. None of this is progressing us much and I have what I came for, a closure of sorts. Although now I've spoken to Keith, I realize I already had closure. I haven't loved him for so long, I made my peace with the end of us long before I left.

"What did you ask me here for?" I say, trying not to grumble.

"I came to say sorry. I know I wasn't a great husband, I promised you the world and never delivered. I also came to say that Declan won't be bothering you anymore. He's gone away. To his aunts. Apparently they're putting him in some fancy rehab place to help with the drinking."

"That will be good for him, hopefully," I reply.

Keith nods. "The other thing, I'm not contesting the divorce. It should be through soon."

I raise my eyebrows. "Wait, what? I stopped proceeding because I didn't have the money," I explain.

"Yeah, I know, my attorney told me. I paid for it." His reply shocks me and I sit back.

"What, wait… what?" I almost shriek, happy that the divorce has been progressing but confused about the money situation. "Where have you got money to pay for it?" I demand.

Keith looks sheepish. "Yeah, well, that's the condition of the divorce. You have to sign the papers." He brings out divorce papers from his back pocket. "These state that you give up any right to money from me. It also says you're fully aware of Ashley and Bobby."

"What?" I'm still confused.

Keith pulls his hand down his face. "I have money. Not loads but my folks left me some. By signing that…" he points to the papers, "…we'll be divorced. But you'll also be agreeing to give up any rights to my money." I look between the paper and his face.

"Why all these years did we live the way we did, if you have money? I'm not talking about the lap of luxury, but we had nothing, I barely scraped together food sometimes." I'm exasperated, shocked, hurt. This man was supposed to love me, yet he allowed me to live barely humanely and treated me like dirt. I look back to him and know, I've lost any respect I still had for him. Just like that, the town I'd always lived in, the one that once held everything I wanted now has nothing. I don't want to be here anymore. I stand up and grab the pen next to the papers. I sign everywhere that the little yellow stickie's point to, just glad to be rid of this man. Finally getting his poison out of my life.

"You don't want to know how much you're giving up?" he asks, surprised.

"Did I ever in all our years together give you a reason to think that I cared about money? *Ever*?" I growl.

Keith looks down at the papers, checking they're all signed in the right places.

"Whatever! You can move on with Danny the dick now," he sneers.

"Yeah, that's where my happily ever after lies, Keith. I suggest you try and find yours," I answer and walk out. I'm barely to the other side of the road to Amanda's car, when the bitch twins walk out of the salon.

"Well, lookie here, little miss perfect, Anabel Vincent," Jenny spits out and my shoulders drop turning to face them, this isn't what I need right now.

"It's Anabel Adams," I reply coldly.

"Oh, yeah. Keith traded you in I heard," Samantha spits.

"Is there something the two of you want?" I snap.

Both their eyes widen. "Well, look who got a backbone." Jenny smirks.

"Is there a reason you both still act like a pair of teenagers? All bitchy and pouty?" I ask shaking my head. Jenny says nothing while Samantha splutters at my question. "You're both ridiculous, you know that, right? Both aging, still spitting your bitchy gossip to the world. You know what I say? Carry on talking about me. That's what I say. Because if you're talking about me, then you're not talking about anyone else, right? And I truly don't care. I don't care what you say, who you say it to and most of all, I don't care what you or anyone else thinks about me. It only matters what I think of myself. When you two idiots realize that, it will be a better day for the world. Because you talking about other people, says nothing about them, and everything about you." Their mouths gape open, but I don't have time to enjoy it. Pulling the door of the car open, I make my way home. The house I'm traveling to isn't my home. It's taken me years to realize what's important.

I'll never forget again.
Danny is my home.

Chapter TWENTY NINE

Danny Quinn

“I asked Bel to marry me, Mom,” I tell her down the phone line.

“What! Dennis… Dennis, listen to this!” my mom screeches down my ear while hollering the news to my pop. I hear him muttering in the background, then my ma covers the phone with her hand. I don’t get it, why cover the phone? She’s not telling him something I don’t already know. I hear my pop cheering and then Mom moves back to the phone. “Oh, darling boy, we’re so happy for you. That girl always belonged to you. I remember when she came to us crying on her wedding day. Such a shame that things got so confused.”

“They didn’t get confused, Ma, I was just a dick.” I chuckle.

"Danny! Language!" Mom scolds. "Oh, I can't wait to call and tell your sister, she'll be so happy. Glad you got rid of that Shannon. Ugh, gold digger that one, I said so from day one. I said *'Dennis that Shannon ain't no more than a gold digger.'*"

I sigh, having heard this a million times, it's nothing new. I knew my parents would be happy when I told them about Bel. They loved her when we were younger when we were friends. I think my mom always knew I had feelings for her, and I told my pop the truth. He'd said I was stupid for sending her away, based on the worry of leaving her in this town. He said, *'Love doesn't come around every day.'* I never knew how true his words were back then. "Tell me about the ring," Mom demands excitedly.

"I haven't got her one," I reply hanging my head, aware of what's coming.

"What! Why ever not?" she complains. Anyone would think it was something for her.

"I asked her on the spur of the moment, I didn't have a ring." My explanation doesn't go down well when Mom coughs and splutters down the line.

"You asked her on the spur of the moment! Are you crazy? You took Shannon for a meal and proposed, yet with Bel it's a spur of the moment thing? I have no words, son of mine." I can imagine her shaking her head and I chuckle. "Do not laugh at me, Danny. You're not too big for me to spank you."

I laugh now. "Yeah Mom, I started being too big for a spanking when I was about eight. Anyway. You know Bel. She's never cared about money, showing off or anything flash, it came from the heart and that's all that matters. Besides, I'm taking her to buy a ring tomorrow. We're going to a hotel in the city tonight, it's a surprise, I'm treating her Mom so park your handbag, okay?" I suppress laughter this time.

Saying my goodbyes and promising to bring Bel to visit with them soon, I then make some final arrangements with Layla for what I want sorted tonight. Luckily, I didn't rent anywhere before I started staying at Amanda's house. I'm itching to get back, just to take a look over everything. I know Layla is more than capable, but I miss it. It's something I'm good at. I'm also aware that the new venture I wanted to start has stalled since Gabrielle was cut out. There's been no real estate that I've been happy with. I've been thinking of alternatives, and keeping myself as fresh as possible with the ice cream store, but it's only a small venture and it won't keep me busy for long. If I'm going to stay here, I need to set something up, somewhere that I can use as a headquarters. I can't sit around doing nothing every day. Although, burying myself inside Bel seems like a pretty good use of my time. From what she told me the other night, though, things need to go gently. I have plans for tonight. Bel said she wanted soon. Tonight I want to do everything in a way that's truly beautiful.

Hearing the front door creak open I move to meet her.

"Hey," her sweet voice always fills me with warmth, and even now I have to pinch myself to remember this is real, that I finally have the woman I've always wanted. She's mine. And I'm fucking keeping her forever.

"Hey, baby. How did things go with Keith?" I'm asking gently, slipping my arms around her and kissing her mouth softly. In truth, I want to rip his fucking throat out for even asking her to meet him.

"It was fine. He told me about Ashley and Bobby, which was nothing more than I already knew. He then produced divorce papers." I feel myself jerk and her head jolts from my movement.

"Sorry Bel, but what?" I ask surprised.

"Yeah, that was pretty much my reaction. I stopped the divorce because I'd run out of spare funds." I contain the frustration I feel. Knowing that she might not be getting divorced right now due to money and yet hadn't told me, and knowing Bel she'd also argue if I offered to pay for it. This money situation has to be addressed. "He told me he'd continued with it, and paid for it. Turns out he has money, I don't know how much and I don't care. He's had us living like that all these years when he could have made my life easier. Whatever, it's done now. So he offered me the divorce as long as I signed to say I give up any right on the money."

"So what did you do?" I ask… stupidly when I realize Bel is glaring at me.

"What do you think, you ass," she snaps and I chuckle. "Not funny douche canoe."

"Douche canoe… really?" I mock her.

She gives me a dirty look and I figure now's a good time to shut up. "Listen, baby," I tell her kissing the end of her nose. "You know I've secured a couple of jewelers to go visit tomorrow."

"You mean Layla secured them." She smirks.

"Yeah, well, that's what I pay her for," I reply, with my own smirk.

"Pig." She returns then laughs. I watch her, really watch her. It feels like forever since she genuinely laughed. I love her laugh, I always have. This, right here, is what's been missing from my life.

"Okay, baby. So I thought tonight, I'd treat you. We're going to go stay in a hotel in the city, have dinner out and then tomorrow we can pick out your engagement ring.

Bel squeaks and stands on her toes. She kisses the hinge of my jaw and I only just stop myself from taking her upstairs and ruining my plans for tonight, when she leans forward her hot breath in my ear and she whispers, "Thank you, Danny."

Anabel Adams

I stand on the balcony of the incredible hotel Danny has brought us to. The lights sparkle all around the city but we're high enough up that I can still see the stars in the sky. "I feel like you're giving me everything I ever wanted, yet you can't be here to enjoy it with me. I miss you every day." My soft words, as usual, go unrequited as the sadness spreads through me. I still talk to Amanda every day. I don't think that will ever change. She's in everything I do because a part of her will always be inside me.

"You ready?" Danny asks from behind, slipping his arms around me and kissing my neck where it meets my shoulder.

"Yeah," I whisper. I'm wearing the navy satin dress that Amanda got for me. The one I never got to wear for her wedding. It's beautiful and it deserves to be worn. Danny threads his fingers through mine and leads us out of the room, down the hall to the elevator, where we travel with another couple to the ground floor. Once there he pulls me through the foyer and out to a waiting limousine.

"I've never been in one of these," I breathe out, looking at everything.

"Get used to it, baby," Danny says and I let out a little scream when he lifts me into his lap.

"Danny, there's room in here for ten people. I don't need to sit on your lap," I say with a smile.

"Yes you do," he answers and pulls my blonde hair away from my shoulder allowing him access to my neck. He nuzzles his mouth into me peppering soft kisses along my collarbone. I'm transported somewhere because within what feels like seconds, we stop and there's a voice crackling through an intercom telling Mr. Quinn that we've arrived at our destination. The car door opens and Danny gets out, turning immediately to me. I slip my hand into his and he guides me out and into the restaurant. After speaking to the hostess, we move through a busy front room until we come to a small, secluded table at the back, next to a beautiful fireplace. "There have been so many times over the years sitting in nice restaurants, or even in mine on business, when I've wished I could be sitting across from you. Wondering what you were doing, how your life was. You know this kind of thing never really happens," he says pointing between us.

"What, real love?" I say confused.

"No, second chances with love." He chuckles and it goes straight to my lady bits like I'm being tickled there. I'm not sure how much longer I can go without at least trying with this man. I'm still scared of sex, but after talking to him about it, I've wanted it more and more. I trust him. He told me he had me, that I come first. I know he's telling the truth. We've done everything else, that's the only thing left. Deciding that if he doesn't make his move tonight, then I will settle my mind, and I feel calm for about twenty minutes until it starts sinking in that I'm going to have sex tonight. "What's wrong? You've just turned pale," Danny asks, grabbing my hand across the table just as our starters are served.

I'm thrown from my panic and all thoughts of sex disappear when I register that I didn't order anything. "I haven't ordered yet," I reply and Danny's lips twitch at my sudden change in conversation.

"No, I pre-ordered our food," he replies with a smirk.

"Oh, I didn't even know you could do that." I'm not sure whether to be happy or annoyed.

"You can. I hope you don't mind. I ordered the French Onion soup to start, the chicken risotto for main, and the honeycomb cheesecake for desert. If you want to change any of that say the word and I'll have it amended."

I look down at my soup. The aroma wafts up to my nose assaulting me with its delicious smells. "No, you did well. I think I'll keep you," I say with a smile while relaxing.

"So, have you thought any more about the ice cream parlor? I'm ready to get started when you are," Danny tells me before starting on his food. I consider how to answer him. This is a shop he's bought. He owns it and he's basically giving it to me. I place my spoon back down. Danny sees this and does the same, recognizing that I need his attention. "Bel? What is it?" he asks concerned.

"I don't want you to be angry."

"Not possible, baby. Tell me."

I nod my head in reply. "I don't want to stay here." Danny looks around, so quickly I continue talking. "Not here… I mean in our town. I want to leave. Leave the town, the house, the shop, I want to leave it all." I look down into my soup.

"Eyes babe," Danny demands and I look at him instantly. "You want to leave, we'll leave. We can go to my place in San Francisco, which has been home for me for five years. I have a place in New York. One in Florida and a couple in Europe. You want somewhere new? Then we can make that happen. This is a new start for us both. We've had challenges from the beginning, I'm not about to make them harder. I love you, Bel. I'm easily pleased. For me, I'm happy if you're happy," he tells me. His face is full of warmth and love.

"I'd like to go to San Francisco and get to know Layla a bit. Although, not if we're going to bump into your ex-wife," I tell him, chewing on my bottom lip.

He chuckles and I feel it run through me again. "Shannon has moved back to be near her parents in Idaho. You won't see her. Anyway, even if she hadn't, part of the divorce settlement was that she can't contact me, *or you*, or any of my family or friends. So she wouldn't have been a bother," he explains and I feel a slow exhale escape from my chest and out through my nose.

"Okay, but there's something else. I'm worried about... Rubén." I watch as Danny's face contorts in pain. "I don't like him being alone. I know his momma moved in with her sister recently, Pastor Wilson told me. He also said that she had the beginnings of Alzheimer's. Rubén has no one now, except us."

Danny nods. "He's gone to Seattle. We could head there first. Check in on him, stay a while? If we can convince him to move back to his New York office, I can move us to my New York apartment. Then we can be in contact regularly. Would that make you feel better?" he asks.

"Yeah. Plus Christmas in New York. Wow!" I say excitedly.

We chat throughout the rest of the meal. Catching up on all the little things we haven't had time to focus on. We also make plans. I decide to keep the shop exactly as it is for now—closed, but empty. I also decide that I don't want to give the house up. But I do have an idea of how it could be useful. I never plan on moving back here, but I simply cannot let the house go completely. My whole future is tied up in this man that sits opposite me. I explain my thought processes to Danny, in that I want to pass the keys to Pastor Wilson. Then if any family happen upon hard times, if anyone is about to be put on the street, he has that house should he need to temporarily give someone refuge. Danny shakes his head, telling me that I never cease to amaze him. I take that as a compliment and can't wipe the smile off my face, even when I don't like the dessert.

Now we're back in the hotel suite. A huge two bedroom place that has more square feet than anywhere I've ever lived. I'm once again drawn to the balcony and the stars.

"Here you go, baby," Danny says, passing me a glass of champagne. Taking the glass from him, I smile. It's awkward and I know why because I'm obsessing about having sex with him. About getting naked with Danny Quinn. "Hey, just relax," Danny tells me. I shake my head with a smile.

"I don't know why I'm so worried. It's probably because it's you," I tell him. Danny steps forward just as I take a sip from my glass. He pulls it away from my lips and replaces it with his mouth.

"Mmm. Remember this works both ways. It's always been you, Bel, even when I thought it never would be." The words slide around my heart giving it a squeeze telling me I'm alive, I'm loved, and I'm safe. I throw my arms around his neck and push my hands into his hair. Danny kisses me again. Softly at first, then moving into a deeper, intense kiss. A kiss that makes me forget my name. Warmth heats my cheeks and continues down my body, filling every crevice, until I'm hot and happy everywhere.

He must place the glass on the table because suddenly he runs his hands up my back until they reach my neck, his forearms run down the length of my spine and he uses his strength to pull me up against him until my feet aren't touching the floor anymore. He walks forward taking me backward, but not missing a beat or the connection between our mouths. I feel my back pressed against a wall and Danny tears his lips away from mine, which makes me mewl at the loss. "Tell me you still want this, before we go any further," he whispers, looking straight into my eyes.

Without looking away or getting embarrassed I give him my reply, "I want this, I want you."

That's all he needs before reconnecting our mouths and picking me back up, carrying me against him into the bedroom. He gently lowers me until my feet touch the floor and I can feel my calves pressing against the bed. Danny stops kissing my mouth. Instead, exploring my throat, taking his time to cover me with gentle kisses and nips all the way to my chest. Then his mouth moves toward my neck, edging his way up the right side until he meets my ear.

Once there, he gently bites my earlobe sending a shiver through my body. Then he whispers. "I've wanted to be inside you since I hit puberty, Bel. I'm going to be doing this for the rest of our lives. *A lot*." His words sink into me. Seeping into my blood, flowing through my veins. I know. *I know*, I can be *me* with him. I'm safe.

That's when I let everything go, all the anxiety that I was still holding, the worry, pain and fear.

I believe in him, in us.

He's my path, my destination and my journey.

Every. Single. Moment.

Danny runs his fingers over the straps of my dress from my shoulders and reaches around my back unzipping me, while kissing from one collarbone across my chest to the other. Once the zip is open, he picks the straps back up and pulls them off my shoulders. Then he steps back as he lets go and my dress drops, pooling on the floor. I have no bra on, and having slipped my shoes off earlier, I now stand before him in just a pair of navy lace panties. I'm not uncomfortable, we've done everything but sex, so he's seen me naked.

"You really are too good to be true," he whispers to himself as he looks down my body. He steps back to me and runs his fingertips up my sides, starting at my thighs, until he gets to my stomach. Then, reaching further up, he cups both my breasts while running his thumbs over my nipples. Kissing me again he pulls his hands away, slipping one around my back, the other he places on the bed and lowers us down until I'm underneath him.

As we continue kissing, I unbuckle his pants. Then move to his shirt pulling away from his mouth. Instead kissing his neck, feeling the roughness from his stubble grazing my skin, setting me on fire and making me feel alive. While I kiss him, I sense his hands removing his clothes. I know he's naked. I can feel the heat coming from his body, not to mention his hardness pressed against me. Just my lace separates us now.

Internally, I've gone from chastity belt to hotter than the seventh circle of hell. All I want is to feel him inside me. Danny moves down covering me with his tongue. He travels between my breasts, stopping to give some attention to each one, then he moves lower, kissing me over my panties. He looks up and I meet his eyes. Watching me intently, he hooks his fingers into the lace and pulls them down my legs, stopping only to kiss behind my knees. His eyes never leaving mine. Once they're off he pushes up, pulling his body over mine, then coming back to meet my mouth with his. He kisses me again as our naked bodies press together. I feel his hand slip down between us and one finger, then two push inside me.

"You're ready," he whispers into my mouth. I want to speak, to say I've been ready forever. But I can't think past the pleasure spiral, I'm currently traveling in. I feel him line up against me. His center at my center. Our last divide, finally crumbling down.

"Danny," I gasp. "I…" my words die as I feel him right at my entrance. He stops kissing me, and I open my eyes to see his, looking down adoringly at me. He says nothing and doesn't move, allowing me to take my time to compose myself. "Danny, I don't want to use a… I want it to be just us nothing between us. I'm c-clean," I say, my cheeks pinking.

Danny's hooded eyes flare. "I am too. And Bel, I know you said you couldn't have kids, but if I plant one inside you tonight then that would be a beautiful thing," he tells me and I smile. Then my eyes close as he surprises me by pushing all the way inside. "Eyes," he growls and I open them, looking straight into his. I can see he's barely controlling himself. "This is going to be slow. This isn't sex. I'm not going to fuck you, Bel. I'm going to love you," he says softly, before kissing my closed lips.

Keeping his eyes trained on mine, he starts moving slowly, back and forth. His sedate lovemaking is intense, it's like he's savoring every moment and it creates a buzzing sensation throughout my body, like it's finally coming alive. He keeps the rhythm up, pulling all the way out, then sliding back in. It's everything I was always missing, and as our bodies become sweaty and his eyes stay burning into mine, I feel all the emotion I've never felt before as tears slip out of my eyes.

With no warning, and having never happened to me during sex before, it's a shock when my orgasm unexpectedly explodes inside me. Danny continues moving slowly, prolonging the beautiful feeling. When I start coming down, he brings his hand up to wipe away hair that's stuck to my forehead. He pushes his thumb into my mouth.

"I love you, Anabel," he tells me as I bite down on his thumb, then his eyes close as he groans out his release which I feel filling me up inside.

Chapter THIRTY

Danny Quinn

As we walk into the boutique jewelers, my fingers interlocked with Bel's proudly, I'm ready to slip a ring onto her finger. If I had my way, I'd be putting two on her delicate digit today. She gave me everything last night because she truly gave me *her*, no holds barred. I felt it, the moment she let go, my love for her in those quiet seconds became unconditional. Everlasting. Finite.

"Wow," Bel breathes out and my focus returns to the room, looking down I see her staring at a simple ring.

"This is a Princess cut solitaire ring with an elegant twist claw," the assistant tells us.

Bel reaches out to touch the ring, which sits on a black velvet stand, nestled alongside five other rings. It's just one of the six stands sitting on the counter top awaiting our very personal perusal. Just before her fingers meet the dazzling platinum band, she stops, pulling her hand back like the ring might burn her. Concern instantly zips around inside.

Wondering if she's gotten cold feet, scared of being married again. All sorts of thoughts to her behavior enter my mind in the three seconds it takes for me to ask, "What's the matter?"

Bel looks at me, like a deer in the headlights then back to the assistant, who still wears a soft smile. "H-how much is it?" Her question allows me to breathe out a sigh of relief. The assistant who, looking at her name tag is called Judy, doesn't remove the fixed smile. She looks to me, then back to Bel.

"Ma'am, we were told to put out only the best. These are all one karat diamonds, at least, most are more." She coughs. "We were also told to remove the price tags."

Bel's eyes snap to me and they're narrowed. It takes everything in me not to smile, I know this is important to her. But she also needs to know that this business with money is going to cause *us* problems if we don't sort it out now. I look back to Judy. "May we have a minute?" She glances at the security guard, situated by the locked front door and nods. Moving through a back door, giving us privacy at least from her.

"Bel, you need to stop with the money issue." She moves to speak, but I place my finger over her soft, plump lips. "If it were the other way around, how would you feel?" I ask and immediately a look of confusion passes over her face. "If you had money and tried to buy me something nice, or do something nice for me, would you expect anything in return?" Her eyebrows pull in and she shakes her head. "Okay, would you throw it in my face should we have an argument?" Immediately she jerks her head left and right, her nonverbal no, once again answering me. "Okay, would you be hurt if I kept turning things down, or pushing things away, based on how much they cost every time you tried to do something nice for me?" This time, she thinks for a moment, her index finger finds its way to her closed mouth and she unknowingly taps it against her lips.

"I guess," the whisper is her surrender.

"Listen, you've known me forever. That works both ways, I've known you forever too. You're no more a gold digger than you are a pimp." Her eyes go wide and I struggle, once again, not to laugh. "I have money, I've worked hard for it, that's true. But if you had been with me from the beginning, I'm fairly sure you would never have questioned money being spent on you, because you'd be used to it. Every time you refuse or argue about money, it hits home that I lived my life without you for far too long. You and me… this is forever. We know this. We've also known it for all the years we haven't been together, but should have been. I have money and

I'm not about to stop living the way I do because you're worried about what's being spent." She nods and I need to push my point home. "Let me ask you one more question, just in case you're still unsure?" I gaze into her eyes, hoping I'm not ruining this special moment. This should be all about us picking out the ring. The last person I want to bring into our day is Keith, but this is important, I need to know she gets this. Our future depends on her getting it. I'm not about to live the rest of my life in a battle over money. That's why I've been successful, because I don't want to worry or argue about money. "If you were still with Keith, and he told you about that money he mentioned the other night. Said he was going to get a better house, or buy you a car, or maybe a new wedding ring. Would you have told him no? Told him not to spend his money, or worried about the cost if it was within his price range?" I know it's below the belt, but she needs to think about it like that, she needs to be clear in her head before we move forward.

"Okay, I get it," she rasps out the words. "I'm sorry. You know I've never been in this kind of a position, I'm not used to anything but struggling," she tells me grabbing my hands, which I didn't realize until she touched them are clenched tight. I release the fists and my hands hold hers.

"Get used to it. There is to be no prenup." She opens her mouth, but I don't allow her to speak when

I reiterate firmly. "No prenup." Rolling her eyes, she bites her lip and I want to chuckle again. "I will be setting up a bank account in your married name. I want to make you Mrs. Quinn as soon as your divorce is final. In writing. Then you'll have your own money. I'll make sure money is fed into it every month. Still if you ever need more, you tell me and we'll sort it out. You want to work, then work. You want to stay at home all day, then you do that. It's your choice, but that money is my way of knowing my wife always has what she needs at her disposal. I don't want you feeling like you have to come to me every time you need something. You're not a child, not an employee or another family member. You're Bel. *You're everything*," I sigh out the last words as I lay my forehead against hers. We stand silently for a moment just listening to each other breathing. Until I hear a small clearing of a throat behind me. Closing my eyes, I pull back then kiss Bel's head, before turning her with me to face Judy again.

"Can you take that one out, please?" I ask, pointing to the one that Bel couldn't—and still can't—take her eyes off. The moment she passes it to me, I turn to Bel and slip it onto her ring finger. I'm slightly shocked it actually fits, but I'm not complaining when I watch Bel's eyes fill with tears. "This is it, isn't it?" I ask and Bel just nods as happy tears flow out of her beautiful eyes. "That's it," I tell Judy, who smiles and starts putting the others away.

"Can you get out wedding bands, for both of us?" I ask and she again nods and goes about her business. "Bel," I whisper and she looks up to me, tearing her eyes away from the ring on her finger.

"Oh," she says wiping her tears away with the back of her hand. "I guess I should take it off, so the lady can put it in the box and put it through the register," she says and I smile.

"That's never coming off your finger baby," I tell her with a smirk. I run my knuckles down her wet cheek. "Listen, how do you want to get married?"

"What do you mean?" she questions.

"Well, big, small, here, somewhere else?" I give her some options.

"I hadn't really thought about it. But I guess I'd love a wedding on the beach, just you and me, Mike, Simone and Rubén. Oh, and of course, your parents and sister." Her answer makes me happy.

"How about Florida? You said the other day that you wanted to see my parents and sister again, and they sure as hell want to see you. If you want, we can go there and see if we can get a beach wedding organized for while we visit?" I ask her. I know weddings are a big deal for women, I just want her to be mine in every possible way. I don't care what it takes or how she wants to do it.

"How about…" she whispers, rubbing her thumb along my lips, "…we ask your mom if she would arrange a small beach wedding? Now I know I haven't spoken to her in years, and I know she gets carried away about things, but I also remember she's the kind of woman if you tell her I want small, she will do it small. If I only want those people I mentioned on the invite list, that's all that she'll invite. Then I can concentrate on buying a dress and some underwear." Her words heat me instantly and I want to drag her back to our hotel room.

"Yeah, if I lay it out to Mom, she'll do exactly what you want. She'll just be so pleased that you want her to organize it in the first place. Do you know when your divorce is expected?"

"I called my lawyer yesterday. Should be any day now. Definitely by next week," she tells me.

"So we'll get it arranged for three weeks from now." She nods back at me, smiling. "In three weeks, you'll be Mrs. Anabel Quinn," I say, kissing her lips again. I watch as another tear falls, then she pushes up on her toes kissing me, longer, harder, until I take over. It's not until I hear a purposefully placed cough that I pull back with a smile. Bel looks slightly dazed and that makes me want to puff out my chest and stalk around like a peacock. "Come on, baby." I turn her around so her back is against my front, then lean down, placing my mouth at her ear. "Let's get our wedding bands, then we can go back to the hotel so I can get you naked, except for the ring," I whisper and watch as her cheeks pink and she bites her lip.

Later that night, as I watch Bel sleep, laying on her front the cover just over her butt, I think about the journey we've all had to go through to get here. The broken pieces we've had to remold or stick back together, hoping they'd gel forever.

We should have always been here.

Right here.

Although we should have Amanda too.

Taking one last glance at Bel, I walk out to the balcony and stare up at the stars. "You gave her everything all your life, but in those last couple of months you freed her. That's when you gave her more than anyone ever has, you gave her back herself. She's gone through hell and she's still suffering at your loss Amanda… but I think… *no, I'm sure*, because of what you gave her. Because you were her best friend, her sister, her strength, and her soulmate, because of you, because of your love, she's finally unbroken."

Epilogue

Anabel Quinn

"Mummy?" I look over at Amanda, sitting on the window ledge watching the stars.

"Yes, sweetheart?" I ask, sitting next to her and sweeping her beautiful dark brown hair away from her cheek.

"Do you think one day we could reach the stars, like in a helicopter?"

"Copter, copter, brrr." I glance behind me at Kyle as he runs around shouting with a mini helicopter grasped in his chubby fingers.

Bringing my attention back to Amanda, I smile. "Maybe one day we could. How amazing would it be? To travel far and wide? Explore new things?"

She looks at her lap and then back to the sky. My little over-thinker. "What is it, Mandie?" I question softly.

"I wish we could go up there. I always wish on every birthday candle I've blown out since I was five, that I could meet Auntie Moo."

Her words momentarily throw me, as emotion climbs up my throat. Swallowing, I rein myself in. "Well baby, I'm not sure that will ever be possible. But I can still tell you all about her? Now you're eight baby, you're a big girl. So if I tell you about the naughty things me and your Aunt Moo got up to when we were your age, you have to promise not to do the same with Hope, okay?" I tease.

My girl is good. She will follow the rules, very rarely gets into trouble, not like her six-year-old sister Clara, who suddenly appears naked and wet, screeching at the top of her lungs like a little version of a streaker. She runs through Mandie's bedroom, in through one door and out through the other like a little blur. We all stop for a second, even Kyle, who's a bundle of energy at three and rarely stops for anything. Just as our heads have whipped from one door to the other, they whip back again as Danny appears.

"Was Clara just in here? I was trying to bathe her. Now she's decided she's a spy and I'm the bad guy trying to get her." His hand rubs the back of his neck, as his frustration eases out of his bright blue eyes. I can't help but laugh. Bath time with Clara is always anything but straight forward. "Never mind." He smirks, walking forward and dropping kisses on all our foreheads, before following the water trail on the floor that will undoubtedly lead to Clara at some point.

"Brrr," Kyle waffles, with his mini helicopter. His PJ's have pictures of planes all over them. He runs out the room and thankfully toward his bedroom.

"So, how about tomorrow I tell you some stories?" I say turning to Mandie.

She nods shyly. "Will you show me the photos again too, Momma?"

"Of course, baby girl, now get in bed. Reading for a while then lights out, okay?" I say kissing her cheek, as she reaches her little girl arms around my shoulders and clings on tight. It's safe to say my eldest is a mommy's girl. My other two, though, they're all about their daddy.

I walk into Kyle's room, but he's already fast asleep on his bed, clutching his toy helicopter for dear life. Kissing his cheek, I pull up the covers and turn off the light. Danny passes me with a wriggling Clara in his arms. I manage to kiss her wet cheek and say goodnight, as Danny carries her to her bedroom.

A little while later I hear the back door open then close. This is quickly followed by a pair of warm, strong arms, as usual, wrapping around me. Resting his chin on my shoulder Danny whispers, "They're all asleep now, baby." I nod but say nothing. "You okay?" he questions squeezing me.

"Mandie was asking about Amanda," I reply.

"So tell her, baby. You've never been quiet about Amanda. What is it?" he asks gently.

"I will tell her, it's not talking about Mandie Moo that's the problem. It's just, I'm going to relive all our childhood, and I'm going to tell Mandie all about us. It's both sad and beautiful at the same time. I don't know, maybe it's because this year is my fortieth birthday and would have been hers, too. I get to have mine, and thanks to your super sperm, you managed to give me kids from our very first time. Now we have three of the little monsters," I say smiling. Then my smile drops. "Amanda will never get to have that," I explain.

"Yeah, but you gave her everything she wanted before she died. You and Rubén both did. And you know full well she'll always be looking down, watching you, watching us all. Amanda only ever wanted the best for you. Being happy is your legacy to her, baby," he tells me. I turn in his arms and softly kiss my husband's lips.

"Have I told you how smart you are today?"

"Mmm, I'd rather be hot," he replies and I giggle.

"You're that, too," I tell him before he claims my mouth and I can't say anything else. That's when the heavens open and Amanda showers me in her love.

The End

Playlist

Kate Bush – This Woman's Work
Sarah McLachlan – In The Arms of An Angel
Lisa Stansfield – Tenderly
Rosi Golan – Been A Long Day
James Bay – Let It Go
Heatwave – Always and Forever
Nickelback – Far Away
Red – Not Alone
Hunter Hayes – Wanted
James Bay – If You Ever Want To Be In Love
Bonnie Raitt – I Can't Make You Love Me
Ed Sheeran – Photograph
James Bay – Move Together
Creed – Higher
Madonna – You'll See
Taylor Swift – Begin Again

Katy Perry – The One That Got Away
Avril Lavigne – Keep Holding On
Seether feat. Amy Lee – Broken
Adele – Hello
Otis Redding – I've Been Loving You Too Long
John Parr – St. Elmo's Fire
New Kids on the Block – I Remember When
Guns N' Roses – Paradise City
Sarah McLachlan – I Will Remember You
New Kids on the Block – Cover Girl
Ella Henderson – Beautifully Unfinished

Acknowledgments

I want to start as always by thanking my husband and daughters and family, for supporting me unconditionally. I love you.

To my Beta's – Beth Lemilliere, Annmarie Thomson, Kerry Adamson, Laura Nelson, Stacey Tester, Donna Tutin, Sarah Queen, Laurie Breitsprecher, Giovanna Bovenzi Cruz, Sharon Dawson, Yvette Vega and Emma Louise. For reading my book chapter by chapter, giving me feedback, suggestions and guidance, and loving my characters as much as I do. For supporting me wholeheartedly and believing in me but most of all, for just being my friends. <3

To Maria's Misfits - my Street Team. You know just how important you all are to me. I love you guys. You're an amazing bunch and I'm blessed that you support me wholeheartedly and tirelessly. I adore you! Thank you for making writing so much fun! Mainly, thank you for interacting and becoming friends with me, as well as each other! I love you guys!

A special thank you to Laurie, Laura, Analia, Giovanna and Penny from my Misfits, who pimp me constantly. Love you, ladies!

To my Instagram family. Your support knows no bounds. You are all amazing and I hope one day we can all meet - sorry if I forget anyone!

Booksandbandanas
bookobsessedgirl
am_johnson_author
sucker_for_books
pia_bibliophile
beautyandthebooks83
naliia_
paperback_pixie
abooklover83
doll_face43
shutupshabby
authormandrews
mee_and_my_books
booksare.everything
emmbooks
thereadingruth

To the authors who support me and give me advice, and for the one's who kick my arse and make me sprint. Rochelle Paige, Kirsty Moseley, Nikki Groom, A.M Johnson and G. L Chapple, just to name the ones I mostly harass!

Francessca Webster from Francessca's Romance Reviews, you rock!

Kaylene Osborn from Swish Design & Editing. Thank you for everything!

Amanda Maria thank you for being an awesome proof-reader!

To every single blogger who has been willing to promote me in one way or another, I know how busy you all are. I know you take time away from family life to support authors. I think what you do is truly amazing and that it is a blessing for us authors, as well as readers, to have you there, helping and supporting. So thank you from the bottom of my heart.

Lastly, thank you to all the readers who have taken, and will take a chance on me. You are the ones who will truly make my dreams come true.

Connect WITH ME ONLINE

Thank you for reading Finally Unbroken.

If you enjoyed it, please consider leaving a review at your point of purchase and on Goodreads. It means a lot to me to hear what you think.

Also, feel free to join my street/reader group: https://www.facebook.com/groups/mariasmisfits/

Goodreads

Add to your TBR list.
Love Reflection - An Entwined Hearts Novel Book 1
Love Resisted - An Entwined Hearts Novel Book 2
Love Renewed – An Entwined Hearts Novel Book 3
Finally Unbroken – Finally Unbroken Series Book 1

Maria Macdonald

Website
http://www.mariamacdonaldauthor.com/

Email
mariamacdonaldauthor@gmail.com

Facebook
https://www.facebook.com/maria.macdonald.71?fref=ts

Goodreads
https://www.goodreads.com/author/show/12764874.Maria_Macdonald?from_search=true

About THE AUTHOR

Maria is a full-time working mum, she has two beautiful daughters, both of whom love books as much as she.

She has loved writing since she was a little girl.

Reading and loving books, as well as blogging, has inspired her to write and publish.

Maria, her husband, and children now reside in Wiltshire, England.

61653838R00211

Made in the USA
Lexington, KY
16 March 2017